Initials Only by Anna Katharine Green

Anna Katharine Green was born in Brooklyn, New York on November 11th, 1846.

Anna's initial ambition was to be a poet. However that path failed to ignite any significant interest and she turned to fiction writing. She published her first—and most famous work in 1878—'The Leavenworth Case'. Wilkie Collins praised it and it sold extremely well.

It led to Anna writing 40 novels and to becoming known as 'the mother of the detective novel.'

In helping to shape the genre she brought many other innovations including a series detective: her main character was detective Ebenezer Gryce of the New York Metropolitan Police Force, but in three novels he is assisted by the nosy society spinster Amelia Butterworth, another innovation and a prototype for Miss Marple, Miss Silver and others.

She also invented the 'girl detective': in the character of Violet Strange, a debutante with a secret life as a sleuth. Anna's other innovations included the now familiar dead bodies in libraries, newspaper clippings as "clews," the coroner's inquest, and expert witnesses. Yale Law School once used her books to demonstrate how damaging it can be to rely on circumstantial evidence.

Her career was now well advanced and she was much admired.

On November 25, 1884, Green married the actor and stove designer, and later noted furniture maker, Charles Rohlfs, who was seven years her junior. They had three children; Rosamund, Roland and Sterling.

Although Anna was a progressive she did not approve of many of her feminist contemporaries, and was opposed to women's suffrage.

On November 25, 1884, Anna married the actor and noted furniture maker, Charles Rohlfs, who was seven years her junior. They had three children; Rosamund, Roland and Sterling.

Anna Katharine Green died on April 11, 1935 in Buffalo, New York, at the age of 88.

Index of Contents

BOOK I

AS SEEN BY TWO STRANGERS

CHAPTER I

POINSETTIAS

"A remarkable man!"

It was not my husband speaking, but some passerby. However, I looked up at George with a smile, and found him looking down at me with much the same humour. We had often spoken of the odd phrases one hears in the street, and how interesting it would be sometimes to hear a little more of the conversation.

"That's a case in point," he laughed, as he guided me through the crowd of theatre-goers which invariably block this part of Broadway at the hour of eight. "We shall never know whose eulogy we have just heard. 'A remarkable man!' There are not many of them."

"No," was my somewhat indifferent reply. It was a keen winter night and snow was packed upon the walks in a way to throw into sharp relief the figures of such pedestrians as happened to be walking alone. "But it seems to me that, so far as general appearance goes, the one in front answers your description most admirably."

I pointed to a man hurrying around the corner just ahead of us.

"Yes, he's remarkably well built. I noticed him when he came out of the Clermont." This was a hotel we had just passed.

"But it's not only that. It's his height, his very striking features, his expression—" I stopped suddenly, gripping George's arm convulsively in a surprise he appeared to share. We had turned the corner immediately behind the man of whom we were speaking and so had him still in full view.

"What's he doing?" I asked, in a low whisper. We were only a few feet behind. "Look! look! don't you call that curious?"

My husband stared, then uttered a low, "Rather." The man ahead of us, presenting in every respect the appearance of a gentleman, had suddenly stooped to the kerb and was washing his hands in the snow, furtively, but with a vigour and purpose which could not fail to arouse the strangest conjectures in any chance onlooker.

"Pilate!" escaped my lips, in a sort of nervous chuckle. But George shook his head at me.

"I don't like it," he muttered, with unusual gravity. "Did you see his face?" Then as the man rose and hurried away from us down the street, "I should like to follow him. I do believe—"

But here we became aware of a quick rush and sudden clamour around the corner we had just left, and turning quickly, saw that something had occurred on Broadway which was fast causing a tumult.

"What's the matter?" I cried. "What can have happened? Let's go see, George. Perhaps it has something to do with our man."

My husband, with a final glance down the street at the fast disappearing figure, yielded to my importunity, and possibly to some new curiosity of his own.

"I'd like to stop that man first," said he. "But what excuse have I? He may be nothing but a crank, with some crack-brained idea in his head. We'll soon know; for there's certainly something wrong there on Broadway."

"He came out of the Clermont," I suggested.

"I know. If the excitement isn't there, what we've just seen is simply a coincidence." Then, as we retraced our steps to the corner "Whatever we hear or see, don't say anything about this man. It's after eight, remember, and we promised Adela that we would be at the house before nine."

"I'll be quiet."

"Remember."

It was the last word he had time to speak before we found ourselves in the midst of a crowd of men and women, jostling one another in curiosity or in the consternation following a quick alarm. All were looking one way, and, as this was towards the entrance of the Clermont, it was evident enough to us that the alarm had indeed had its origin in the very place we had anticipated. I felt my husband's arm press me closer to his side as we worked our way towards the entrance, and presently caught a warning sound from his lips as the oaths and confused cries everywhere surrounding us were broken here and there by articulate words and we heard:

"Is it murder?"

"The beautiful Miss Challoner!"

"A millionairess in her own right!"

"Killed, they say."

"No, no! suddenly dead; that's all."

"George, what shall we do?" I managed to cry into my husband's ear.

"Get out of this. There is no chance of our reaching that door, and I can't have you standing round any longer in this icy slush."

"But—but is it right?" I urged, in an importunate whisper. "Should we go home while he—"

"Hush! My first duty is to you. We will go make our visit; but to-morrow—"

"I can't wait till to-morrow," I pleaded, wild to satisfy my curiosity in regard to an event in which I naturally felt a keen personal interest.

He drew me as near to the edge of the crowd as he could. There were new murmurs all about us.

"If it's a case of heart-failure, why send for the police?" asked one.

"It is better to have an officer or two here," grumbled another.

"Here comes a cop."

"Well, I'm going to vamoose."

"I'll tell you what I'll do," whispered George, who, for all his bluster was as curious as myself. "We will try the rear door where there are fewer persons. Possibly we can make our way in there, and if we can, Slater will tell us all we want to know."

Slater was the assistant manager of the Clermont, and one of George's oldest friends.

"Then hurry," said I. "I am being crushed here."

George did hurry, and in a few minutes we were before the rear entrance of the great hotel. There was a mob gathered here also, but it was neither so large nor so rough as the one on Broadway. Yet I doubt if we should have been able to work our way through t if Slater had not, at that very instant, shown himself in the doorway, in company with an officer to whom he was giving some final instructions. George caught his eye as soon as he was through with the man, and ventured on what I thought a rather uncalled for plea.

"Let us in, Slater," he begged. "My wife feels a little faint; she has been knocked about so by the crowd."

The manager glanced at my face, and shouted to the people around us to make room. I felt myself lifted up, and that is all I remember of this part of our adventure. For, affected more than I realised by the excitement of the event, I no sooner saw the way cleared for our entrance than I made good my husband's words by fainting away in earnest.

When I came to, it was suddenly and with perfect recognition of my surroundings. The small reception room to which I had been taken was one I had often visited, and its familiar features did not hold my attention for a moment. What I did see and welcome was my husband's face bending close over me, and to him I spoke first. My words must have sounded oddly to those about. "Have they told you anything about it?" I asked. "Did he—"

A quick pressure on my arm silenced me, and then I noticed that we were not alone. Two or three ladies stood near, watching me, and one had evidently been using some restorative, for she held a small vinaigrette in her hand. To this lady, George made haste to introduce me, and from her I presently learned the cause of the disturbance in the hotel.

It was of a somewhat different nature from what I expected, and during the recital, I could not prevent myself from casting furtive and inquiring glances at George.

Edith, the well-known daughter of Moses Challoner, had fallen suddenly dead on the floor of the mezzanine. She was not known to have been in poor health, still less in danger of a fatal attack, and the shock was consequently great to her friends, several of whom were in the building. Indeed, it was likely to prove a shock to the whole community, for she had great claims to general admiration, and her death must be regarded as a calamity to persons in all stations of life.

I realised this myself, for I had heard much of the young lady's private virtues, as well as of her great beauty and distinguished manner. A heavy loss, indeed, but—

"Was she alone when she fell?" I asked.

"Virtually alone. Some persons sat on the other side of the room, reading at the big round table. They did not even hear her fall. They say that the band was playing unusually loud in the musicians' gallery."

"Are you feeling quite well, now?"

"Quite myself," I gratefully replied as I rose slowly from the sofa. Then, as my kind informer stepped aside, I turned to George with the proposal we should go now.

He seemed as anxious as myself to leave and together we moved towards the door, while the hum of excited comment which the intrusion of a fainting woman had undoubtedly interrupted, recommenced behind us till the whole room buzzed.

In the hall we encountered Mr. Slater, whom I have before mentioned. He was trying to maintain order while himself in a state of great agitation. Seeing us, he could not refrain from whispering a few words into my husband's ear.

"The doctor has just gone up—her doctor, I mean. He's simply dumbfounded. Says that she was the healthiest woman in New York yesterday—I think—don't mention it, that he suspects something quite different from heart failure."

"What do you mean?" asked George, following the assistant manager down the broad flight of steps leading to the office. Then, as I pressed up close to Mr. Slater's other side, "She was by herself, wasn't she, in the half floor above?"

"Yes, and had been writing a letter. She fell with it still in her hand."

"Have they carried her to her room?" I eagerly inquired, glancing fearfully up at the large semi-circular openings overlooking us from the place where she had fallen.

"Not yet. Mr. Hammond insists upon waiting for the coroner." (Mr. Hammond was the proprietor of the hotel.) "She is lying on one of the big couches near which she fell. If you like, I can give you a glimpse of her. She looks beautiful. It's terrible to think that she is dead."

I don't know why we consented. We were under a spell, I think. At all events, we accepted his offer and followed him up a narrow staircase open to very few that night. At the top, he turned upon us with a warning gesture which I hardly think we needed, and led us down a narrow hall flanked by openings corresponding to those we had noted from below. At the furthest one he paused and, beckoning us to his side, pointed across the lobby into the large writing-room which occupied the better part of the mezzanine floor.

We saw people standing in various attitudes of grief and dismay about a couch, one end of which only was visible to us at the moment. The doctor had just joined them, and every head was turned towards him and every body bent forward in anxious expectation. I remember the face of one grey haired old man. I shall never forget it. He was probably her father. Later, I knew him to be so. Her face, even her form, was entirely hidden from us, but as we watched (I have often thought with what heartless curiosity) a sudden movement took place in the whole group—and for one instant a startling picture presented itself to our gaze. Miss Challoner was stretched out upon the couch. She was dressed as she came from dinner, in a gown of ivory-tinted satin, relieved at the breast by a large bouquet of scarlet poinsettias. I mention this adornment, because it was what first met and drew our eyes and the eyes of every one about her, though the face, now quite revealed, would seem to have the greater attraction. But the cause was evident and one not to be resisted. The doctor was pointing at these poinsettias in horror and with awful meaning, and though we could not hear his words, we knew almost instinctively, both from his attitude and the cries which burst from the lips of those about him, that something more than broken petals and disordered laces had met his eyes; that blood was there—slowly oozing drops from the heart—which for some reason had escaped all eyes till now.

Miss Challoner was dead, not from unsuspected disease, but from the violent attack of some murderous weapon; As the realisation of this brought fresh panic and bowed the old father's head with emotions even more bitter than those of grief, I turned a questioning look up at George's face.

It was fixed with a purpose I had no trouble in understanding.

CHAPTER II

"I KNOW THE MAN"

Yet he made no effort to detain Mr. Slater, when that gentleman, under this renewed excitement, hastily left us. He was not the man to rush into anything impulsively, and not even the presence of murder could change his ways.

"I want to feel sure of myself," he explained. "Can you bear the strain of waiting around a little longer, Laura? I mustn't forget that you fainted just now."

"Yes, I can bear it; much better than I could bear going to Adela's in my present state of mind. Don't you think the man we saw had something to do with this? Don't you believe—"

"Hush! Let us listen rather than talk. What are they saying over there? Can you hear?"

"No. And I cannot bear to look. Yet I don't want to go away. It's all so dreadful."

"It's devilish. Such a beautiful girl! Laura, I must leave you for a moment. Do you mind?"

"No, no; yet—"

I did mind; but he was gone before I could take back my word. Alone, I felt the tragedy much more than when he was with me. Instead of watching, as I had hitherto done, every movement in the room opposite, I drew back against the wall and hid my eyes, waiting feverishly for George's return.

He came, when he did come, in some haste and with certain marks of increased agitation.

"Laura," said he, "Slater says that we may possibly be wanted and proposes that we stay here all night. I have telephoned Adela and have made it all right at home. Will you come to your room? This is no place for you."

Nothing could have pleased me better; to be near and yet not the direct observer of proceedings in which we took so secret an interest! I showed my gratitude by following George immediately. But I could not go without casting another glance at the tragic scene I was leaving. A stir was perceptible there, and I was just in time to see its cause. A tall, angular gentleman was approaching from the direction of the musicians' gallery, and from the manner of all present, as well as from the whispered comment of my husband, I recognised in him the special official for whom all had been waiting.

"Are you going to tell him?" was my question to George as we made our way down to the lobby.

"That depends. First, I am going to see you settled in a room quite remote from this business."

"I shall not like that."

"I know, my dear, but it is best."

I could not gainsay this.

Nevertheless, after the first few minutes of relief, I found it very lonesome upstairs. The pictures which crowded upon me of the various groups of excited and wildly gesticulating men and women through which we had passed on our way up, mingled themselves with the solemn horror of the scene in the writing-room, with its fleeting vision of youth and beauty lying pulseless in sudden death. I could not escape the one without feeling the immediate impress of the other, and if by chance they both yielded for an instant to that earlier scene of a desolate street, with its solitary lamp shining down on the crouched figure of a man washing his shaking hands in a drift of freshly fallen snow, they immediately rushed back with a force and clearness all the greater for the momentary lapse.

I was still struggling with these fancies when the door opened, and George came in. There was news in his face as I rushed to meet him.

"Tell me—tell," I begged.

He tried to smile at my eagerness, but the attempt was ghastly.

"I've been listening and looking," said he, "and this is all I have learned. Miss Challoner died, not from a stroke or from disease of any kind, but from a wound reaching the heart. No one saw the attack, or even the approach or departure of the person inflicting this wound. If she was killed by a pistol-shot, it was at a distance, and almost over the heads of the persons sitting at the table we saw there. But the doctors shake their heads at the word pistol-shot, though they refuse to explain themselves or to express any opinion till the wound has been probed. This they are going to do at once, and when that question is decided, I may feel it my duty to speak and may ask you to support my story."

"I will tell what I saw," said I.

"Very good. That is all that will be required. We are strangers to the parties concerned, and only speak from a sense of justice. It may be that our story will make no impression, and that we shall be dismissed with but few thanks. But that is nothing to us. If the woman has been murdered, he is the murderer. With such a conviction in my mind, there can be no doubt as to my duty."

"We can never make them understand how he looked."

"No. I don't expect to."

"Or his manner as he fled."

"Nor that either."

"We can only describe what we saw him do."

"That's all."

"Oh, what an adventure for quiet people like us! George, I don't believe he shot her."

"He must have."

"But they would have seen—have heard—the people around, I mean."

"So they say; but I have a theory—but no matter about that now. I'm going down again to see how things have progressed. I'll be back for you later. Only be ready."

Be ready! I almost laughed,—a hysterical laugh, of course, when I recalled the injunction. Be ready! This lonely sitting by myself, with nothing to do but think was a fine preparation for a sudden appearance before those men—some of them police-officers, no doubt.

But that's enough about myself; I'm not the heroine of this story. In a half hour or an hour—I never knew which—George reappeared only to tell me that no conclusions had as yet been reached; an element of great mystery involved the whole affair, and the most astute detectives on the force had been sent for. Her father, who had been her constant companion all winter, had not the least suggestion to offer in way of its solution. So far as he knew—and he believed himself to have been in perfect accord with his daughter—she had injured no one. She had just lived the even, happy and useful life of a young woman of means, who sees duties beyond those of her own household and immediate surroundings. If, in the fulfillment of those duties, she had encountered any obstacle to content, he did not know it; nor could he mention a friend of hers—he would even say lovers, since that was what he meant—who to his knowledge could be accused of harbouring any such passion of revenge as was manifested in this secret and diabolical attack. They were all gentlemen and respected her as heartily as they appeared to admire her. To no living being, man or woman, could he point as possessing any motive for such a deed. She had been the victim of some mistake, his lovely and ever kindly disposed daughter, and while the loss was irreparable he would never make it unendurable by thinking otherwise.

Such was the father's way of looking at the matter, and I own that it made our duty a trifle hard. But George's mind, when once made up, was persistent to the point of obstinacy, and while he was yet talking he led me out of the room and down the hall to the elevator.

"Mr. Slater knows we have something to say, and will manage the interview before us in the very best manner," he confided to me now with an encouraging air. "We are to go to the blue reception room on the parlour floor."

I nodded, and nothing more was said till we entered the place mentioned. Here we came upon several gentlemen, standing about, of a more or less professional appearance. This was not very agreeable to one of my retiring disposition, but a look from George brought back my courage, and I found myself waiting rather anxiously for the questions I expected to hear put.

Mr. Slater was there according to his promise, and after introducing us, briefly stated that we had some evidence to give regarding the terrible occurrence which had just taken place in the house.

George bowed, and the chief spokesman—I am sure he was a police-officer of some kind—asked him to tell what it was.

George drew himself up—George is not one of your tall men, but he makes a very good appearance at times. Then he seemed suddenly to collapse. The sight of their expectation made him feel how flat and childish his story would sound. I, who had shared his adventure, understood his embarrassment, but the others were evidently at a loss to do so, for they glanced askance at each other as he hesitated, and only looked back when I ventured to say:

"It's the peculiarity of the occurrence which affects my husband. The thing we saw may mean nothing."

"Let us hear what it was and we will judge."

Then my husband spoke up, and related our little experience. If it did not create a sensation, it was because these men were well accustomed to surprises of all kinds.

"Washed his hands—a gentleman—out there in the snow—just after the alarm was raised here?" repeated one.

"And you saw him come out of this house?" another put in.

"Yes, sir; we noticed him particularly."

"Can you describe him?"

It was Mr. Slater who put this question; he had less control over himself, and considerable eagerness could be heard in his voice.

"He was a very fine-looking man; unusually tall and unusually striking both in his dress and appearance. What I could see of his face was bare of beard, and very expressive. He walked with the swing of an athlete, and only looked mean and small when he was stooping and dabbling in the snow."

"His clothes. Describe his clothes." There was an odd sound in Mr. Slater's voice.

"He wore a silk hat and there was fur on his overcoat. I think the fur was black."

Mr. Slater stepped back, then moved forward again with a determined air.

"I know the man," said he.

CHAPTER III

THE MAN

"You know the man?"

"I do; or rather, I know a man who answers to this description. He comes here once in a while. I do not know whether or not he was in the building to-night, but Clausen can tell you; no one escapes Clausen's eye."

"His name."

"Brotherson. A very uncommon person in many respects; quite capable of such an eccentricity, but incapable, I should say, of crime. He's a gifted talker and so well read that he can hold one's attention for hours. Of his tastes, I can only say that they appear to be mainly scientific. But he is not averse to society, and is always very well dressed."

"A taste for science and for fine clothing do not often go together."

"This man is an exception to all rules. The one I'm speaking of, I mean. I don't say that he's the fellow seen pottering in the snow."

"Call up Clausen."

The manager stepped to the telephone.

Meanwhile, George had advanced to speak to a man who had beckoned to him from the other side of the room, and with whom in another moment I saw him step out. Thus deserted, I sank into a chair near one of the windows. Never had I felt more uncomfortable. To attribute guilt to a totally unknown person—a person who is little more to you than a shadowy silhouette against a background of snow—is easy enough and not very disturbing to the conscience. But to hear that person named; given positive attributes; lifted from the indefinite into a living, breathing actuality, with a man's hopes, purposes and responsibilities, is an entirely different proposition. This Brotherson might be the most innocent person alive; and, if so, what had we done? Nothing to congratulate ourselves upon, certainly. And George was not present to comfort and encourage me. He was—

Where was he? The man who had carried him off was the youngest in the group. What had he wanted of George? Those who remained showed no interest in the matter. They had enough to say among themselves. But I was interested—naturally so, and, n my uneasiness, glanced restlessly from the window, the shade of which was up. The outlook was a very peaceful one. This room faced a side street, and, as my eyes fell upon the whitened pavements, I received an answer to one, and that the most anxious, of my queries. This was the street into which we had turned, in the wake of the handsome stranger they were trying at this very moment to identify with Brotherson. George had evidently been asked to point out the exact spot where the man had stopped, for I could see from my vantage point two figures bending near the kerb, and even pawing at the snow which lay there. It gave me a slight turn when one of them—I do not think it was George—began to rub his hands together in much the way the unknown gentleman had done, and, in my excitement, I probably uttered some sort of an ejaculation, for I was suddenly conscious of a silence in the room, and when I turned saw all the men about me looking my way.

I attempted to smile, but instead, shuddered painfully, as I raised my hand and pointed down at the street.

"They are imitating the man," I cried; "my husband and—and the person he went out with. It looked dreadful to me; that is all."

One of the gentlemen immediately said some kind words to me, and another smiled in a very encouraging way. But their attention was soon diverted, and so was mine by the entrance of a man in semi-uniform, who was immediately addressed as Clausen.

I knew his face. He was one of the doorkeepers; the oldest employee about the hotel, and the one best liked. I had often exchanged words with him myself.

Mr. Slater at once put his question:

"Has Mr. Brotherson passed your door at any time to-night?"

"Mr. Brotherson! I don't remember, really I don't," was the unexpected reply. "It's not often I forget. But so many people came rushing in during those few minutes, and all so excited—"

"Before the excitement, Clausen. A little while before, possibly just before."

"Oh, now I recall him! Yes, Mr. Brotherson went out of my door not many minutes before the cry upstairs. I forgot because I had stepped back from the door to hand a lady the muff she had dropped, and it was at that minute he went out. I just got a glimpse of his back as he passed into the street."

"But you are sure of that back?"

"I don't know another like it, when he wears that big coat of his. But Jim can tell you, sir. He was in the cafe up to that minute, and that's where Mr. Brotherson usually goes first."

"Very well; send up Jim. Tell him I have some orders to give him."

The old man bowed and went out.

Meanwhile, Mr. Slater had exchanged some words with the two officials, and now approached me with an expression of extreme consideration. They were about to excuse me from further participation in this informal inquiry. This I saw before he spoke. Of course they were right. But I should greatly have preferred to stay where I was till George came back.

However, I met him for an instant in the hall before I took the elevator, and later I heard in a round-about way what Jim and some others about the house had to say of Mr. Brotherson.

He was an habitue of the hotel, to the extent of dining once or twice a week in the cafe, and smoking, afterwards, in the public lobby. When he was in the mood for talk, he would draw an ever-enlarging group about him, but at other times he would be seen sitting quite alone and morosely indifferent to all who approached him. There was no mystery about his business. He was an inventor, with one or two valuable patents already on the market. But this was not his only interest. He was an all round sort of man, moody but brilliant in many ways—a character which at once attracted and repelled, odd in that he seemed to set little store by his good looks, yet was most careful to dress himself in a way to show them off to advantage. If he had means beyond the ordinary no one knew it, nor could any man say that he had not. On all personal matters he was very close-mouthed, though he would talk about other men's riches in a way to show that he cherished some very extreme views.

This was all which could be learned about him off-hand, and at so late an hour. I was greatly interested, of course, and had plenty to think of till I saw George again and learned the result of the latest investigations.

Miss Challoner had been shot, not stabbed. No other deduction was possible from such facts as were now known, though the physicians had not yet handed in their report, or even intimated what that report would be. No assailant could have approached or left her, without attracting the notice of some one, if not all of the persons seated at a table in the same room. She could only have been reached by a bullet sent from a point near the head of a small winding staircase connecting the mezzanine floor with a coat-room adjacent to the front door. This has already been insisted on, as you will remember, and if you will glance at the diagram which George hastily scrawled for me, you will see why.

A. B., as well as C. D., are half circular openings into the office lobby. E. F. are windows giving upon Broadway, and G. the party wall, necessarily unbroken by window, door or any other opening.

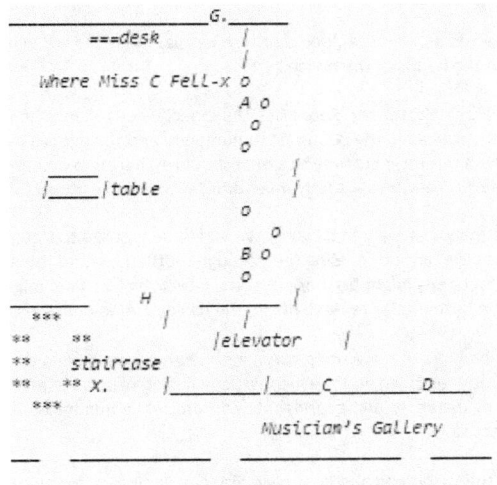

```
_____G._____
      ===desk         |
                      |
   Where Miss C Fell-x o
                    A o
                      o
                      o
                             |
   _____| table         |
   |_____|               o
                           o
                      B o
                         o
              H       |
   _____        |  _____   |
   ***        |       |
   **    **       | elevator   |
   **   staircase  |_____|_____C_____D____
   **   ** X.   |
   ***

              Musician's Gallery

   ___    _____    _____

        Dining Room Level with Lobby
```

It follows then that the only possible means of approach to this room lies through the archway H., or from the elevator door. But the elevator made no stop at the mezzanine on or near the time of the attack upon Miss Challoner; nor did any one leave the table or pass by it in either direction till after the alarm given by her fall.

But a bullet calls for no approach. A man at X. might raise and fire his pistol without attracting any attention to himself. The music, which all acknowledge was at its full climax at this moment, would drown the noise of the explosion, and the staircase, out of view of all but the victim, afford the same means of immediate escape, which it must have given of secret and unseen approach. The coat-room into which it descended communicated with the lobby very near the main entrance, and if Mr. Brotherson were the man, his sudden appearance there would thus be accounted for.

To be sure, this gentleman had not been noticed in the coatroom by the man then in charge, but if the latter had been engaged at that instant, as he often was, in hanging up or taking down a coat from the rack, a person might easily pass by him and disappear into the lobby without attracting his attention. So many people passed that way from the dining-room beyond, and so many of these were tall, fine-looking and well-dressed.

It began to look bad for this man, if indeed he were the one we had seen under the street-lamp; and, as George and I reviewed the situation, we felt our position to be serious enough for us severally to set down our impressions of this man before we lost our first vivid idea. I do not know what George wrote, for he sealed his words up as soon as he had finished writing, but this is what I put on paper while my memory was still fresh and my excitement unabated:

He had the look of a man of powerful intellect and determined will, who shudders while he triumphs; who outwardly washes his hands of a deed over which he inwardly gloats. This was when he first rose from the snow. Afterwards he had a moment of fear; plain, human, everyday fear. But this was evanescent. Before he had turned to go, he showed the self-possession of one who feels himself so secure, or is so well-satisfied with himself, that he is no longer conscious of other emotions.

"Poor fellow," I commented aloud, as I folded up these words; "he reckoned without you, George. By to-morrow he will be in the hands of the police."

"Poor fellow?" he repeated. "Better say 'Poor Miss Challoner!' They tell me she was one of those perfect women who reconcile even the pessimist to humanity and the age we live in. Why any one should want to kill her is a mystery; but why this man should—There! no one professes to explain it. They simply go by the facts. To-morrow surely must bring strange revelations."

And with this sentence ringing in my mind, I lay down and endeavoured to sleep. But it was not till very late that rest came. The noise of passing feet, though muffled beyond their wont, roused me in spite of myself. These footsteps might be those of some late arrival, or they might be those of some wary detective intent on business far removed from the usual routine of life in this great hotel.

I recalled the glimpse I had had of the writing-room in the early evening, and imagined it as it was with Miss Challoner's body removed and the incongruous flitting of strange and busy figures across its fatal floors, measuring distances and peering into corners, while hundreds slept above and about them in undisturbed repose.

Then I thought of him, the suspected and possibly guilty one. In visions over which I had little if any control, I saw him in all the restlessness of a slowly dying down excitement—the surroundings strange and unknown to me, the figure not—seeking for quiet; facing the past; facing the future; knowing, perhaps, for the first time in his life what it was for crime and remorse to murder sleep. I could not think of him as lying still—slumbering like the rest of mankind, in the hope and expectation of a busy morrow. Crime perpetrated looms so large in the soul, and this man had a soul as big as his body; of that I was assured. That its instincts were cruel and inherently evil, did not lessen its capacity for suffering. And he was suffering now; I could not doubt it, remembering the lovely face and fragrant memory of the noble woman he had, under some unknown impulse, sent to an unmerited doom.

At last I slept, but it was only to rouse again with the same quick realisation of my surroundings, which I had experienced on my recovery from my fainting fit of hours before. Someone had stopped at our door before hurrying by down the hall. Who was that someone? I rose on my elbow, and endeavoured to peer through the dark. Of course, I could see nothing. But when I woke a second time, there was enough light in the room, early as it undoubtedly was, for me to detect a letter lying on the carpet just inside the door.

Instantly I was on my feet. Catching the letter up, I carried it to the window. Our two names were on it—Mr. and Mrs. George Anderson: the writing, Mr. Slater's.

I glanced over at George. He was sleeping peacefully. It was too early to wake him, but I could not lay that letter down unread; was not my name on it? Tearing it open, devoured its contents,—the exclamation I made on reading it, waking George.

The writing was in Mr. Slater's hand, and the words were:

"I must request, at the instance of Coroner Heath and such of the police as listened to your adventure, that you make no further mention of what you saw in the street under our windows last night. The doctors find no bullet in the wound. This clears Mr. Brotherson."

CHAPTER IV

SWEET LITTLE MISS CLARKE

When we took our seats at the breakfast-table, it was with the feeling of being no longer looked upon as connected in any way with this case. Yet our interest in it was, if anything, increased, and when I saw George casting furtive glances at a certain table behind me, I leaned over and asked him the reason, being sure that the people whose faces I saw reflected in the mirror directly before us had something to do with the great matter then engrossing us. His answer conveyed the somewhat exciting information that the four persons seated in my rear were the same four who had been reading at the round table in the mezzanine at the time of Miss Challoner's death.

Instantly they absorbed all my attention, though I dared not give them a direct look, and continued to observe them only in the glass.

"Is it one family?" I asked.

"Yes, and a very respectable one. Transients, of course, but very well known in Denver. The lady is not the mother of the boys, but their aunt. The boys belong to the gentleman, who is a widower."

"Their word ought to be good."

George nodded.

"The boys look wide-awake enough if the father does not. As for the aunt, she is sweetness itself. Do they still insist that Miss Challoner was the only person in the room with them at this time?"

"They did last night. I don't know how they will meet this statement of the doctor's."

"George?"

He leaned nearer.

"Have you ever thought that she might have been a suicide? That she stabbed herself?"

"No, for in that case a weapon would have been found."

"And are you sure that none was?"

"Positive. Such a fact could not have been kept quiet. If a weapon had been picked up there would be no mystery, and no necessity for further police investigation."

"And the detectives are still here?"

"I just saw one."

"George?"

Again his head came nearer.

"Have they searched the lobby? I believe she had a weapon."

"Laura!"

"I know it sounds foolish, but the alternative is so improbable. A family like that cannot be leagued together in a conspiracy to hide the truth concerning a matter so serious. To be sure, they may all be short-sighted, or so little given to observation that they didn't see what passed before their eyes. The boys look wide-awake enough, but who can tell? I would sooner believe that—"

I stopped short so suddenly that George looked startled. My attention had been caught by something new I saw in the mirror upon which my attention was fixed. A man was looking in from the corridor behind, at the four persons we were just discussing. He was watching them intently, and I thought I knew his face.

"What kind of a looking person was the man who took you outside last night?" I inquired of George, with my eyes still on this furtive watcher.

"A fellow to make you laugh. A perfect character, Laura; hideously homely but agreeable enough. I took quite a fancy to him. Why?"

"I am looking at him now."

"Very likely. He's deep in this affair. Just an everyday detective, but ambitious, I suppose, and quite alive to the importance of being thorough."

"He is watching those people. No, he isn't. How quickly he disappeared!"

"Yes, he's mercurial in all his movements. Laura, we must get out of this. There happens to be something else in the world for me to do than to sit around and follow up murder clews."

But we began to doubt if others agreed with him, when on passing out we were stopped in the lobby by this same detective, who had something to say to George, and drew him quickly aside.

"What does he want?" I asked, as soon as George had returned to my side.

"He wants me to stand ready to obey any summons the police may send me."

"Then they still suspect Brotherson?"

"They must."

My head rose a trifle as I glanced up at George.

"Then we are not altogether out of it?" I emphasised, complacently.

He smiled which hardly seemed apropos. Why does George sometimes smile when I am in my most serious moods.

As we stepped out of the hotel, George gave my arm a quiet pinch which served to direct my attention to an elderly gentleman who, was just alighting from a taxicab at the kerb. He moved heavily and with some appearance of pain, but from the crowd collected on the sidewalk many of whom nudged each other as he passed, he was evidently a person of some importance, and as he disappeared within the hotel entrance, I asked George who this kind-faced, bright-eyed old gentleman could be.

He appeared to know, for he told me at once that he was Detective Gryce; a man who had grown old in solving just such baffling problems as these.

"He gave up work some time ago, I have been told," my husband went on; "but evidently a great case still has its allurement for him. The trail here must be a very blind one for them to call him in. I wish we had not left so soon. It would have been quite an experience to see him at work."

"I doubt if you would have been given the opportunity. I noticed that we were slightly de trop towards the last."

"I wouldn't have minded that; not on my own account, that is. It might not have been pleasant for you. However, the office is waiting. Come, let me put you on the car."

That night I bided his coming with an impatience I could not control. He was late, of course, but when he did appear, I almost forgot our usual greeting in my hurry to ask him if he had seen the evening papers.

"No," he grumbled, as he hung up his overcoat. "Been pushed about all day. No time for anything."

"Then let me tell you—"

But he would have dinner first.

However, a little later we had a comfortable chat. Mr. Gryce had made a discovery, and the papers were full of it. It was one which gave me a small triumph over George. The suggestion he had laughed at was not so entirely foolish as he had been pleased to consider it. But let me tell the story of that day, without any further reference to myself.

The opinion had become quite general with those best acquainted with the details of this affair, that the mystery was one of those abnormal ones for which no solution would ever be found, when the aged detective showed himself in the building and was taken to the room, where an Inspector of Police awaited him. Their greeting was cordial, and the lines on the latter's face relaxed a little as he met the still bright eye of the man upon whose instinct and judgment so much reliance had always been placed.

"This is very good of you," he began, glancing down at the aged detective's bundled up legs, and gently pushing a chair towards him. "I know that it was a great deal to ask, but we're at our wits' end, and so I telephoned. It's the most inexplicable—There! you have heard that phrase before. But clews—there are absolutely none. That is, we have not been able to find any. Perhaps you can. At least, that is what we hope. I've known you more than once to succeed where others have failed."

The elderly man thus addressed, glanced down at his legs, now propped up on a stool which someone had brought him, and smiled, with the pathos of the old who sees the interests of a lifetime slipping gradually away.

"I am not what I was. I can no longer get down on my hands and knees to pick up threads from the nap of a rug, or spy out a spot of blood in the crimson woof of a carpet."

"You shall have Sweetwater here to do the active work for you. What we want of you is the directing mind—the infallible instinct. It's a case in a thousand, Gryce. We've never had anything just like it. You've never had anything at all like it. It will make you young again."

The old man's eyes shot fire and unconsciously one foot slipped to the floor. Then he bethought himself and painfully lifted it back again.

"What are the points? What's the difficulty?" he asked. "A woman has been shot—"

"No, not shot, stabbed. We thought she had been shot, for that was intelligible and involved no impossibilities. But Drs. Heath and Webster, under the eye of the Challoners' own physician, have made an examination of the wound—an official one, thorough and quite final so far as they are concerned, and they declare that no bullet is to be found in the body. As the wound extends no further than the heart, this settles one great point, at least."

"Dr. Heath is a reliable man and one of our ablest coroners."

"Yes. There can be no question as to the truth of his report. You know the victim? Her name, I mean, and the character she bore?"

"Yes; so much was told me on my way down."

"A fine girl unspoiled by riches and seeming independence. Happy, too, to all appearance, or we should be more ready to consider the possibility of suicide."

"Suicide by stabbing calls for a weapon. Yet none has been found, I hear."

"None."

"Yet she was killed that way?"

"Undoubtedly, and by a long and very narrow blade, larger than a needle but not so large as the ordinary stiletto."

"Stabbed while by herself, or what you may call by herself? She had no companion near her?"

"None, if we can believe the four members of the Parrish family who were seated at the other end of the room."

"And you do believe them?"

"Would a whole family lie—and needlessly? They never knew the woman—father, maiden aunt and two boys, clear-eyed, jolly young chaps whom even the horror of this tragedy, perpetrated as it were under their very nose, cannot make serious for more than a passing moment."

"It wouldn't seem so."

"Yet they swear up and down that nobody crossed the room towards Miss Challoner."

"So they tell me."

"She fell just a few feet from the desk where she had been writing. No word, no cry, just a collapse and sudden fall. In olden days they would have said, struck by a bolt from heaven. But it was a bolt which drew blood; not much blood, I hear, but sufficient to end life almost instantly. She never looked up or spoke again. What do you make of it, Gryce?"

"It's a tough one, and I'm not ready to venture an opinion yet. I should like to see the desk you speak of, and the spot where she fell."

A young fellow who had been hovering in the background at once stepped forward. He was the plain-faced detective who had spoken to George.

"Will you take my arm, sir?"

Mr. Gryce's whole face brightened. This Sweetwater, as they called him, was, I have since understood, one of his proteges and more or less of a favourite.

"Have you had a chance at this thing?" he asked. "Been over the ground—studied the affair carefully?"

"Yes, sir; they were good enough to allow it."

"Very well, then, you're in a position to pioneer me. You've seen it all and won't be in a hurry."

"No; I'm at the end of my rope. I haven't an idea, sir."

"Well, well, that's honest at all events." Then, as he slowly rose with the other's careful assistance, "There's no crime without its clew. The thing is to recognise that clew when seen. But I'm in no position, to make promises. Old days don't return for the asking."

Nevertheless, he looked ten years younger than when he came in, or so thought those who knew him.

The mezzanine was guarded from all visitors save such as had official sanction. Consequently, the two remained quite uninterrupted while they moved about the place in quiet consultation. Others had preceded them; had examined the plain little desk and found nothing; had paced off the distances; had looked with longing and inquiring eyes at the elevator cage and the open archway leading to the little staircase and the musicians' gallery. But this was nothing to the old detective. The locale was what he wanted, and he got it. Whether he got anything else it would be impossible to say from his manner as he finally sank into a chair by one of the openings, and looked down on the lobby below. It was full of people coming and going on all sorts of business, and presently he drew back, and, leaning on Sweetwater's arm, asked him a few questions.

"Who were the first to rush in here after the Parrishes gave the alarm?"

"One or two of the musicians from the end of the hall. They had just finished their programme and were preparing to leave the gallery. Naturally they reached her first."

"Good! their names?"

"Mark Sowerby and Claus Hennerberg. Honest Germans—men who have played here for years."

"And who followed them? Who came next on the scene?"

"Some people from the lobby. They heard the disturbance and rushed up pell-mell. But not one of these touched her. Later her father came."

"Who did touch her? Anybody, before the father came in?"

"Yes; Miss Clarke, the middle-aged lady with the Parrishes. She had run towards Miss Challoner as soon as she heard her fall, and was sitting there with the dead girl's head in her lap when the musicians showed themselves."

"I suppose she has been carefully questioned?"

"Very, I should say."

"And she speaks of no weapon?"

"No. Neither she nor any one else at that moment suspected murder or even a violent death. All thought it a natural one—sudden, but the result of some secret disease."

"Father and all?"

"Yes."

"But the blood? Surely there must have been some show of blood?"

"They say not. No one noticed any. Not till the doctor came—her doctor who was happily in his office in this very building. He saw the drops, and uttered the first suggestion of murder."

"How long after was this? Is there any one who has ventured to make an estimate of the number of minutes which elapsed from the time she fell, to the moment when the doctor first raised the cry of murder?"

"Yes. Mr. Slater, the assistant manager, who was in the lobby at the time, says that ten minutes at least must have elapsed."

"Ten minutes and no blood! The weapon must still have been there. Some weapon with a short and inconspicuous handle. I think they said there were flowers over and around the place where it struck?"

"Yes, great big scarlet ones. Nobody noticed—nobody looked. A panic like that seems to paralyse people."

"Ten minutes! I must see every one who approached her during those ten minutes. Every one, Sweetwater, and I must myself talk with Miss Clarke."

"You will like her. You will believe every word she says."

"No doubt. All the more reason why I must see her. Sweetwater, someone drew that weapon out. Effects still have their causes, notwithstanding the new cult. The question is who? We must leave no stone unturned to find that out."

"The stones have all been turned over once."

"By you?"

"Not altogether by me."

"Then they will bear being turned over again. I want to be witness of the operation."

"Where will you see Miss Clarke?"

"Wherever she pleases—only I can't walk far."

"I think I know the place. You shall have the use of this elevator. It has not been running since last night or it would be full of curious people all the time, hustling to get a glimpse of this place. But they'll put a man on for you."

"Very good; manage it as you will. I'll wait here till you're ready. Explain yourself to the lady. Tell her I'm an old and rheumatic invalid who has been used to asking his own questions. I'll not trouble her much. But there is one point she must make clear to me."

Sweetwater did not presume to ask what point, but he hoped to be fully enlightened when the time came.

And he was. Mr. Gryce had undertaken to educate him for this work, and never missed the opportunity of giving him a lesson. The three met in a private sitting-room on an upper floor, the detectives entering first and the lady coming in soon after. As her quiet figure appeared in the doorway, Sweetwater stole a glance at Mr. Gryce. He was not looking her way, of course; he never looked directly at anybody; but he formed his impressions for all that, and Sweetwater was anxious to make sure of these impressions. There was no doubting them in this instance. Miss Clarke was not a woman to rouse an unfavourable opinion in any man's mind. Of slight, almost frail build, she had that peculiar animation which goes with a speaking eye and a widely sympathetic nature. Without any substantial claims to beauty, her expression was so womanly and so sweet that she was invariably called lovely.

Mr. Gryce was engaged at the moment in shifting his cane from the right hand to the left, but his manner was never more encouraging or his smile more benevolent.

"Pardon me," he apologised, with one of his old-fashioned bows, "I'm sorry to trouble you after all the distress you must have been under this morning. But there is something I wish especially to ask you in regard to the dreadful occurrence in which you played so kind a part. You were the first to reach the prostrate woman, I believe."

"Yes. The boys jumped up and ran towards her, but they were frightened by her looks and left it for me to put my hands under her and try to lift her up."

"Did you manage it?"

"I succeeded in getting her head into my lap, nothing more."

"And sat so?"

"For some little time. That is, it seemed long, though I believe it was not more than a minute before two men came running from the musicians' gallery. One thinks so fast at such a time—and feels so much."

"You knew she was dead, then?"

"I felt her to be so."

"How felt?"

"I was sure—I never questioned it."

"You have seen women in a faint?"

"Yes, many times."

"What made the difference? Why should you believe Miss Challoner dead simply because she lay still and apparently lifeless?"

"I cannot tell you. Possibly, death tells its own story. I only know how I felt."

"Perhaps there was another reason? Perhaps, that, consciously or unconsciously, you laid your palm upon her heart?"

Miss Clarke started, and her sweet face showed a moment's perplexity.

"Did I?" she queried, musingly. Then with a sudden access of feeling, "I may have done so, indeed, I believe I did. My arms were around her; it would not have been an unnatural action."

"No; a very natural one, I should say. Cannot you tell me positively whether you did this or not?"

"Yes, I did. I had forgotten it, but I remember now." And the glance she cast him while not meeting his eye showed that she understood the importance of the admission. "I know," she said, "what you are going to ask me now. Did I feel anything there but the flowers and the tulle? No, Mr. Gryce, I did not. There was no poniard in the wound."

Mr. Gryce felt around, found a chair and sank into it.

"You are a truthful woman," said he. "And," he added more slowly, "composed enough in character I should judge not to have made any mistake on this very vital point."

"I think so, Mr. Gryce. I was in a state of excitement, of course; but the woman was a stranger to me, and my feelings were not unduly agitated."

"Sweetwater, we can let my suggestion go in regard to those ten minutes I spoke of. The time is narrowed down to one, and in that one, Miss Clarke was the only person to touch her."

"The only one," echoed the lady, catching perhaps the slight rising sound of query in his voice.

"I will trouble you no further." So said the old detective, thoughtfully. "Sweetwater, help me out of this." His eye was dull and his manner betrayed exhaustion. But vigour returned to him before he had well reached the door, and he showed some of his old spirit as he thanked Miss Clarke and turned to take the elevator.

"But one possibility remains," he confided to Sweetwater, as they stood waiting at the elevator door. "Miss Challoner died from a stab. The next minute she was in this lady s arms. No weapon protruded from the wound, nor was any found on or near her in the mezzanine. What follows? She struck the blow herself, and the strength of purpose which led her to do this, gave her the additional force to pull the weapon out and fling it from her. It did not fall upon the floor around her; therefore, it flew through one of those openings into the lobby, and there it either will be, or has been found."

It was this statement, otherwise worded, which gave me my triumph over George.

CHAPTER V

THE RED CLOAK

"What results? Speak up, Sweetwater."

"None. Every man, woman and boy connected with the hotel has been questioned; many of them routed out of their beds for the purpose, but not one of them picked up anything from the floor of the lobby, or knows of any one who did."

"There now remain the guests."

"And after them—(pardon me, Mr. Gryce) the general public which rushed in rather promiscuously last night."

"I know it; it's a task, but it must be carried through. Put up bulletins, publish your wants in the papers;—do anything, only gain your end."

A bulletin was put up.

Some hours later, Sweetwater re-entered the room, and, approaching Mr. Gryce with a smile, blurted out:

"The bulletin is a great go. I think—of course, I cannot be sure—that it's going to do the business. I've watched every one who stopped to read it. Many showed interest and many, emotion; she seems to have had a troop of friends. But embarrassment! only one showed that. I thought you would like to know."

"Embarrassment? Humph! a man?"

"No, a woman; a lady, sir; one of the transients. I found out in a jiffy all they could tell me about her."

"A woman! We didn't expect that. Where is she? Still in the lobby?"

"No, sir. She took the elevator while I was talking with the clerk."

"There's nothing in it. You mistook her expression."

"I don't think so. I had noticed her when she first came into the lobby. She was talking to her daughter who was with her, and looked natural and happy. But no sooner had she seen and read that bulletin, than the blood shot up into her face and her manner became furtive and hasty. There was no mistaking the difference, sir. Almost before I could point her out, she had seized her daughter by the arm and hurried her towards the elevator. I wanted to follow her, but you may prefer to make your own inquiries. Her room is on the seventh floor, number 712, and her name is Watkins. Mrs. Horace Watkins of Nashville."

Mr. Gryce nodded thoughtfully, but made no immediate effort to rise.

"Is that all you know about her?" he asked.

"Yes; this is the first time she has stopped at this hotel. She came yesterday. Took a room indefinitely. Seems all right; but she did blush, sir. I ever saw its beat in a young girl."

"Call the desk. Say that I'm to be told if Mrs. Watkins of Nashville rings up during the next ten minutes. We'll give her that long to take some action. If she fails to make any move, I'll make my own approaches."

Sweetwater did as he was bid, then went back to his place in the lobby.

But he returned almost instantly.

"Mrs. Watkins has just telephoned down that she is going to—to leave, sir."

"To leave?"

The old man struggled to his feet. "No. 712, do you say? Seven stories," he sighed. But as he turned with a hobble, he stopped. "There are difficulties in the way of this interview," he remarked. "A blush is not much to go upon. I'm afraid we shall have to resort to the shadow business and that is your work, not mine."

But here the door opened and a boy brought in a line which had been left at the desk. It related to the very matter then engaging them, and ran thus:

"I see that information is desired as to whether any person was seen to stoop to the lobby floor last night at or shortly after the critical moment of Miss Challoner's fall in the half story above. I can give such information. I was in the lobby at the time, and in the height of the confusion following this alarming incident, I remember seeing a lady,—one of the new arrivals (there were several coming in at the time)—stoop quickly down and pick up something from the floor. I thought nothing of it at the time, and so paid little attention to her appearance. I can only recall the suddenness with which she stooped and the colour of the cloak she wore. It was red, and the whole garment was voluminous. If you wish further particulars, though in truth, I have no more to give, you can find me in 356.

"HENRY A. MCELROY."

"Humph! This should simplify our task," was Mr. Gryce's comment, as he handed the note over to Sweetwater. "You can easily find out if the lady, now on the point of departure, can be identified with the one described by Mr. McElroy. If she can, I am ready to meet her anywhere."

"Here goes then!" cried Sweetwater, and quickly left the room.

When he returned, it was not with his most hopeful air.

"The cloak doesn't help," he declared. "No one remembers the cloak. But the time of Mrs. Watkins' arrival was all right. She came in directly on the heels of this catastrophe."

"She did! Sweetwater, I will see her. Manage it for me at once."

"The clerk says that it had better be upstairs. She is a very sensitive woman. There might be a scene, if she were intercepted on her way out."

"Very well." But the look which the old detective threw at his bandaged legs was not without its pathos.

And so it happened that just as Mrs. Watkins was watching the wheeling out of her trunks, there appeared in the doorway before her, an elderly gentleman, whose expression, always benevolent, save at moments when benevolence would be quite out of keeping with the situation, had for some reason, so marked an effect upon her, that she coloured under his eye, and, indeed, showed such embarrassment, that all doubt of the propriety of his intrusion vanished from the old man's mind, and with the ease of one only too well accustomed to such scenes, he kindly remarked:

"Am I speaking to Mrs. Watkins of Nashville?"

"You are," she faltered, with another rapid change of colour. "I—I am just leaving. I hope you will excuse me. I—"

"I wish I could," he smiled, hobbling in and confronting her quietly in her own room. "But circumstances make it quite imperative that I should have a few words with you on a topic which need not be disagreeable to you, and probably will not be. My name is Gryce. This will probably convey nothing to you, but I am not unknown to the management below, and my years must certainly give you confidence in the propriety of my errand. A beautiful and charming young woman died here last night. May I ask if you knew her?"

"I?" She was trembling violently now, but whether with indignation or some other more subtle emotion, it would be difficult to say. "No, I'm from the South. I never saw the young lady. Why do you ask? I do not recognise your right. I—I—"

Certainly her emotion must be that of simple indignation. Mr. Gryce made one of his low bows, and propping himself against the table he stood before, remarked civilly:—

"I had rather not force my rights. The matter is so very ordinary. I did not suppose you knew Miss Challoner, but one must begin somehow, and as you came in at the very moment when the alarm was raised in the lobby, I thought perhaps you could tell me something which would aid me in my effort to elicit the real facts of the case. You were crossing the lobby at the time—"

"Yes." She raised her head. "So were a dozen others—"

"Madam,"—the interruption was made in his kindliest tones, but in a way which nevertheless suggested authority. "Something was picked up from the floor at that moment. If the dozen you mention were witnesses to this act we do not know it. But we do know that it did not pass unobserved by you. Am I not correct? Didn't you see a certain person—I will mention no names—stoop and pick up something from the lobby floor?"

"No." The word came out with startling violence. "I was conscious of nothing but the confusion." She was facing him with determination and her eyes were fixed boldly on his face. But her lips quivered, and her cheeks were white, too white now for simple indignation.

"Then I have made a big mistake," apologised the ever-courteous detective. "Will you pardon me? It would have settled a very serious question if it could be found that the object thus picked up was the weapon which killed Miss Challoner. That is my excuse for the trouble I have given you."

He was not looking at her; he was looking at her hand which rested on the table before which he himself stood. Did the fingers tighten a little and dig into the palm they concealed? He thought so, and was very slow in turning limpingly about towards the door. Meanwhile, would she speak? No. The silence was so marked, he felt it an excuse for stealing another glance in her direction. She was not looking his way but at a door in the partition wall on her right; and the look was one very akin to anxious fear. The next moment he understood it. The door burst open, and a young girl bounded into the room, with the merry cry:

"All ready, mother. I'm glad we are going to the Clarendon. I hate hotels where people die almost before your eyes."

What the mother said at this outburst is immaterial. What the detective did is not. Keeping on his way, he reached the door, but not to open it wider; rather to close it softly but with unmistakable decision. The cloak which enveloped the girl was red, and full enough to be called voluminous.

"Who is this?" demanded the girl, her indignant glances flashing from one to the other.

"I don't know," faltered the mother in very evident distress. "He says he has a right to ask us questions and he has been asking questions about—about—"

"Not about me," laughed the girl, with a toss of her head Mr. Gryce would have corrected in one of his grandchildren. "He can have nothing to say about me." And she began to move about the room in an aimless, half-insolent way.

Mr. Gryce stared hard at the few remaining belongings of the two women, lying in a heap on the table, and half musingly, half deprecatingly, remarked:

"The person who stooped wore a long red cloak. Probably you preceded your daughter, Mrs. Watkins."

The lady thus brought to the point made a quick gesture towards the girl who suddenly stood still, and, with a rising colour in her cheeks, answered, with some show of resolution on her own part:

"You say your name is Gryce and that you have a right to address me thus pointedly on a subject which you evidently regard as serious. That is not exact enough for me. Who are you, sir? What is your business?"

"I think you have guessed it. I am a detective from Headquarters. What I want of you I have already stated. Perhaps this young lady can tell me what you cannot. I shall be pleased if this is so."

"Caroline"—Then the mother broke down. "Show the gentleman what you picked up from the lobby floor last night."

The girl laughed again, loudly and with evident bravado, before she threw the cloak back and showed what she had evidently been holding in her hand from the first, a sharp-pointed, gold-handled paper-cutter.

"It was lying there and I picked it up. I don't see any harm in that."

"You probably meant none. You couldn't have known the part it had just played in this tragic drama," said the old detective looking carefully at the cutter which he had taken in his hand, but not so carefully that he failed to note that the look of distress was not lifted from the mother's face either by her daughter's words or manner.

"You have washed this?" he asked.

"No. Why should I wash it? It was clean enough. I was just going down to give it in at the desk. I wasn't going to carry it away." And she turned aside to the window and began to hum, as though done with the whole matter.

The old detective rubbed his chin, glanced again at the paper-cutter, then at the girl in the window, and lastly at the mother, who had lifted her head again and was facing him bravely.

"It is very important," he observed to the latter, "that your daughter should be correct in her statement as to the condition of this article when she picked it up. Are you sure she did not wash it?"

"I don't think she did. But I'm sure she will tell you the truth about that. Caroline, this is a police matter. Any mistake about it may involve us in a world of trouble and keep you from getting back home in time for your coming-out party. Did you—did you wash this cutter when you got upstairs, or—or—" she added, with a propitiatory glance at Mr. Gryce—"wipe it off at any time between then and now? Don't answer hastily. Be sure. No one can blame you for that act. Any girl, as thoughtless as you, might do that."

"Mother, how can I tell what I did?" flashed out the girl, wheeling round on her heel till she faced them both. "I don't remember doing a thing to it. I just brought it up. A thing found like that belongs to the finder. You needn't hold it out towards me like that. I don't want it now; I'm sick of it. Such a lot of talk about a paltry thing which couldn't have cost ten dollars." And she wheeled back.

"It isn't the value." Mr. Gryce could be very patient. "It's the fact that we believe it to have been answerable for Miss Challoner's death—that is, if there was any blood on it when you picked it up."

"Blood!" The girl was facing them again, astonishment struggling with disgust on her plain but mobile features. "Blood! is that what you mean. No wonder I hate it. Take it away," she cried.

"Oh, mother, I'll never pick up anything again which doesn't belong to me! Blood!" she repeated in horror, flinging herself into her mother's arms.

Mr. Gryce thought he understood the situation. Here was a little kleptomaniac whose weakness the mother was struggling to hide. Light was pouring in. He felt his body's weight less on that miserable foot of his.

"Does that frighten you? Are you so affected by the thought of blood?"

"Don't ask me. And I put the thing under my pillow! I thought it was so—so pretty."

"Mrs. Watkins," Mr. Gryce from that moment ignored the daughter, "did you see it there?"

"Yes; but I didn't know where it came from. I had not seen my daughter stoop. I didn't know where she got it till I read that bulletin."

"Never mind that. The question agitating me is whether any stain was left under that pillow. We want to be sure of the connection between this possible weapon and the death by stabbing which we all deplore—if there is a connection."

"I didn't see any stain, but you can look for yourself. The bed has been made up, but there was no change of linen. We expected to remain here; I see no good to be gained by hiding any of the facts now."

"None whatever, Madam."

"Come, then. Caroline, sit down and stop crying. Mr. Gryce believes that your only fault was in not taking this object at once to the desk."

"Yes, that's all," acquiesced the detective after a short study of the shaking figure and distorted features of the girl. "You had no idea, I'm sure, where this weapon came from, or for what it had been used. That's evident."

Her shudder, as she seated herself, was very convincing. She was too young to simulate so successfully emotions of this character.

"I'm glad of that," she responded, half fretfully, half gratefully, as Mr. Gryce followed her mother into the adjoining room. "I've had a bad enough time of it without being blamed for what I didn't know and didn't do."

Mr. Gryce laid little stress upon these words, but much upon the lack of curiosity she showed in the minute and careful examination he now made of her room. There was no stain on the pillow-cover and none on the bureau-spread where she might very naturally have laid the cutter down on first coming into her room. The blade was so polished that it must have been rubbed off somewhere, either purposely or by accident. Where then, since not here? He asked to see her gloves—the ones she had worn the previous night.

"They are the same she is wearing now," the anxious mother assured him. "Wait, and I will get them for you."

"No need. Let her hold out her hands in token of amity. I shall soon see."

They returned to where the girl still sat, wrapped in her cloak, sobbing still, but not so violently.

"Caroline, you may take off your things," said the mother, drawing the pins from her own hat. "We shall not go to-day."

The child shot her mother one disappointed look, then proceeded to follow suit. When her hat was off, she began to take off her gloves. As soon as they were on the table, the mother pushed them over to Mr. Gryce. As he looked at them, the girl lifted off her cloak.

"Will—will he tell?" she whispered behind its ample folds into her mother's ear.

The answer came quickly, but not in the mother's tones. Mr. Gryce's ears had lost none of their ancient acuteness.

"I do not see that I should gain much by doing so. The one discovery which would link this find of yours indissolubly with Miss Challoner's death, I have failed to make. If I am equally unsuccessful below—if I can establish no closer connection there than here between this cutter and the weapon which killed Miss Challoner, I shall have no cause to mention the matter. It will be too extraneous to the case. Do you remember the exact spot where you stooped, Miss Watkins?"

"No, no. Somewhere near those big chairs; I didn't have to step out of my way; I really didn't."

Mr. Gryce's answering smile was a study. It seemed to convey a two-fold message, one for the mother and one for the child, and both were comforting. But he went away, disappointed. The clew which promised so much was, to all appearance, a false one

He could soon tell.

CHAPTER VI

INTEGRITY

Mr. Gryce's fears were only too well founded. Though Mr. McElroy was kind enough to point out the exact spot where he saw Miss Watkins stoop, no trace of blood was found upon the rug which had lain there, nor had anything of the kind been washed up by the very careful man who scrubbed the lobby floor in the early morning. This was disappointing, as its presence would have settled the whole question. When, these efforts all exhausted, the two detectives faced each other again in the small room given up to their use, Mr. Gryce showed his discouragement. To be certain of a fact you cannot prove has not the same alluring quality for the old that it has for the young. Sweetwater watched him in some concern, then with the persistence which was one of his strong points, ventured finally to remark:

"I have but one idea left on the subject."

"And what is that?" Old as he was, Mr. Gryce was alert in a moment.

"The girl wore a red cloak. If I mistake not, the lining was also red. A spot on it might not show to the casual observer. Yet it would mean much to us."

"Sweetwater!"

A faint blush rose to the old man's cheek.

"Shall I request the privilege of looking that garment over?"

"Yes."

The young fellow ducked and left the room. When he returned, it was with a downcast air.

"Nothing doing," said he.

And then there was silence.

"We only need to find out now that this cutter was not even Miss Challoner's property," remarked Mr. Gryce, at last, with a gesture towards the object named, lying openly on the table before him.

"That should be easy. Shall I take it to their rooms and show it to her maid?"

"If you can do so without disturbing the old gentleman."

But here they were themselves disturbed. A knock at the door was followed by the immediate entrance of the very person just mentioned. Mr. Challoner had come in search of the inspector, and showed some surprise to find his place occupied by an unknown old man.

But Mr. Gryce, who discerned tidings in the bereaved father's face, was all alacrity in an instant. Greeting his visitor with a smile which few could see without trusting the man, he explained the inspector's absence and introduced himself in his own capacity.

Mr. Challoner had heard of him. Nevertheless, he did not seem inclined to speak.

Mr. Gryce motioned Sweetwater from the room. With a woeful look the young detective withdrew, his last glance cast at the cutter still lying in full view on the table.

Mr. Gryce, not unmindful himself of this object, took it up, then laid it down again, with an air of seeming abstraction.

The father's attention was caught.

"What is that?" he cried, advancing a step and bestowing more than an ordinary glance at the object thus brought casually, as it were, to his notice. "I surely recognise this cutter. Does it belong here or—"

Mr. Gryce, observing the other's emotion, motioned him to a chair. As his visitor sank into it, he remarked, with all the consideration exacted by the situation:

"It is unknown property, Mr. Challoner. But we have some reason to think it belonged to your daughter. Are we correct in this surmise?"

"I have seen it, or one like it, often in her hand." Here his eyes suddenly dilated and the hand stretched forth to grasp it quickly drew back. "Where—where was it found?" he hoarsely demanded. "O God! am I to be crushed to the very earth by sorrow!"

Mr. Gryce hastened to give him such relief as was consistent with the truth.

"It was picked up—last night—from the lobby floor. There is seemingly nothing to connect it with her death. Yet—"

The pause was eloquent. Mr. Challoner gave the detective an agonised look and turned white to the lips. Then gradually, as the silence continued, his head fell forward, and he muttered almost unintelligibly:

"I honestly believe her the victim of some heartless stranger. I do now; but—but I cannot mislead the police. At any cost I must retract a statement I made under false impressions and with no desire to deceive. I said that I knew all of the gentlemen who admired her and aspired to her hand, and that they were all reputable men and above committing a crime of this or any other kind. But it seems that I did not know her secret heart as thoroughly as I had supposed. Among her effects I have just come upon a batch of letters—love letters I am forced to acknowledge—signed by initials totally strange to me. The letters are manly in tone—most of them—but one—"

"What about the one?"

"Shows that the writer was displeased. It may mean nothing, but I could not let the matter go without setting myself right with the authorities. If it might be allowed to rest here—if those letters can remain sacred, it would save me the additional pang of seeing her inmost concerns—the secret and holiest recesses of a woman's heart, laid open to the public. For, from the tenor of most of these letters, she—she was not averse to the writer."

Mr. Gryce moved a little restlessly in his chair and stared hard at the cutter so conveniently placed under his eye. Then his manner softened and he remarked:

"We will do what we can. But you must understand that the matter is not a simple one. That, in fact, it contains mysteries which demand police investigation. We do not dare to trifle with any of the facts. The inspector, and, if not he, the coroner, will have to be told about these letters and will probably ask to see them."

"They are the letters of a gentleman."

"With the one exception."

"Yes, that is understood." Then in a sudden heat and with an almost sublime trust in his daughter notwithstanding the duplicity he had just discovered:

"Nothing—not the story told by these letters, or the sight of that sturdy paper-cutter with its long and very slender blade, will make me believe that she willingly took her own life. You do not know, cannot know, the rare delicacy of her nature. She was a lady through and through. If she had meditated death—if the breach suggested by the one letter I have mentioned, should have so preyed upon her spirits as to lead her to break her old father's heart and outrage the feelings of all who knew her, she could not, being the woman she was, choose a public place for such an act—an hotel writing-room—in face of a lobby full of hurrying men. It was out of nature. Every one who knows her will tell you so. The deed was an accident—incredible—but still an accident."

Mr. Gryce had respect for this outburst. Making no attempt to answer it, he suggested, with some hesitation, that Miss Challoner had been seen writing a letter previous to taking those fatal steps from the desk which ended so tragically. Was this letter to one of her lady friends, as reported, and was it as far from suggesting the awful tragedy which followed, as he had been told?

"It was a cheerful letter. Such a one as she often wrote to her little protegees here and there. I judge that this was written to some girl like that, for the person addressed was not known to her maid, any more than she was to me. It expressed an affectionate interest, and it breathed encouragement— encouragement! and she meditating her own death at the moment! Impossible! That letter should exonerate her if nothing else does."

Mr. Gryce recalled the incongruities, the inconsistencies and even the surprising contradictions which had often marked the conduct of men and women, in his lengthy experience with the strange, the sudden, and the tragic things of life, and slightly shook his head. He pitied Mr. Challoner, and admired even more his courage in face of the appalling grief which had overwhelmed him, but he dared not encourage a false hope. The girl had killed herself and with this weapon. They might not be able to prove it absolutely, but it was nevertheless true, and this broken old man would some day be obliged to acknowledge it. But the detective said nothing of this, and was very patient with the further arguments the other advanced to prove his point and the lofty character of the girl to whom, misled by appearance, the police seemed inclined to attribute the awful sin of self-destruction.

But when, this topic exhausted, Mr. Challoner rose to leave the room, Mr. Gryce showed where his own thoughts still centred, by asking him the date of the correspondence discovered between his daughter and her unknown admirer.

"Some of the letters were dated last summer, some this fall. The one you are most anxious to hear about only a month back," he added, with unconquerable devotion to what he considered his duty.

Mr. Gryce would like to have carried his inquiries further, but desisted. His heart was full of compassion for this childless old man, doomed to have his choicest memories disturbed by cruel doubts which possibly would never be removed to his own complete satisfaction.

But when he was gone, and Sweetwater had returned, Mr. Gryce made it his first duty to communicate to his superiors the hitherto unsuspected fact of a secret romance in Miss Challoner's seemingly calm and well-guarded life. She had loved and been loved by one of whom her family knew nothing. And the two had quarrelled, as certain letters lately found could be made to show.

CHAPTER VII

THE LETTERS

Before a table strewn with papers, in the room we have already mentioned as given over to the use of the police, sat Dr. Heath in a mood too thoughtful to notice the entrance of Mr. Gryce and Sweetwater from the dining-room where they had been having dinner.

However as the former's tread was somewhat lumbering, the coroner's attention was caught before they had quite crossed the room, and Sweetwater, with his quick eye, noted how his arm and hand immediately fell so as to cover up a portion of the papers lying nearest to him.

"Well, Gryce, this is a dark case," he observed, as at his bidding the two detectives took their seats.

Mr. Gryce nodded; so did Sweetwater.

"The darkest that has ever come to my knowledge," pursued the coroner.

Mr. Gryce again nodded; but not so, Sweetwater. For some reason this simple expression of opinion seemed to have given him a mental start.

"She was not shot. She was not struck by any other hand; yet she lies dead from a mortal wound in the breast. Though there is no tangible proof of her having inflicted this wound upon herself, the jury will have no alternative, I fear, than to pronounce the case one of suicide."

"I'm sorry that I've been able to do so little," remarked Mr. Gryce.

The coroner darted him a quick look.

"You are not satisfied? You have some different idea?" he asked.

The detective frowned at his hands crossed over the top of his cane, then shaking his head, replied:

"The verdict you mention is the only natural one, of course. I see that you have been talking with Miss Challoner's former maid?"

"Yes, and she has settled an important point for us. There was a possibility, of course, that the paper-cutter which you brought to my notice had never gone with her into the mezzanine. That she, or some other person, had dropped it in passing through the lobby. But this girl assures me that her mistress did not enter the lobby that night. That she accompanied her down in the elevator, and saw her step off at the mezzanine. She can also swear that the cutter was in a book she carried—the book we found lying on the desk. The girl remembers distinctly seeing its peculiarly chased handle projecting from its pages. Could anything be more satisfactory if—I was going to say, if the young lady had been of the impulsive type and the provocation greater. But Miss Challoner's nature was calm, and were it not for these letters—" here his arm shifted a little—"I should not be so sure of my jury's future verdict. Love—" he went on, after a moment of silent consideration of a letter he had chosen from those before him, "disturbs the most equable natures. When it enters as a factor, we can expect anything—as you know. And Miss Challoner evidently was much attached to her correspondent, and naturally felt the reproach conveyed in these lines."

And Dr. Heath read:

"Dear Miss Challoner:

"Only a man of small spirit could endure what I endured from you the other day. Love such as mine would be respectable in a clod-hopper, and I think that even you will acknowledge that I stand somewhat higher than that. Though I was silent under yourdisapprobation, you shall yet have your answer. It will not lack point because of its necessary delay."

"A threat!"

The words sprang from Sweetwater, and were evidently involuntary. Dr. Heath paid no notice, but Mr. Gryce, in shifting his hands on his cane top, gave them a sidelong look which was not without a hint of fresh interest in a case concerning which he had believed himself to have said his last word.

"It is the only letter of them all which conveys anything like a reproach," proceeded the coroner. "The rest are ardent enough and, I must acknowledge that, so far as I have allowed myself to look into them, sufficiently respectful. Her surprise must consequently have been great at receiving these lines, and her resentment equally so. If the two met afterwards—But I have not shown you the signature. To the poor father it conveyed nothing—some facts have been kept from him—but to us—" here he whirled the letter about so that Sweetwater, at least, could see the name, "it conveys a hope that we may yet understand Miss Challoner."

"Brotherson!" exclaimed the young detective in loud surprise. "Brotherson! The man who—"

"The man who left this building just before or simultaneously with the alarm caused by Miss Challoner's fall. It clears away some of the clouds befogging us. She probably caught sight of him in the lobby, and in the passion of the moment forgot her usual instincts and drove the sharp-pointed weapon into her heart."

"Brotherson!" The word came softly now, and with a thoughtful intonation. "He saw her die."

"Why do you say that?"

"Would he have washed his hands in the snow if he had been in ignorance of the occurrence? He was the real, if not active, cause of her death and he knew it. Either he—Excuse me, Dr. Heath and Mr. Gryce, it is not for me to obtrude my opinion."

"Have you settled it beyond dispute that Brotherson is really the man who was seen doing this?"

"No, sir. I have not had a minute for that job, but I'm ready for the business any time you see fit to spare me."

"Let it be to-morrow, or, if you can manage it, to-night. We want the man even if he is not the hero of that romantic episode. He wrote these letters, and he must explain the last one. His initials, as you see, are not ordinary ones, and you will find them at the bottom of all these sheets. He was brave enough or arrogant enough to sign the questionable one with his full name. This may speak well for him, and it may not. It is for you to decide that. Where will you look for him, Sweetwater? No one here knows his address."

"Not Miss Challoner's maid?"

"No; the name is a new one to her. But she made it very evident that she was not surprised to hear that her mistress was in secret correspondence with a member of the male sex. Much can be hidden from servants, but not that."

"I'll find the man; I have a double reason for doing that now; he shall not escape me."

Dr. Heath expressed his satisfaction, and gave some orders. Meanwhile, Mr. Gryce had not uttered a word.

CHAPTER VIII

STRANGE DOINGS FOR GEORGE

That evening George sat so long over the newspapers that in spite of my absorbing interest in the topic engrossing me, I fell asleep in my cozy little rocking chair. I was awakened by what seemed like a kiss falling very softly on my forehead, though, to be sure, it may have been only the flap of George's coat sleeve as he stooped over me.

"Wake up, little woman," I heard, "and trot away to bed. I'm going out and may not be in till daybreak."

"You! going out! at ten o'clock at night, tired as you are—as we both are! What has happened—Oh!"

This broken exclamation escaped me as I perceived in the dim background by the sitting-room door, the figure of a man who called up recent, but very thrilling experiences.

"Mr. Sweetwater," explained George. "We are going out together. It is necessary, or you may be sure I should not leave you."

I was quite wide awake enough by now to understand. "Oh, I know. You are going to hunt up the man. How I wish—"

But George did not wait for me to express my wishes. He gave me a little good advice as to how I had better employ my time in his absence, and was off before I could find words to answer.

This ends all I have to say about myself; but the events of that night carefully related to me by George are important enough for me to describe them, with all the detail which is their rightful due. I shall tell the story as I have already been led to do in other portions of this narrative, as though I were present and shared the adventure.

As soon as the two were in the street, the detective turned towards George and said:

"Mr. Anderson, I have a great deal to ask of you. The business before us is not a simple one, and I fear that I shall have to subject you to more inconvenience than is customary in matters like this. Mr.

Brotherson has vanished; that is, in his own proper person, but I have an idea that I am on the track of one who will lead us very directly to him if we manage the affair carefully. What I want of you, of course, is mere identification. You saw the face of the man who washed his hands in the snow, and would know it again, you say. Do you think you could be quite sure of yourself, if the man were differently dressed and differently occupied?"

"I think so. There's his height and a certain strong look in his face. I cannot describe it."

"You don't need to. Come! we're all right. You don't mind making a night of it?"

"Not if it is necessary."

"That we can't tell yet." And with a characteristic shrug and smile, the detective led the way to a taxicab which stood in waiting at the corner.

A quarter of an hour of rather fast riding brought them into a tangle of streets on the East side. As George noticed the swarming sidewalks and listened to the noises incident to an over-populated quarter, he could not forbear, despite the injunction he had received, to express his surprise at the direction of their search.

"Surely," said he, "the gentleman I have described can have no friends here." Then, bethinking himself, he added: "But if he has reasons to fear the law, naturally he would seek to lose himself in a place as different as possible from his usual haunts."

"Yes, that would be some men's way," was the curt, almost indifferent, answer he received. Sweetwater was looking this way and that from the window beside him, and now, leaning out gave some directions to the driver which altered their course.

When they stopped, which was in a few minutes, he said to George:

"We shall have to walk now for a block or two. I'm anxious to attract no attention, nor is it desirable for you to do so. If you can manage to act as if you were accustomed to the place and just leave all the talking to me, we ought to get along first-rate. Don't be astonished at anything you see, and trust me for the rest; that's all."

They alighted, and he dismissed the taxicab. Some clock in the neighbourhood struck the hour of ten. "Good! we shall be in time," muttered the detective, and led the way down the street and round a corner or so, till they came to a block darker than the rest, and much less noisy.

It had a sinister look, and George, who is brave enough under all ordinary circumstances, was glad that his companion wore a badge and carried a whistle. He was also relieved when he caught sight of the burly form of a policeman in the shadow of one of the doorways. Yet the houses he saw before him were not so very different from those they had already passed. His uneasiness could not have sprung from them. They had even an air of positive respectability, as though inhabited by industrious workmen. Then, what was it which made the close companionship of a member of the police so uncommonly welcome? Was it a certain aspect of solitariness which clung to the block, or was it the sudden appearance here and there of strangely gliding figures, which no sooner loomed up against the snowy perspective, than they disappeared again in some unseen doorway?

"There's a meeting on to-night, of the Associated Brotherhood of the Awl, the Plane and the Trowel (whatever that means), and it is the speaker we want to see: the man who is to address them promptly at ten o'clock. Do you object to meetings?"

"Is this a secret one?"

"It wasn't advertised."

"Are we carpenters or masons that we can count on admittance?"

"I am a carpenter. Don't you think you can be a mason for the occasion?"

"I doubt it, but—"

"Hush! I must speak to this man."

George stood back, and a few words passed between Sweetwater and a shadowy figure which seemed to have sprung up out of the sidewalk.

"Balked at the outset," were the encouraging words with which the detective rejoined George. "It seems that a pass-word is necessary, and my friend has been unable to get it. Will the speaker pass out this way?" he inquired of the shadowy figure still lingering in their rear.

"He didn't go in by it; yet I believe he's safe enough inside," was the muttered answer.

Sweetwater had no relish for disappointments of this character, but it was not long before he straightened up and allowed himself to exchange a few more words with this mysterious person. These appeared to be of a more encouraging nature than the last, for it was not long before the detective returned with renewed alacrity to George, and, wheeling him about, began to retrace his steps to the corner.

"Are we going back? Are you going to give up the job?" George asked.

"No; we're going to take him from the rear. There's a break in the fence—Oh, we'll do very well. Trust me."

George laughed. He was growing excited, but not altogether agreeably so. He says that he has seen moments of more pleasant anticipation. Evidently, my good husband is not cut out for detective work.

Where they went under this officer's guidance, he cannot tell. The tortuous tangle of alleys through which he now felt himself led was dark as the nether regions to his unaccustomed eyes. There was snow under his feet and now and then he brushed against some obtruding object, or stumbled against a low fence; but beyond these slight miscalculations on his own part, he was a mere automaton in the hands of his eager guide, and only became his own man again when they suddenly stepped into an open yard and he could discern plainly before him the dark walls of a building pointed out by Sweetwater as their probable destination. Yet even here they encountered some impediment which prohibited a close approach. A wall or shed cut off their view of the building's lower storey; and though somewhat startled at being left unceremoniously alone after just a whispered word of encouragement from the ever ready detective, George could quite understand the necessity which that person must feel for a quiet reconnoitering of the surroundings before the two of them ventured further forward in their possibly hazardous undertaking. Yet the experience was none too pleasing to George, and he was very glad to hear Sweetwater's whisper again at his ear, and to feel himself rescued from the pool of slush in which he had been left to stand.

"The approach is not all that can be desired," remarked the detective as they entered what appeared to be a low shed. "The broken board has been put back and securely nailed in place, and if I am not very much mistaken there is a fellow stationed in the yard who will want the pass-word too. Looks shady to me. I'll have something to tell the chief when I get back."

"But we! What are we going to do if we cannot get in front or rear?"

"We're going to wait right here in the hopes of catching a glimpse of our man as he comes out," returned the detective, drawing George towards a low window overlooking the yard he had described as sentinelled. "He will have to pass directly under this window on his way to the alley," Sweetwater went on to explain, "and if I can only raise it—but the noise would give us away. I can't do that."

"Perhaps it swings on hinges," suggested George. "It looks like that sort of a window."

"If it should—well! it does. We're in great luck, sir. But before I pull it open, remember that from the moment I unlatch it, everything said or done here can be heard in the adjoining yard. So no whispers and no unnecessary movements. When you hear him coming, as sooner or later you certainly will, fall carefully to your knees and lean out just far enough to catch a glimpse of him before he steps down from the porch. If he stops to light his cigar or to pass a few words with some of the men he will leave behind, you may get a plain enough view of his face or figure to identify him. The light is burning low in that rear hall, but it will do. If it does not,—if you can't see him or if you do, don't hang out of the window more than a second. Duck after your first look. I don't want to be caught at this job with no better opportunity for escape than we have here. Can you remember all that?"

George pinched his arm encouragingly, and Sweetwater, with an amused grunt, softly unlatched the window and pulled it wide open.

A fine sleet flew in, imperceptible save for the sensation of damp it gave, and the slight haze it diffused through the air. Enlarged by this haze, the building they were set to watch rose in magnified proportions at their left. The yard between, piled high in the centre with snow-heaps or other heaps covered with snow, could not have been more than forty feet square. The window from which they peered, was half-way down this yard, so that a comparatively short distance separated them from the porch where George had been told to look for the man he was expected to identify. All was dark there at present, but he could hear from time to time some sounds of restless movement, as the guard posted inside shifted in his narrow quarters, or struck his benumbed feet softly together.

But what came to them from above was more interesting than anything to be heard or seen below. A man's voice, raised to a wonderful pitch by the passion of oratory, had burst the barriers of the closed hall in that towering third storey and was carrying its tale to other ears than those within. Had it been summer and the windows open, both George and Sweetwater might have heard every word; for the tones were exceptionally rich and penetrating, and the speaker intent only on the impression he was endeavouring to make upon his audience. That he had not mistaken his power in this direction was evinced by the applause which rose from time to time from innumerable hands and feet. But this uproar would be speedily silenced, and the mellow voice ring out again, clear and commanding. What could the subject be to rouse such enthusiasm in the Associated Brotherhood of the Awl, the Plane and the Trowel? There was a moment when our listening friends expected to be enlightened. A shutter was thrown back in one of those upper windows, and the window hurriedly raised, during which words took the place of sounds and they heard enough to whet their appetite for more. But only that. The shutter was speedily restored to place, and the window again closed. A wise precaution, or so thought George if they wished to keep their doubtful proceedings secret.

A tirade against the rich and a loud call to battle could be gleaned from the few sentences they had heard. But its virulence and pointed attack was not that of the second-rate demagogue or business agent, but of a man whose intellect and culture rang in every tone, and informed each sentence.

Sweetwater, in whom satisfaction was fast taking the place of impatience and regret, pushed the window to before asking George this question:

"Did you hear the voice of the man whose action attracted, your attention outside the Clermont?"

"No."

"Did you note just now the large shadow dancing on the ceiling over the speaker's head?"

"Yes, but I could judge nothing from that."

"Well, he's a rum one. I shan't open this window again till he gives signs of reaching the end of his speech. It's too cold."

But almost immediately he gave a start and, pressing George's arm, appeared to listen, not to the speech which was no longer audible, but to something much nearer—a step or movement in the adjoining yard. At least, so George interpreted the quick turn which this impetuous detective made, and the pains he took to direct George's attention to the walk running under the window beneath which they crouched. Someone was stealing down upon the house at their left, from the alley beyond. A big man, whose shoulder brushed the window as he went by. George felt his hand seized again and pressed as this happened, and before he had recovered from this excitement, experienced another quick pressure and still another as one, two, three additional figures went slipping by. Then his hand was suddenly dropped, for a cry had shot up from the door where the sentinel stood guard, followed by a sudden loud slam, and the noise of a shooting bolt, which, proclaiming as it did that the invaders were not friends but enemies to the cause which was being vaunted above, so excited Sweetwater that he pulled the window wide open and took a bold look out. George followed his example and this was what they saw:

Three men were standing flat against the fence leading from the shed directly to the porch. The fourth was crouching within the latter, and in another moment they heard his fist descend upon the door inside in a way to rouse the echoes. Meantime, the voice in the audience hall above had ceased, and there could be heard instead the scramble of hurrying feet and the noise of overturning benches. Then a window flew up and a voice called down:

"Who's that? What do you want down there?"

But before an answer could be shouted back, this man was drawn fiercely inside, and the scramble was renewed, amid which George heard Sweetwater's whisper at his ear:

"It's the police. The chief has got ahead of me. Was that the man we're after—the one who shouted down?"

"No. Neither was he the speaker. The voices are very different."

"We want the speaker. If the boys get him, we're all right; but if they don't—wait, I must make the matter sure."

And with a bound he vaulted through the window, whistling in a peculiar way. George, thus left quite alone, had the pleasure of seeing his sole protector mix with the boys, as he called them, and ultimately crowd in with them through the door which had finally been opened for their admittance. Then came a wait, and then the quiet re-appearance of the detective alone and in no very, amiable mood.

"Well?" inquired George, somewhat breathlessly. "Do you want me? They don't seem to be coming out."

"No; they've gone the other way. It was a red hot anarchist meeting, and no mistake. They have arrested one of the speakers, but the other escaped. How, we have not yet found out; but I think there's a way out somewhere by which he got the start of us. He was the man I wanted you to see. Bad luck, Mr. Anderson, but I'm not at the end of my resources. If you'll have patience with me and accompany me a little further, I promise you that I'll only risk one more failure. Will you be so good, sir?"

CHAPTER IX

THE INCIDENT OF THE PARTLY LIFTED SHADE

The fellow had a way with him, hard to resist. Cold as George was and exhausted by an excitement of a kind to which he was wholly unaccustomed, he found himself acceding to the detective's request; and after a quick lunch and a huge cup of coffee in a restaurant which I wish I had time to describe, the two took a car which eventually brought them into one of the oldest quarters of the Borough of Brooklyn. The sleet which had stung their faces in the streets of New York had been left behind them somewhere on the bridge, but the chill was not gone from the air, and George felt greatly relieved when Sweetwater paused in the middle of a long block before a lofty tenement house of mean appearance, and signified that here they were to stop, and that from now on, mum was to be their watchword.

George was relieved I say, but he was also more astonished than ever. What kind of haunts were these for the cultured gentleman who spent his evenings at the Clermont? It was easy enough in these days of extravagant sympathies, to understand such a man addressing the uneasy spirits of lower New York—he had been called an enthusiast, and an enthusiast is very often a social agitator—but to trace him afterwards to a place like this was certainly a surprise. A tenement—such a tenement as this—meant home—home for himself or for those he counted his friends, and such a supposition seemed inconceivable to my poor husband, with the memory of the gorgeous parlour of the Clermont in his mind. Indeed, he hinted something of the kind to his affable but strangely reticent companion, but all the answer he got was a peculiar smile whose humorous twist he could barely discern in the semi-darkness of the open doorway into which they had just plunged.

"An adventure! certainly an adventure!" flashed through poor George's mind, as he peered, in great curiosity down the long hall before him, into a dismal rear, opening into a still more dismal court. It was truly a novel experience for a business man whose philanthropy was carried on entirely by proxy—that is, by his wife. Should he be expected to penetrate into those dark, ill-smelling recesses, or would he be led up the long flights of naked stairs, so feebly illuminated that they gave the impression of extending indefinitely into dimmer and dimmer heights of decay and desolation?

Sweetwater seemed to decide for the rear, for leaving George, he stepped down the hall into the court beyond, where George could see him casting inquiring glances up at the walls above him. Another tenement, similar to the one whose rear end he was contemplating, towered behind but he paid no attention to that. He was satisfied with the look he had given and came quickly back, joining George at the foot of the staircase, up which he silently led the way.

It was a rude, none-too-well-cared-for building, but it seemed respectable enough and very quiet, considering the mass of people it accommodated. There were marks of poverty everywhere, but no squalor. One flight—two flights—three—and then George's guide stopped, and, looking back at him, made a gesture. It appeared to be one of caution, but when the two came together at the top of the staircase, Sweetwater spoke quite naturally as he pointed out a door in their rear:

"That's the room. We'll keep a sharp watch and when any man, no matter what his dress or appearance comes up these stairs and turns that way, give him a sharp look. You understand?"

"Yes; but-"

"Oh, he hasn't come in yet. I took pains to find that out. You saw me go into the court and look up. That was to see if his window was lighted. Well, it wasn't."

George felt non-plussed.

"But surely," said he, "the gentleman named Brotherson doesn't live here."

"The inventor does."

"Oh!"

"And—but I will explain later."

The suppressed excitement contained in these words made George stare. Indeed, he had been wondering for some time at the manner of the detective which showed a curious mixture of several opposing emotions. Now, the fellow was actually in a tremble of hope or impatience;—and, not content with listening, he peered every few minutes down the well of the staircase, and when he was not doing that, tramped from end to end of the narrow passage-way separating the head of the stairs from the door he had pointed out, like one to whom minutes were hours. All this time he seemed to forget George who certainly had as much reason as himself for finding the time long. But when, after some half hour of this tedium and suspense, there rose from below the faint clatter of ascending footsteps, he remembered his meek companion and beckoning him to one side, began a studied conversation with him, showing him a note-book in which he had written such phrases as these:

Don't look up till he is fairly in range with the light.

There's nothing to fear; he doesn't know either of us.

If it is a face you have seen before;—if it is the one we are expecting to see, pull your necktie straight. It's a little on one side.

These rather startling injunctions were read by George, with no very perceptible diminution of the uneasiness which it was only natural for him to feel at the oddity of his position. But only the demand last made produced any impression on him. The man they were waiting for was no further up than the second floor, but instinctively George's hand had flown to his necktie, and he was only stopped from its premature re-arrangement by a warning look from Sweetwater.

"Not unless you know him," whispered the detective; and immediately launched out into an easy talk about some totally different business which George neither understood, nor was expected to, I dare say.

Suddenly the steps below paused, and George heard Sweetwater draw in his breath in irrepressible dismay. But they were immediately resumed, and presently the head and shoulders of a workingman of uncommon proportions appeared in sight on the stairway.

George cast him a keen look, and his hand rose doubtfully to his neck and then fell back again. The approaching man was tall, very well-proportioned and easy of carriage; but the face—such of it as could be seen between his cap and the high collar he had pulled up about his ears, conveyed no exact impression to George's mind, and he did not dare to give the signal Sweetwater expected from him. Yet as the man went by with a dark and sidelong glance at them both, he felt his hand rise again, though he did not complete the action, much to his own disgust and to the evident disappointment of the watchful detective.

"You're not sure?" he now heard, oddly interpolated in the stream of half-whispered talk with which the other endeavoured to carry off the situation.

George shook his head. He could not rid himself of the old impression he had formed of the man in the snow.

"Mr. Dunn, a word with you," suddenly spoke up Sweetwater, to the man who had just passed them. "That's your name, isn't it?"

"Yes, that is my name," was the quiet response, in a voice which was at once rich and resonant; a voice which George knew—the voice of the impassioned speaker he had heard resounding through the sleet as he cowered within hearing in the shed behind the Avenue A tenement. "Who are you who wish to speak to me at so late an hour?"

He was returning to them from the door he had unlocked and left slightly ajar.

"Well, we are—You know what," smiled the ready detective, advancing half-way to greet him. "We're not members of the Associated Brotherhood, but possibly have hopes of being so. At all events, we should like to talk the matter over, if, as you say, it's not too late."

"I have nothing to do with the club—"

"But you spoke before it."

"Yes."

"Then you can give us some sort of an idea how we are to apply for membership."

Mr. Dunn met the concentrated gaze of his two evidently unwelcome visitors with a frankness which dashed George's confidence in himself, but made little visible impression upon his daring companion.

"I should rather see you at another time," said he. "But—" his hesitation was inappreciable save to the nicest ear—"if you will allow me to be brief, I will tell you what I know—which is very little."

Sweetwater was greatly taken aback. All he had looked for, as he was careful to tell my husband later, was a sufficiently prolonged conversation to enable George to mark and study the workings of the face he was not yet sure of. Nor did the detective feel quite easy at the readiness of his reception; nor any too well pleased to accept the invitation which this man now gave them to enter his room.

But he suffered no betrayal of his misgivings to escape him, though he was careful to intimate to George, as they waited in the doorway for the other to light up, that he should not be displeased at his refusal to accompany him further in this adventure, and even advised him to remain in the hall till he received his summons to enter.

But George had not come as far as this to back out now, and as soon as he saw Sweetwater advance into the now well-lighted interior, he advanced too and began to look around him.

The room, like many others in these old-fashioned tenements, had a jog just where the door was, so that on entering they had to take several steps before they could get a full glimpse of its four walls. When they did, both showed surprise. Comfort, if not elegance, confronted them, which impression, however, was immediately lost in the evidences of work, manual, as well as intellectual, which were everywhere scattered about.

The man who lived here was not only a student, as was evinced by a long wall full of books, but he was an art-lover, a musician, an inventor and an athlete.

So much could be learned from the most cursory glance. A more careful one picked up other facts fully as startling and impressive. The books were choice; the invention to all appearance a practical one; the art of a high order and the music, such as was in view, of a character of which the nicest taste need not be ashamed. George began to feel quite conscious of the intrusion of which they had been guilty, and was amazed at the ease with which the detective carried himself in the presence of such manifestations of culture and good, hard work. He was trying to recall the exact appearance of the figure he had seen stooping in the snowy street two nights before, when he found himself staring at the occupant of the room, who had taken up his stand before them and was regarding them while they were regarding the room.

He had thrown aside his hat and rid himself of his overcoat, and the fearlessness of his aspect seemed to daunt the hitherto dauntless Sweetwater, who, for the first time in his life, perhaps, hunted in vain for words with which to start conversation.

Had he made an awful mistake? Was this Mr. Dunn what he seemed an unknown and careful genius, battling with great odds in his honest struggle to give the world something of value in return for what it had given him? The quick, almost deprecatory glance he darted at George betrayed his dismay; a dismay which George had begun to share, notwithstanding his growing belief that the man's face was not wholly unknown to him even if he could not recognise it as the one he had seen outside the Clermont.

"You seem to have forgotten your errand," came in quiet, if not good-natured, sarcasm from their patiently waiting host.

"It's the room," muttered Sweetwater, with an attempt at his old-time ease which was not as fully successful as usual. "What an all-fired genius you must be. I never saw the like. And in a tenement house too! You ought to be in one of those big new studio buildings in New York where artists be and everything you see is beautiful. You'd appreciate it, you would."

The detective started, George started, at the gleam which answered him from a very uncommon eye. It was a temporary flash, however, and quickly veiled, and the tone in which this Dunn now spoke was anything but an encouraging one.

"I thought you were desirous of joining a socialistic fraternity," said he; "a true aspirant for such honours don't care for beautiful things unless all can have them. I prefer my tenement. How is it with you, friends?"

Sweetwater found some sort of a reply, though the thing which this man now did must have startled him, as it certainly did George. They were so grouped that a table quite full of anomalous objects stood at the back of their host, and consequently quite beyond their own reach. As Sweetwater began to speak, he whom he had addressed by the name of Dunn, drew a pistol from his breast pocket and laid it down barrel towards them on this table top. Then he looked up courteously enough, and listened till Sweetwater was done. A very handsome man, but one not to be trifled with in the slightest degree. Both recognised this fact, and George, for one, began to edge towards the door.

"Now I feel easier," remarked the giant, swelling out his chest. He was unusually tall, as well as unusually muscular. "I never like to carry arms; but sometimes it is unavoidable. Damn it, what hands!" He was looking at his own, which certainly showed soil. "Will you pardon me?" he pleasantly apologised, stepping towards a washstand and plunging his hands into the basin. "I cannot think with dirt on me like that. Humph, hey! did you speak?"

He turned quickly on George who had certainly uttered an ejaculation, but receiving no reply, went on with his task, completing it with a care and a disregard of their presence which showed him up in still another light.

But even his hardihood showed shock, when, upon turning round with a brisk, "Now I'm ready to talk," he encountered again the clear eye of Sweetwater. For, in the person of this none too welcome intruder, he saw a very different man from the one upon whom he had just turned his back with so little ceremony; and there appeared to be no good reason for the change. He had not noted in his preoccupation, how George, at sight of his stooping figure, had made a sudden significant movement, and if he had, the pulling of a necktie straight, would have meant nothing to him. But to Sweetwater it meant every thing, and it was in the tone of one fully at ease with himself that he now dryly remarked: "Mr. Brotherson, if you feel quite clean; and if you have sufficiently warmed yourself, I would suggest that we start out at once, unless you prefer to have me share this room with you till the morning."

There was silence. Mr. Dunn thus addressed attempted no answer; not for a full minute. The two men were measuring each other—George felt that he did not count at all—and they were quite too much occupied with this task to heed the passage of time. To George, who knew little, if anything, of what this silent struggle meant to either, it seemed that the detective stood no show before this Samson of physical strength and intellectual power, backed by a pistol just within reach of his hand. But as George continued to look and saw the figure of the smaller man gradually dilate, while that of the larger, the more potent and the better guarded, gave unmistakable signs of secret wavering, he slowly changed his mind and, ranging himself with the detective, waited for the word or words which should explain this situation and render intelligible the triumph gradually becoming visible in the young detective's eyes.

But he was not destined to have his curiosity satisfied so far. He might witness and hear, but it was long before he understood.

"Brotherson?" repeated their host, after the silence had lasted to the breaking-point. "Why do you call me that?"

"Because it is your name."

"You called me Dunn a minute ago."

"That is true."

"Why Dunn if Brotherson is my name?"

"Because you spoke under the name of Dunn at the meeting to-night. and if I don't mistake, that is the name by which you are known here."

"And you? By what name are you known?"

"It is late to ask, isn't it? But I'm willing to speak it now, and I might not have been so a little earlier in our conversation. I am Detective Sweetwater of the New York Department of Police, and my errand here is a very simple one. Some letters signed by you have been found among the papers of the lady whose mysterious death at the hotel Clermont is just now occupying the attention of the New York authorities. If you have any information to give which will in any way explain that death, your presence will be welcome at Coroner Heath's office in New York. If you have not, your presence will still be welcome. At all events, I was told to bring you. You will be on hand to accompany me in the morning, I am quite sure, pardoning the unconventional means I have taken to make sure of my man?"

The humour with which this was said seemed to rob it of anything like attack, and Mr. Brotherson, as we shall hereafter call him, smiled with an odd acceptance of the same, as he responded:

"I will go before the police certainly. I haven't much to tell, but what I have is at their service. It will not help you, but I have no secrets. What are you doing?"

He bounded towards Sweetwater, who had simply stepped to the window, lifted the shade and looked across at the opposing tenement.

"I wanted to see if it was still snowing," explained the detective, with a smile, which seemed to strike the other like a blow. "If it was a liberty, please pardon it."

Mr. Brotherson drew back. The cold air of self-possession which he now assumed, presented such a contrast to the unwarranted heat of the moment before that George wondered greatly over it, and later, when he recapitulated to me the whole story of this night, it was this incident of the lifted shade, together with the emotion it had caused, which he acknowledged as being for him the most inexplicable event of the evening and the one he was most anxious to hear explained.

As this ends our connection with this affair, I will bid you my personal farewell. I have often wished that circumstances had made it possible for me to accompany you through the remaining intricacies of this remarkable case.

But you will not lack a suitable guide.

BOOK II

AS SEEN BY DETECTIVE SWEETWATER

CHAPTER X

A DIFFERENCE OF OPINION

At an early hour the next morning, Sweetwater stood before the coroner's desk, urging a plea he feared to hear refused. He wished to be present at the interview soon to be held with Mr. Brotherson, and he had no good reason to advance why such a privilege should be allotted him.

"It's not curiosity," said he. "There's a question I hope to see settled. I can't communicate it—you would laugh at me; but it's an important one, a very important one, and I beg that you will let me sit in one of the corners and hear what he says. I won't bother and I'll be very still, so still that he'll hardly notice me. Do grant me this favour, sir."

The coroner, who had had some little experience with this man, surveyed him with a smile less forbidding than the poor fellow expected.

"You seem to lay great store by it," said he; "if you want to sort those papers over there, you may."

"Thank you. I don't understand the job, but I promise you not to increase the confusion. If I do; if I rattle the leaves too loudly, it will mean, 'Press him further on this exact point,' but I doubt if I rattle them, sir. No such luck."

The last three words were uttered sotto voce, but the coroner heard him, and followed his ungainly figure with a glance of some curiosity, as he settled himself at the desk on the other side of the room.

"Is the man—" he began, but at this moment the man entered, and Dr. Heath forgot the young detective, in his interest in the new arrival.

Neither dressed with the elegance known to the habitues of the Clermont, nor yet in the workman's outfit in which he had thought best to appear before the Associated Brotherhood, the newcomer advanced, with an aspect of open respect which could not fail to make a favourable impression upon the critical eye of the official awaiting him. So favourable, indeed, was this impression that that gentleman half rose, infusing a little more consideration into his greeting than he was accustomed to show to his prospective witnesses. Such a fearless eye he had seldom encountered, nor was it often his pleasure to confront so conspicuous a specimen of physical and intellectual manhood.

"Mr. Brotherson, I believe," said he, as he motioned his visitor to sit.

"That is my name, sir."

"Orlando Brotherson?"

"The same, sir."

"I'm glad we have made no mistake," smiled the doctor. "Mr. Brotherson, I have sent for you under the supposition that you were a friend of the unhappy lady lately dead at the Hotel Clermont."

"Miss Challoner?"

"Certainly; Miss Challoner."

"I knew the lady. But—" here the speaker's eye took on a look as questioning as that of his interlocutor—"but in a way so devoid of all publicity that I cannot but feel surprised that the fact should be known."

At this, the listening Sweetwater hoped that Dr. Heath would ignore the suggestion thus conveyed and decline the explanation it apparently demanded. But the impression made by the gentleman's good looks had been too strong for this coroner's proverbial caution, and, handing over the slip of a note which had been found among Miss Challoner's effects by her father, he quietly asked:

"Do you recognise the signature?"

"Yes, it is mine."

"Then you acknowledge yourself the author of these lines?"

"Most certainly. Have I not said that this is my signature?"

"Do you remember the words of this note, Mr. Brotherson?'

"Hardly. I recollect its tenor, but not the exact words."

"Read them."

"Excuse me, I had rather not. I am aware that they were bitter and should be the cause of great regret. I was angry when I wrote them."

"That is evident. But the cause of your anger is not so clear, Mr. Brotherson. Miss Challoner was a woman of lofty character, or such was the universal opinion of her friends. What could she have done to a gentleman like yourself to draw forth such a tirade?"

"You ask that?"

"I am obliged to. There is mystery surrounding her death;—the kind of mystery which demands perfect frankness on the part of all who were near her on that evening, or whose relations to her were in any way peculiar. You acknowledge that your friendship was of such a guarded nature that it surprised you greatly to hear it recognised. Yet you could write her a letter of this nature. Why?"

"Because—" the word came glibly; but the next one was long in following. "Because," he repeated, letting the fire of some strong feeling disturb for a moment his dignified reserve, "I offered myself to Miss Challoner, and she dismissed me with great disdain."

"Ah! and so you thought a threat was due her?"

"A threat?"

"These words contain a threat, do they not?"

"They may. I was hardly master of myself at the time. I may have expressed myself in an unfortunate manner."

"Read the words, Mr. Brotherson. I really must insist that you do so."

There was no hesitancy now. Rising, he leaned over the table and read the few words the other had spread out for his perusal. Then he slowly rose to his full height, as he answered, with some slight display of compunction:

"I remember it perfectly now. It is not a letter to be proud of. I hope—"

"Pray finish, Mr. Brotherson."

"That you are not seeking to establish a connection between this letter and her violent death?"

"Letters of this sort are often very mischievous, Mr. Brotherson. The harshness with which this is written might easily rouse emotions of a most unhappy nature in the breast of a woman as sensitive as Miss Challoner."

"Pardon me, Dr. Heath; I cannot flatter myself so far. You overrate my influence with the lady you name."

"You believe, then, that she was sincere in her rejection of your addresses?"

A start, too slight to be noted by any one but the watchful Sweetwater, showed that this question had gone home. But the self-poise and mental control of this man were perfect, and in an instant he was facing the coroner again, with a dignity which gave no clew to the disturbance into which his thoughts had just been thrown. Nor was this disturbance apparent in his tones when he made his reply:

"I have never allowed myself to think otherwise. I have seen no reason why I should. The suggestion you would convey by such a question is hardly welcome, now. I pray you to be careful in your judgment of such a woman's impulses. They often spring from sources not to be sounded even by her dearest friends."

Just; but how cold! Dr. Heath, eyeing him with admiration rather than sympathy, hesitated how to proceed; while Sweetwater, peering up from his papers, sought in vain for some evidence of the bereaved lover in the impressive but wholly dispassionate figure of him who had just spoken. Had pride got the better of his heart? or had that organ always been subordinate to the will in this man of instincts so varying, that at one time he impressed you simply as a typical gentleman of leisure; at another, as no more than a fiery agitator with powers absorbed by, if not limited to the one cause he advocated; and again—and this seemed the most contradictory of all—just the ardent inventor, living in a tenement, with Science for his goddess and work always under his hand? As the young detective weighed these possibilities and marvelled over the contradictions they offered, he forgot the papers now lying quiet under his hand. He was too interested to remember his own part— something which could not often be said of Sweetwater.

Meantime, the coroner had collected his thoughts. With an apology for the extremely personal nature of his inquiry, he asked Mr. Brotherson if he would object to giving him some further details of his acquaintanceship with Miss Challoner; where he first met her and under what circumstances their friendship had developed.

"Not at all," was the ready reply. "I have nothing to conceal in the matter. I only wish that her father were present that he might listen to the recital of my acquaintanceship with his daughter. He might possibly understand her better and regard with more leniency the presumption into which I was led by my ignorance of the pride inherent in great families."

"Your wish can very easily be gratified," returned the official, pressing an electric button on his desk.

"Mr. Challoner is in the adjoining room." Then, as the door communicating with the room he had mentioned swung ajar and stood so, Dr. Heath added, without apparent consciousness of the dramatic character of this episode, "You will not need to raise your voice beyond its natural pitch. He can hear perfectly from where he sits."

"Thank you. I am glad to speak in his presence," came in undisturbed self-possession from this not easily surprised witness. "I shall relate the facts exactly as they occurred, adding nothing and concealing nothing. If I mistook my position, or Miss Challoner's position, it is not for me to apologise. I never hid my business from her, nor the moderate extent of my fortune. If she knew me at all, she knew me for what I am; a man of the people who glories in work and who has risen by it to a position somewhat unique in this city. I feel no lack of equality even with such a woman as Miss Challoner."

A most unnecessary preamble, no doubt, and of doubtful efficacy in smoothing his way to a correct understanding with the deeply bereaved father. But he looked so handsome as he thus asserted himself and made so much of his inches and the noble poise of his head—though cold of eye and always cold of manner—that those who saw, as well as heard him, forgave this display of egotism in consideration of its honesty and the dignity it imparted to his person.

"I first met Miss Challoner in the Berkshires," he began, after a moment of quiet listening for any possible sound from the other room. "I had been on the tramp, and had stopped at one of the great hotels for a seven days' rest. I will acknowledge that I chose this spot at the instigation of a relative who knew my tastes and how perfectly they might be gratified there. That I should mingle with the guests may not have been in his thought, any more than it was in mine at the beginning of my stay. The panorama of beauty spread out before me on every side was sufficient in itself for my enjoyment, and might have continued so to the end if my attention had not been very forcibly drawn on one memorable morning to a young lady—Miss Challoner—by the very earnest look she gave me as I was crossing the office from one verandah to another. I must insist on this look, even if it shock the delicacy of my listeners, for without the interest it awakened in me, I might not have noticed the blush with which she turned aside to join her friends on the verandah. It was an overwhelming blush which could not have sprung from any slight embarrassment, and, though I hate the pretensions of those egotists who see in a woman's smile more than it by right conveys, I could not help being moved by this display of feeling in one so gifted with every grace and attribute of the perfect woman. With less caution than I usually display, I approached the desk where she had been standing and, meeting the eyes of the clerk, asked the young lady's name. He gave it, and waited for me to express the surprise he expected it to evoke. But I felt none and showed none. Other feelings had seized me. I had heard of this gracious woman from many sources, in my life among the suffering masses of New York, and now that I had seen her and found her to be not only my ideal of personal loveliness but seemingly approachable and not uninterested in myself, I allowed my fancy to soar and my heart to become touched. A fact which the clerk now confided to me naturally deepened the impression. Miss Challoner had seen my name in the guest-book and asked to have me pointed out to her. Perhaps she had heard my name spoken in the same quarter where I had heard hers. We have never exchanged confidences on the subject, and I cannot say. I can only give you my reason for the interest I felt in Miss Challoner and why I forgot, in the glamour of this episode, the aims and purposes of a not unambitious life and the distance which the world and the so-called aristocratic class put between a woman of her wealth and standing and a simple worker like myself.

"I must be pardoned. She had smiled upon me once, and she smiled again. Days before we were formally presented, I caught her softened look turned my way, as we passed each other in hall or corridor. We were friends, or so it appeared to me, before ever a word passed between us, and when fortune favoured us and we were duly introduced, our minds met in a strange sympathy which made this one interview a memorable one to me. Unhappily, as I then considered it, this was my last day at the hotel, and our conversation, interrupted frequently by passing acquaintances, was never resumed. I exchanged a few words with her by way of good-bye but nothing more. I came to New York, and she remained in Lenox. A month after and she too came to New York."

"This good-bye—do you remember it? The exact language, I mean?"

"I do; it made a great impression on me. 'I shall hope for our further acquaintance,' she said. 'We have one very strong interest in common.' And if ever a human face spoke eloquently, it was hers at that moment. The interest, as I understood it, was our mutual sympathy for our toiling, half-starved, down-trodden brothers and sisters in the lower streets of this city; but the eloquence—that I probably mistook. I thought it sprang from personal interest, and it gave me courage to pursue the intention which had taken the place of every other feeling and ambition by which I had hitherto been moved. Here was a woman in a thousand; one who could make a man of me indeed. If she could ignore the social gulf between us, I felt free to take the leap. Cowardice had never been a fault of mine. But I was no fool even then. I realised that I must first let her see the manner of man I was and what life meant to me and must mean to her if the union I contemplated should become an actual fact. I wrote letters to her, but I did not give her my address or even request a reply. I was not ready for any word from her. I am not like other men and I could wait. And I did, for weeks, then I suddenly appeared at her hotel."

The change of voice—the bitterness which he infused into this final sentence made every one look up. Hitherto he had spoken calmly, almost monotonously, as if no present heart-beat responded to this tale of vanished love; but with the words, "Then I suddenly appeared at her hotel," he showed himself human again, and betrayed a passion which though curbed was of the fiery quality, befitting his extraordinary attributes of mind and person.

"This was when?" put in Dr. Heath, anxious to bridge the pause which must have been very painful to the listening father.

"The week after Thanksgiving. I did not see her the first day, and only casually the second. But she knew I was in the building, and when I came upon her one evening seated at the very desk in the mezzanine which we all have such bitter cause to remember, I could not forbear expressing myself in a way she could not misunderstand. The result was of a kind to drive a man like myself to an extremity of self-condemnation and rage. She rose up as if insulted, and flung me one sentence and one sentence only before she hailed the elevator and left my presence. A cur could not have been dismissed with less ceremony."

"That is not like my daughter. What was the sentence you allude to? Let me hear the very words." Mr. Challoner had come forward and now stood awaiting his reply, a dignified but pathetic figure, which all must view with respect.

"I hate the memory of them, but since you demand it, I will repeat them just as they fell from her lips," was Mr. Brotherson's bitter retort. "She said, 'You of all men should recognise the unseemliness of these proposals. Had your letters given me any hint of the feelings you have just expressed, you would never have had this opportunity of approaching me.' That was all; but her indignation was scathing. Ladies who have supped exclusively off silver, show a fine scorn for the common ware of the cottager."

Mr. Challoner bowed. "There is some mistake," said he. "My daughter might be averse to your addresses, but she would never show indignation to any aspirant for her hand, simply on account of extraneous conditions. She had wide sympathies—wider than I often approved. Something in your conduct or the confidence you showed shocked her nicer sense; not your lack of the luxuries she often misprised. This much I feel obliged to say, out of justice to her character, which was uniformly considerate."

"You have seen her with men of her own world and yours," was the harsh response. "She had another side to her nature for the man of a different sphere. And it killed my love—that you can see—and led to my sending her the injudicious letter with which you have confronted me. The hurt bull utters one bellow before he dies. I bellowed, and bellowed loudly, but I did not die. I'm my own man still and mean to remain so."

The assertive boldness—some would call it bravado—with which he thus finished the story of his relations with the dead heiress, seemed to be more than Mr. Challoner could stand. With a look of extreme pain and perplexity he vanished from the doorway, and it fell to Dr. Heath to inquire:

"Is this letter—a letter of threat you will remember—the only communication which passed between you and Miss Challoner after this unfortunate passage of arms at the Clermont?"

"Yes. I had no wish to address her again. I had exhausted in this one outburst whatever humiliation I felt."

"And she? Did she give no sign, make you no answer?"

"None whatever." Then, as if he found it impossible to hide this hurt to his pride, "She did not even seem to consider me worthy the honour of an added rebuke. Such arrogance is, no doubt, commendable in a Challoner."

This time his bitterness did not pass unrebuked by the coroner:

"Remember the grey hairs of the only Challoner who can hear you, and respect his grief."

Mr. Brotherson bowed.

"I have finished," said he. "I shall have nothing more to say on the subject." And he drew himself up in expectation of the dismissal he evidently thought pending.

But the coroner was not done with him by any means. He had a theory in regard to this lamentable suicide which he hoped to establish by this man's testimony, and, in pursuit of this plan, he not only motioned to Mr. Brotherson to reseat himself, but began at once to open a fresh line of examination by saying:

"You will pardon me, if I press this matter. I have been given to understand that notwithstanding your break with Miss Challoner, you have kept up your visits to the Clermont and were even on the spot at the time of her death."

"On the spot?"

"In the hotel, I mean."

"There you are right; I was in the hotel."

"At the time of her death?"

"Very near the time. I remember hearing some disturbance in the lobby behind me, just as I was passing out at the Broadway entrance."

"You did, and did not return?"

"Why should I return? I am not a man of much curiosity. There was no reason why I should connect a sudden alarm in the lobby of the Clermont with any cause of special interest to myself."

This was so true and the look which accompanied the words was so frank that the coroner hesitated a moment before he said:

"Certainly not, unless—well, to be direct, unless you had just seen Miss Challoner and knew her state of mind and what was likely to follow your abrupt departure."

"I had no interview with Miss Challoner."

"But you saw her? Saw her that evening and just before the accident?"

Sweetwater's papers rattled; it was the only sound to be heard in that moment of silence. Then— "What do you mean by those words?" inquired Mr. Brotherson, with studied composure. "I have said that I had no interview with Miss Challoner. Why do you ask me then, if I saw her?"

"Because I believe that you did. From a distance possibly, but yet directly and with no possibility of mistake."

"Do you put that as a question?"

"I do. Did you see her figure or face that night?"

"I did."

Nothing—not even the rattling of Sweetwater's papers—disturbed the silence which followed this admission.

"From where?" Dr. Heath asked at last.

"From a point far enough away to make any communication between us impossible. I do not think you will require me to recall the exact spot."

"If it were one which made it possible for her to see you as clearly as you could see her, I think it would be very advisable for you to say so."

"It was—such—a spot."

"Then I think I can locate it for you, or do you prefer to locate it yourself?"

"I will locate it myself. I had hoped not to be called upon to mention what I cannot but consider a most unfortunate coincidence. As a gentleman you will understand my reticence and also why it is a matter of regret to me that with an acumen worthy of your position, you should have discovered a fact which, while it cannot explain Miss Challoner's death, will drag our little affair before the public, and possibly give it a prominence in some minds which I am sure does not belong to it. I met Miss Challoner's eye for one instant from the top of the little staircase running up to the mezzanine. I had yielded thus far to an impulse I had frequently combated, to seek by another interview to retrieve the bad effect which must have been made upon her by my angry note. I knew that she frequently wrote letters in the mezzanine at this hour, and got as far as the top of the staircase in my effort to join her. But got no further. When I saw her on her feet, with her face turned my way, I remembered the scorn with which she had received my former heart-felt proposals and, without taking another step forward, I turned away from her and fled down the steps and so out of the building by the main entrance. She saw me, for her hand flew up with a startled gesture, but I cannot think that my presence on the same floor with her could have caused her to strike the blow which terminated her life. Why should I? No woman sacrifices her life out of mere regret for the disdain she has shown a man she has taken no pains to understand."

His tone and his attitude seemed to invite the concurrence of Dr. Heath in this statement. But the richness of the one and the grace of the other showed the handsome speaker off to such advantage that the coroner was rather inclined to consider how a woman, even of Miss Challoner's fine taste and careful breeding, might see in such a situation much for regret, if not for active despair and the suicidal act. He gave no evidence of his thought, however, but followed up the one admission made by Mr. Brotherson which he and others must naturally view as of the first importance.

"You saw Miss Challoner lift her hand, you say. Which hand. and what was in it? Anything?"

"She lifted her right hand, but it would be impossible for me to tell you whether there was anything in it or not. I simply saw the movement before I turned away. It looked like one of alarm to me. I felt that she had some reason for this. She could not know that it was in repentance I came rather than in fulfilment of my threat."

A sigh from the adjoining room. Mr. Brotherson rose, as he heard it, and in doing so met the clear eye of Sweetwater fixed upon his own. Its language was, no doubt, peculiar and it seemed to fascinate him for a moment, for he started as if to approach the detective, but forsook this intention almost immediately, and addressing the coroner, gravely remarked:

"Her death following so quickly upon this abortive attempt of mine at an interview startled me by its coincidence as much as it does you. If in the weakness of her woman's nature, it was more than this—if the scorn she had previously shown me was a cloak she instinctively assumed to hide what she was not ready to disclose, my remorse will be as great as any one here could wish. But the proof of all this will have to be very convincing before my present convictions will yield to it. Some other and more poignant source will have to be found for that instant's impulsive act than is supplied by this story of my unfortunate attachment."

Dr. Heath was convinced, but he was willing to concede something to the secret demand made upon him by Sweetwater, who was bundling up his papers with much clatter.

Looking up with a smile which had elements in it he was hardly conscious of perhaps himself, he asked in an off-hand way:

"Then why did you take such pains to wash your hands of the affair the moment you had left the hotel?"

"I do not understand."

"You passed around the corner into—street, did you not?"

"Very likely. I could go that way as well as another."

"And stopped at the first lamp-post?"

"Oh, I see. Someone saw that childish action of mine."

"What did you mean by it?"

"Just what you have suggested. I did go through the pantomime of washing my hands of an affair I considered definitely ended. I had resisted an irrepressible impulse to see and talk with Miss Challoner again, and was pleased with my firmness. Unaware of the tragic blow which had just fallen, I was full of self-congratulations at my escape from the charm which had lured me back to this hotel again and again in spite of my better judgment, and I wished to symbolise my relief by an act of which I was, in another moment, ashamed. Strange that there should have been a witness to it. (Here he stole a look at Sweetwater.) Stranger still, that circumstances by the most extraordinary of coincidences, should have given so unforeseen a point to it."

"You are right, Mr. Brotherson. The whole occurrence is startling and most strange. But life is made up of the unexpected, as none know better than we physicians, whether our practice be of a public or private character."

As Mr. Brotherson left the room, the curiosity to which he had yielded once before, led him to cast a glance of penetrating inquiry behind him full at Sweetwater, and if either felt embarrassment, it was not the hunted but the hunter.

But the feeling did not last.

"I've simply met the strongest man I've ever encountered," was Sweetwater's encouraging comment to himself. "All the more glory if I can find a joint in his armour or a hidden passage to his cold, secretive heart."

CHAPTER XI

ALIKE IN ESSENTIALS

"Mr. Gryce, I am either a fool or the luckiest fellow going. You must decide which."

The aged detective, thus addressed, laid down his evening paper and endeavoured to make out the dim form he could just faintly discern standing between him and the library door.

"Sweetwater, is that you?"

"No one else. Sweetwater, the fool, or Sweetwater, much too wise for his own good. I don't know which. Perhaps you can find out and tell me."

A grunt from the region of the library table, then the sarcastic remark:

"I'm just in the mood to settle that question. This last failure to my account ought to make me an excellent judge of another's folly. I've meddled with the old business for the last time, Sweetwater. You'll have to go it lone from now on. The Department has no more work for Ebenezar Gryce, or rather Ebenezar Gryce will make no more fool attempts to please them. Strange that a man don't know when his time has come to quit. I remember how I once scored Yeardsley for hanging on after he had lost his grip; and here am I doing the same thing. But what's the matter with you? Speak out, my boy. Something new in the wind?"

"No, Mr. Gryce; nothing new. It's the same old business. But, if what I suspect is true, this same old business offers opportunities for some very interesting and unusual effort. You're not satisfied with the coroner's verdict in the Challoner case?"

"No. I'm satisfied with nothing that leaves all ends dangling. Suicide was not proved. It seemed the only presumption possible, but it was not proved. There was no blood-stain on that cutter-point."

"Nor any evidence that it had ever been there."

"No. I'm not proud of the chain which lacks a link where it should be strongest."

"We shall never supply that link."

"I quite agree with you."

"That chain we must throw away."

"And forge another?"

Sweetwater approached and sat down.

"Yes; I believe we can do it; yet I have only one indisputable fact for a starter. That is why I want you to tell me whether I'm growing daft or simply adventurous. Mr. Gryce, I don't trust Brotherson. He has pulled the wool over Dr. Heath's eyes and almost over those of Mr. Challoner. But he can't pull it over mine. Though he should tell a story ten times more plausible than the one with which he has satisfied the coroner's jury, I would still listen to him with more misgiving than confidence. Yet I have caught him in no misstatement, and his eye is steadier than my own. Perhaps it is simply a deeply rooted antipathy on my part, or the rage one feels at finding he has placed his finger on the wrong man. Again it may be—"

"What, Sweetwater?"

"A well-founded distrust. Mr. Gryce, I'm going to ask you a question."

"Ask away. Ask fifty if you want to."

"No; the one may involve fifty, but it is big enough in itself to hold our attention for a while. Did you ever hear of a case before, that in some of its details was similar to this?"

"No, it stands alone. That's why it is so puzzling."

"You forget. The wealth, beauty and social consequence of the present victim has blinded you to the strong resemblance which her case bears to one you know, in which the sufferer had none of the worldly advantages of Miss Challoner. I allude to—"

"Wait! the washerwoman in Hicks Street! Sweetwater, what have you got up your sleeve? You do mean that Brooklyn washerwoman, don't you?"

"The same. The Department may have forgotten it, but I haven't. Mr. Gryce, there's a startling similarity in the two cases if you study the essential features only. Startling, I assure you."

"Yes, you are right there. But what if there is? We were no more successful in solving that case than we have been in solving this. Yet you look and act like a hound which has struck a hot scent." The young man smoothed his features with an embarrassed laugh.

"I shall never learn," said he, "not to give tongue till the hunt is fairly started. If you will excuse me we'll first make sure of the similarity I have mentioned. Then I'll explain myself. I have some notes here, made at the time it was decided to drop the Hicks Street case as a wholly inexplicable one. As you know, I never can bear to say 'die,' and I sometimes keep such notes as a possible help in case any such unfinished matter should come up again. Shall I read them?"

"Do. Twenty years ago it would not have been necessary. I should have remembered every detail of an affair so puzzling. But my memory is no longer entirely reliable. So fire away, my boy, though I hardly see your purpose or what real bearing the affair in Hicks Street has upon the Clermont one. A poor washerwoman and the wealthy Miss Challoner! True, they were not unlike in their end."

"The connection will come later," smiled the young detective, with that strange softening of his features which made one at times forget his extreme plainness. "I'm sure you will not consider the time lost if I ask you to consider the comparison I am about to make, if only as a curiosity in criminal annals."

And he read:

"'On the afternoon of December Fourth, 1910, the strong and persistent screaming of a young child in one of the rooms of a rear tenement in Hicks Street, Brooklyn, drew the attention of some of the inmates and led them, after several ineffectual efforts to gain an entrance, to the breaking in of the door which had been fastened on the inside by an old-fashioned door-button.

"'The tenant whom all knew for an honest, hard-working woman, had not infrequently fastened her door in this manner, in order to safeguard her child who was abnormally active and had a way of rattling the door open when it was not thus secured. But she had never refused to open before, and the child's cries were pitiful.

"'This was no longer a matter of wonder, when, the door having been wrenched from its hinges, they all rushed in. Across a tub of steaming clothes lifted upon a bench in the open window, they saw the body of this good woman, lying inert and seemingly dead; the frightened child tugging at her skirts. She was of a robust make, fleshy and fair, and had always been considered a model of health and energy, but at the sight of her helpless figure, thus stricken while at work, the one cry was 'A stroke! till she had been lifted off and laid upon the floor. Then some discoloration in the water at the bottom of the tub led to a closer examination of her body, and the discovery of a bullet-hole in her breast directly over the heart.

"'As she had been standing with face towards the window, all crowded that way to see where the shot had come from. As they were on the fourth storey it could not have come from the court upon which the room looked. It could only have come from the front tenement, towering up before them some twenty feet away. A single window of the innumerable ones confronting them stood open, and this was the one directly opposite.

"'Nobody was to be seen there or in the room beyond, but during the excitement, one man ran off to call the police and another to hunt up the janitor and ask who occupied this room.

"'His reply threw them all into confusion. The tenant of that room was the best, the quietest and most respectable man in either building.

"'Then he must be simply careless and the shot an accidental one. A rush was made for the stairs and soon the whole building was in an uproar. But when this especial room was reached, it was found locked and on the door a paper pinned up, on which these words were written: Gone to New York. Will be back at 6:30! Words that recalled a circumstance to the janitor. He had seen the gentleman go out an hour before. This terminated all inquiry in this direction, though some few of the excited throng were for battering down this door just as they had the other one. But they were overruled by the janitor, who saw no use in such wholesale destruction, and presently the arrival of the police restored order and limited the inquiry to the rear building, where it undoubtedly belonged.'

"Mr. Gryce," (here Sweetwater laid by his notes that he might address the old gentleman more directly), "I was with the boys when they made their first official investigation. This is why you can rely upon the facts as here given. I followed the investigation closely and missed nothing which could in any way throw light on the case. It was a mysterious one from the first, and lost nothing by further inquiry into the details.

"The first fact to startle us as we made our way up through the crowd which blocked halls and staircases was this:—A doctor had been found and, though he had been forbidden to make more than a cursory examination of the body till the coroner came, he had not hesitated to declare after his first look, that the wound had not been made by a bullet but by some sharp and slender weapon thrust home by a powerful hand. (You mark that, Mr. Gryce.) As this seemed impossible in face of the fact that the door had been found buttoned on the inside, we did not give much credit to his opinion and began our work under the obvious theory of an accidental discharge of some gun from one of the windows across the court. But the doctor was nearer right than we supposed. When the coroner came to look into the matter, he discovered that the wound was not only too small to have been made by the ordinary bullet, but that there was no bullet to be found in the woman's body or anywhere else. Her heart had been reached by a thrust and not by a shot from a gun. Mr. Gryce, have you not heard a startling repetition of this report in a case nearer at hand?

"But to go back. This discovery, so important if true, was as yet—that is, at the time of our entering the room,—limited to the off-hand declaration of an irresponsible physician, but the possibility it involved was of so astonishing a nature that it influenced us unconsciously in our investigation and led us almost immediately into a consideration of the difficulties attending an entrance into, as well as an escape from, a room situated as this was.

"Up three flights from the court, with no communication with the adjoining rooms save through a door guarded on both sides by heavy pieces of furniture no one person could handle, the hall door buttoned on the inside, and the fire-escape some fifteen feet to the left, this room of death appeared to be as removed from the approach of a murderous outsider as the spot in the writing-room of the Clermont where Miss Challoner fell.

"Otherwise, the place presented the greatest contrast possible to that scene of splendour and comfort. I had not entered the Clermont at that time, and no, such comparison could have struck my mind. But I have thought of it since, and you, with your experience, will not find it difficult to picture the room where this poor woman lived and worked. Bare walls, with just a newspaper illustration pinned up here and there, a bed—tragically occupied at this moment—a kitchen stove on which a boiler, half-filled with steaming clothes still bubbled and foamed,—an old bureau,—a large pine wardrobe against an inner door which we later found to have been locked for months, and the key lost,—some chairs—and most pronounced of all, because of its position directly before the window, a pine bench supporting a wash-tub of the old sort.

"As it was here the woman fell, this tub naturally received the closest examination. A board projected from its further side, whither it had evidently been pushed by the weight of her falling body; and from its top hung a wet cloth, marking with its lugubrious drip on the boards beneath the first heavy moments of silence which is the natural accompaniment of so serious a survey. On the floor to the right lay a half-used cake of soap just as it had slipped from her hand. The window was closed, for the temperature was at the freezing-point, but it had been found up, and it was put up now to show the height at which it had then stood. As we all took our look at the house wall opposite, a sound of shouting came up from below. A dozen children were sliding on barrel staves down a slope of heaped-up snow. They had been engaged in this sport all the afternoon and were our witnesses later that no one had made a hazardous escape by means of the ladder of the fire-escape, running, as I have said, at an almost unattainable distance towards the left.

"Of her own child, whose cries had roused the neighbours, nothing was to be seen. The woman in the extreme rear had carried it off to her room; but when we came to see it later, no doubt was felt by any of us that this child was too young to talk connectedly, nor did I ever hear that it ever said anything which could in any way guide investigation.

"And that is as far as we ever got. The coroner's jury brought in a verdict of death by means of a stab from some unknown weapon in the hand of a person also unknown, but no weapon was ever found, nor was it ever settled how the attack could have been made or the murderer escape under the conditions described. The woman was poor, her friends few, and the case seemingly inexplicable. So after creating some excitement by its peculiarities, it fell of its own weight. But I remembered it, and in many a spare hour have tried to see my way through the no-thoroughfare it presented. But quite in vain. To-day, the road is as blind as ever, but—" here Sweetwater's face sharpened and his eyes burned as he leaned closer and closer to the older detective—"but this second case, so unlike the first in non-essentials but so exactly like it in just those points which make the mystery, has dropped a thread from its tangled skein into my hand, which may yet lead us to the heart of both. Can you guess—have you guessed—what this thread is? But how could you without the one clew I have not given you? Mr. Gryce, the tenement where this occurred is the same I visited the other night in search of Mr. Brotherson. And the man characterised at that time by the janitor as the best, the quietest and most respectable tenant in the whole building, and the one you remember whose window opened directly opposite the spot where this woman lay dead, was Mr. Dunn himself, or, in other words, our late redoubtable witness, Mr. Orlando Brotherson."

CHAPTER XII

Mr. GRYCE FINDS AN ANTIDOTE FOR OLD AGE

"I thought I should make you sit up. I really calculated upon doing so, sir. Yes, I have established the plain fact that this Brotherson was near to, if not in the exact line of the scene of crime in each of these extraordinary and baffling cases. A very odd coincidence, is it not?" was the dry conclusion of our eager young detective.

"Odd enough if you are correct in your statement. But I thought it was conceded that the man Brotherson was not personally near,—was not even in the building at the time of the woman's death in Hicks Street; that he was out and had been out for hours according to the janitor."

"And so the janitor thought, but he didn't quite know his man. I'm not sure that I do. But I mean to make his acquaintance and make it thoroughly before I let him go. The hero—well, I will say the possible hero of two such adventures—deserves some attention from one so interested in the abnormal as myself."

"Sweetwater, how came you to discover that Mr. Dunn of this ramshackle tenement in Hicks Street was identical with the elegantly equipped admirer of Miss Challoner?"

"Just this way. The night before Miss Challoner's death I was brooding very deeply over the Hicks Street case. It had so possessed me that I had taken this street in on my way from Flatbush; as if staring at the house and its swarming courtyard was going to settle any such question as that! I walked by the place and I looked up at the windows. No inspiration. Then I sauntered back and entered the house with the fool intention of crossing the courtyard and wandering into the rear building where the crime had occurred. But my attention was diverted and my mind changed by seeing a man coming down the stairs before me, of so fine a figure that I involuntarily stopped to look at him. Had he moved a little less carelessly, had he worn his workman's clothes a little less naturally, I should have thought him some college bred man out on a slumming expedition. But he was entirely too much at home where he was, and too unconscious of his jeans for any such conclusion on my part, and when he had passed out I had enough curiosity to ask who he was.

"My interest, you may believe, was in no wise abated when I learned that he was that highly respectable tenant whose window had been open at the time when half the inmates of the two buildings had rushed up to his door, only to find a paper on it displaying these words: Gone to New York; will be back at 6:30. Had he returned at that hour? I don't think anybody had ever asked; and what reason had I for such interference now? But an idea once planted in my brain sticks tight, and I kept thinking of this man all the way to the Bridge. Instinctively and quite against my will, I found myself connecting him with some previous remembrance in which I seemed to see his tall form and strong features under the stress of some great excitement. But there my memory stopped, till suddenly as I was entering the subway, it all came back to me. I had met him the day I went with the boys to investigate the case in Hicks Street. He was coming down the staircase of the rear tenement then, very much as I had just seen him coming down the one in front. Only the Dunn of to-day seemed to have all his wits about him, while the huge fellow who brushed so rudely by me on that occasion had the peculiar look of a man struggling with horror or some other grave agitation. This was not surprising, of course, under the circumstances. I had met more than one man and woman in those halls who had worn the same look; but none of them had put up a sign on his door that he had left for New York and would not be back till 6:30, and then changed his mind so suddenly that he was back in the tenement at three, sharing the curiosity and the terrors of its horrified inmates.

"But the discovery, while possibly suggestive, was not of so pressing a nature as to demand instant action; and more immediate duties coming up, I let the matter slip from my mind, to be brought up again the next day, you may well believe, when all the circumstances of the death at the Clermont came to light and I found myself confronted by a problem very nearly the counterpart of the one then occupying me.

"But I did not see any real connection between the two cases, until, in my hunt for Mr. Brotherson, I came upon the following facts: that he was not always the gentleman he appeared: that the apartment in which he was supposed to live was not his own but a friend's; and that he was only there by spells. When he was there, he dressed like a prince and it was while so clothed he ate his meals in the cafe of the Hotel Clermont.

"But there were times when he had been seen to leave this apartment in a very different garb, and while there was no one to insinuate that he was slack in paying his debts or was given to dissipation or any overt vice, it was generally conceded by such as casually knew him, that there was a mysterious side to his life which no one understood. His friend—a seemingly candid and open-minded gentleman—explained these contradictions by saying that Mr. Brotherson was a humanitarian and spent much of his time in the slums. That while so engaged he naturally dressed to suit the occasion, and if he was to be criticised at all, it was for his zeal which often led him to extremes and kept him to his task for days, during which time none of his up-town friends saw him. Then this enthusiastic gentleman called him the great intellectual light of the day, and—well, if ever I want a character I shall take pains to insinuate myself into the good graces of this Mr. Conway.

"Of Brotherson himself I saw nothing. He had come to Mr. Conway's apartment the night before—the night of Miss Challoner's death, you understand but had remained only long enough to change his clothes. Where he went afterwards is unknown to Mr. Conway, nor can he tell us when to look for his return. When he does show up, my message will be given him, etc., etc. I have no fault to find with Mr. Conway.

"But I had an idea in regard to this elusive Brotherson. I had heard enough about him to be mighty sure that together with his other accomplishments he possessed the golden tongue and easy speech of an orator. Also, that his tendencies were revolutionary and that for all his fine clothes and hankering after table luxuries and the like, he cherished a spite against wealth which made his words under certain moods cut like a knife. But there was another man, known to us of the —— Precinct, who had very nearly these same gifts, and this man was going to speak at a secret meeting that very evening. This we had been told by a disgruntled member of the Associated Brotherhood. Suspecting Brotherson, I had this prospective speaker described, and thought I recognised my man. But I wanted to be positive in my identification, so I took Anderson with me, and—but I'll cut that short. We didn't see the orator and that 'go' went for nothing; but I had another string to my bow in the shape of the workman Dunn who also answered to the description which had been given me; so I lugged poor Anderson over into Hicks Street.

"It was late for the visit I proposed, but not too late, if Dunn was also the orator who, surprised by a raid I had not been let into, would be making for his home, if only to establish an alibi. The subway was near, and I calculated on his using it, but we took a taxicab and so arrived in Hicks Street some few minutes before him. The result you know. Anderson recognised the man as the one whom he saw washing his hands in the snow outside of the Clermont, and the man, seeing himself discovered, owned himself to be Brotherson and made no difficulty about accompanying us the next day to the coroner's office.

"You have heard how he bore himself; what his explanations were and how completely they fitted in with the preconceived notions of the Inspector and the District Attorney. In consequence, Miss Challoner's death is looked upon as a suicide—the impulsive act of a woman who sees the man she may have scouted but whom she secretly loves, turn away from her in all probability forever. A weapon was in her hand—she impulsively used it, and another deplorable suicide was added to the melancholy list. Had I put in my oar at the conference held in the coroner's office; had I recalled to Dr. Heath the curious case of Mrs. Spotts, and then identified Brotherson as the man whose window fronted hers from the opposite tenement, a diversion might have been created and the outcome been different. But I feared the experiment. I'm not sufficiently in with the Chief as yet, nor yet with the Inspector. They might not have called me a fool—you may; but that's different—and they might have listened, but it would doubtless have been with an air I could not have held up against, with that fellow's eyes fixed mockingly on mine. For he and I are pitted for a struggle, and I do not want to give him the advantage of even a momentary triumph. He's the most complete master of himself of any man I ever met, and it will take the united brain and resolution of the whole force to bring him to book—if he ever is brought to book, which I doubt. What do you think about it?"

"That you have given me an antidote against old age," was the ringing and unexpected reply, as the thoughtful, half-puzzled aspect of the old man yielded impulsively to a burst of his early enthusiasm. "If we can get a good grip on the thread you speak of, and can work ourselves along by it, though it be by no more than an inch at a time, we shall yet make our way through this labyrinth of undoubted crime and earn for ourselves a triumph which will make some of these raw and inexperienced young fellows about us stare. Sweetwater, coincidences are possible. We run upon them every day. But coincidence in crime! that should make work for a detective, and we are not afraid of work. There's my hand for my end of the business "

"And here's mine."

Next minute the two heads were closer than ever together, and the business had begun.

TIME, CIRCUMSTANCE, AND A VILLAIN'S HEART

"Our first difficulty is this. We must prove motive. Now, I do not think it will be so very hard to show that this Brotherson cherished feelings of revenge towards Miss Challoner. But I have to acknowledge right here and now that the most skillful and vigourous pumping of the janitor and such other tenants of the Hicks Street tenement as I have dared to approach, fails to show that he has ever held any communication with Mrs. Spotts, or even knew of her existence until her remarkable death attracted his attention. I have spent all the afternoon over this, and with no result. A complete break in the chain at the very start."

"Humph! we will set that down, then, as so much against us."

"The next, and this is a bitter pill too, is the almost insurmountable difficulty already recognised of determining how a man, without approaching his victim, could manage to inflict a mortal stab in her breast. No cloak of complete invisibility has yet been found, even by the cleverest criminals."

"True. The problem is such as a nightmare offers. For years my dreams have been haunted by a gnome who proposes just such puzzles."

"But there's an answer to everything, and I'm sure there's an answer to this. Remember his business. He's an inventor, with startling ideas. So much I've seen for myself. You may stretch probabilities a little in his case; and with this conceded, we may add by way of off-set to the difficulties you mention, coincidences of time and circumstance, and his villainous heart. Oh, I know that I am prejudiced; but wait and see! Miss Challoner was well rid of him even at the cost of her life."

"She loved him. Even her father believes that now. Some lately discovered letters have come to light to prove that she was by no means so heart free as he supposed. One of her friends, it seems, has also confided to him that once, while she and Miss Challoner were sitting together, she caught Miss Challoner in the act of scribbling capitals over a sheet of paper. They were all B's with the exception of here and there a neatly turned O, and when her friend twitted her with her fondness for these two letters, and suggested a pleasing monogram, Miss Challoner answered, 'O. B. (transferring the letters, as you see) are the initials of the finest man in the world.'"

"Gosh! has he heard this story?"

"Who?"

"The gentleman in question."

"Mr. Brotherson?"

"Yes."

"I don't think so. It was told me in confidence."

"Told you, Mr. Gryce? Pardon my curiosity."

"By Mr. Challoner."

"Oh! by Mr. Challoner."

"He is greatly distressed at having the disgraceful suggestion of suicide attached to his daughter's name. Notwithstanding the circumstances,—notwithstanding his full recognition of her secret predilection for a man of whom he had never heard till the night of her death, he cannot believe that she struck the blow she did, intentionally. He sent for me in order to inquire if anything could be done to reinstate her in public opinion. He dared not insist that another had wielded the weapon which laid her low so suddenly, but he asked if, in my experience, it had never been known that a woman, hyper-sensitive to some strong man's magnetic influence, should so follow his thought as to commit an act which never could have arisen in her own mind, uninfluenced. He evidently does not like Brotherson either."

"And what—what did you—say?" asked Sweetwater, with a halting utterance and his face full of thought.

"I simply quoted the latest authority on hypnotism that no person even in hypnotic sleep could be influenced by another to do what was antagonistic to his natural instincts."

"Latest authority. That doesn't mean a final one. Supposing that it was hypnotism! But that wouldn't account for Mrs. Spotts' death. Her wound certainly was not a self-inflicted one."

"How can you be sure?"

"There was no weapon found in the room, or in the court. The snow was searched and the children too. No weapon, Mr. Gryce, not even a paper-cutter. Besides—but how did Mr. Challoner take what you said? Was he satisfied with this assurance?"

"He had to be. I didn't dare to hold out any hope based on so unsubstantial a theory. But the interview had this effect upon me. If the possibility remains of fixing guilt elsewhere than on Miss Challoner's inconsiderate impulse, I am ready to devote any amount of time and strength to the work. To see this grieving father relieved from the worst part of his burden is worth some effort and now you know why I have listened so eagerly to you. Sweetwater, I will go with you to the Superintendent. We may not gain his attention and again we may. If we don't—but we won't cross that bridge prematurely. When will you be ready for this business?"

"I must be at Headquarters to-morrow."

"Good, then let it be to-morrow. A taxicab, Sweetwater. The subway for the young. I can no longer manage the stairs."

CHAPTER XIV

A CONCESSION

"It is true; there seems to be something extraordinary in the coincidence."

Thus Mr. Brotherson, in the presence of the Inspector.

"But that is all there is to it," he easily proceeded. "I knew Miss Challoner and I have already said how much and how little I had to do with her death. The other woman I did not know at all; I did not even know her name. A prosecution based on grounds so flimsy as those you advance would savour of persecution, would it not?"

The Inspector, surprised by this unexpected attack, regarded the speaker with an interest rather augmented than diminished by his boldness. The smile with which he had uttered these concluding words yet lingered on his lips, lighting up features of a mould too suggestive of command to be associated readily with guilt. That the impression thus produced was favourable, was evident from the tone of the Inspector's reply:

"We have said nothing about prosecution, Mr. Brotherson. We hope to avoid any such extreme measures, and that we may the more readily do so, we have given you this opportunity to make such explanations as the situation, which you yourself have characterised as remarkable, seems to call for."

"I am ready. But what am I called upon to explain? I really cannot see, sir. Knowing nothing more about either case than you do, I fear that I shall not add much to your enlightenment."

"You can tell us why with your seeming culture and obvious means, you choose to spend so much time in a second-rate tenement like the one in Hicks Street."

Again that chill smile preceding the quiet answer:

"Have you seen my room there? It is piled to the ceiling with books. When I was a poor man, I chose the abode suited to my purse and my passion for first-rate reading. As I grew better off, my time became daily more valuable. I have never seen the hour when I felt like moving that precious collection. Besides, I am a man of the people. I like the working class, and am willing to be thought one of them. I can find time to talk to a hard-pushed mechanic as easily as to such members of the moneyed class as I encounter on stray evenings at the Hotel Clermont. I have led—I may say that I am leading—a double life; but of neither am I ashamed, nor have I cause to be. Love drove me to ape the gentleman in the halls of the Clermont; a broad human interest in the work of the world, to live as a fellow among the mechanics of Hicks Street."

"But why make use of one name as a gentleman of leisure and quite a different one as the honest workman?"

"Ah, there you touch upon my real secret. I have a reason for keeping my identity quiet till my invention is completed."

"A reason connected with your anarchistic tendencies?"

"Possibly." But the word was uttered in a way to carry little conviction. "I am not much of an anarchist," he now took the trouble to declare, with a careless lift of his shoulders. "I like fair play, but I shall never give you much trouble by my manner of insuring it. I have too much at stake. My invention is dearer to me than the overthrow of present institutions. Nothing must stand in the way of its success, not even the satisfaction of inspiring terror in minds shut to every other species of argument. I have uttered my last speech; you can rely on me for that."

"We are glad to hear it, Mr. Dunn. Physical overthrow carries more than the immediate sufferer with it."

If this were meant as an irritant, it did not act successfully. The social agitator, the political demagogue, the orator whose honeyed tones had rung with biting invective in the ears of the United Brotherhood of the Awl, the Plane and the Trowel, simply bowed and calmly waited for the next attack.

Perhaps it was of a nature to surprise even him.

"We have no wish," continued the Inspector, "to probe too closely into concerns seemingly quite removed from the main issue. You say that you are ready, nay more, are even eager to answer all questions. You will probably be anxious then to explain away a discrepancy between your word and your conduct, which has come to our attention. You were known to have expressed the intention of spending the afternoon of Mrs. Spotts' death in New York and were supposed to have done so, yet you were certainly seen in the crowd which invaded that rear building at the first alarm. Are you conscious of possessing a double, or did you fail to cross the river as you expected to?"

"I am glad this has come up." The tone was one of self-congratulation which would have shaken Sweetwater sorely had he been admitted to this unofficial examination. "I have never confided to any one the story of my doings on that unhappy afternoon, because I knew of no one who would take any interest in them. But this is what occurred. I did mean to go to New York and I even started on my walk to the Bridge at the hour mentioned. But I got into a small crowd on the corner of Fulton Street, in which a poor devil who had robbed a vendor's cart of a few oranges, was being hustled about. There was no policeman within sight, and so I busied myself there for a minute paying for the oranges and dragging the poor wretch away into an alley, where I could have the pleasure of seeing him eat them. When I came out of the alley the small crowd had vanished, but a big one was collecting up the street very near my home. I always think of my books when I see anything suggesting fire, and naturally I returned, and equally natural y, when I heard what had happened, followed the crowd into the court and so up to the poor woman's doorway. But my curiosity satisfied, I returned at once to the street and went to New York as I had planned."

"Do you mind telling us where you went in New York?"

"Not at all. I went shopping. I wanted a certain very fine wire, for an experiment I had on hand, and I found it in a little shop in Fourth Avenue. If I remember rightly, the name over the door was Grippus. Its oddity struck me."

There was nothing left to the Inspector but to dismiss him. He had answered all questions willingly, and with a countenance inexpressive of guile. He even indulged in a parting shot on his own account, as full of frank acceptance of the situation as it was fearless in its attack. As he halted in the doorway before turning his back upon the room, he smiled for the third time as he quietly said:

"I have ceased visiting my friend's apartment in upper New York. If you ever want me again, you will find me amongst my books. If my invention halts and other interests stale, you have furnished me this day with a problem which cannot fail to give continual occupation to my energies. If I succeed in solving it first, I shall be happy to share my knowledge with you. Till then, trust the laws of nature. No man when once on the outside of a door can button it on the inside, nor could any one without the gift of complete invisibility, make a leap of over fifteen feet from the sill of a fourth story window on to an adjacent fire escape, without attracting the attention of some of the many children playing down below."

He was half-way out the door, but his name quickly spoken by the Inspector drew him back.

"Anything more?" he asked.

The Inspector smiled.

"You are a man of considerable analytic power, as I take it, Mr. Brotherson. You must have decided long ago how this woman died."

"Is that a question, Inspector?"

"You may take it as such."

"Then I will allow myself to say that there is but one common-sense view to take of the matter. Miss Challoner's death was due to suicide; so was that of the washerwoman. But there I stop. As for the means—the motive—such mysteries may be within your province but they are totally outside mine! God help us all! The world is full of misery. Again I wish you good-day."

The air seemed to have lost its vitality and the sun its sparkle when he was gone.

"Now, what do you think, Gryce?"

The old man rose and came out of his corner.

"This: that I'm up against the hardest proposition of my lifetime. Nothing in the man's appearance or manner evinces guilt, yet I believe him guilty. I must. Not to, is to strain probability to the point of breakage. But how to reach him is a problem and one of no ordinary nature. Years ago, when I was but little older than Sweetwater, I had just such a conviction concerning a certain man against whom I had even less to work on than we have here. A murder had been committed by an envenomed spring contained in a toy puzzle. I worked upon the conscience of the suspect in that case, by bringing constantly before his eyes a facsimile of that spring. It met him in the folded napkin which he opened at his restaurant dinner. He stumbled upon it in the street, and found it lying amongst his papers at home. I gave him no relief and finally he succumbed. He had been almost driven mad by remorse. But this man has no conscience. If he is not innocent as the day, he's as hard as unquarried marble. He might be confronted with reminders of his crime at every turn without weakening or showing by loss of appetite or interrupted sleep any effect upon his nerves. That's my opinion of the gentleman. He is either that, or a man of uncommon force and self-restraint."

"I'm inclined to believe him the latter."

"And so give the whole matter the go-by?"

"Possibly."

"It will be a terrible disappointment to Sweetwater."

"That's nothing."

"And to me."

"That's different. I'm disposed to consider you, Gryce—after all these years."

"Thank you; I have done the state some service."

"What do you want? You say the mine is unworkable."

"Yes, in a day, or in a week, possibly in a month. But persistence and a protean adaptability to meet his moods might accomplish something. I don't say will, I only say might. If Sweetwater had the job, with unlimited time in which to carry out any plan he may have, or even for a change of plans to suit a changed idea, success might be his, and both time, effort and outlay justified."

"The outlay? I am thinking of the outlay."

"Mr. Challoner will see to that. I have his word that no reasonable amount will daunt him."

"But this Brotherson is suspicious. He has an inventor's secret to hide, if none other. We can't saddle him with a guy of Sweetwater's appearance and abnormal loquaciousness."

"Not readily, I own. But time will bring counsel. Are you willing to help the boy, to help me and possibly yourself by this venture in the dark? The Department shan't lose money by it; that's all I can promise."

"But it's a big one. Gryce, you shall have your way. You'll be the only loser if you fail; and you will fail; take my word for it."

"I wish I could speak as confidently to the contrary, but I can't. I can give you my hand though, Inspector, and Sweetwater's thanks. I can meet the boy now. An hour ago I didn't know how I was to do it."

CHAPTER XV

THAT'S THE QUESTION

"How many times has he seen you?"

"Twice."

"So that he knows your face and figure?"

"I'm afraid so. He cannot help remembering the man who faced him in his own room."

"That's unfortunate."

"Damned unfortunate; but one must expect some sort of a handicap in a game like this. Before I'm done with him, he'll look me full in the face and wonder if he's ever seen me before. I wasn't always a detective. I was a carpenter once, as you know, and I'll take to the tools again. As soon as I'm handy with them I'll hunt up lodgings in Hicks Street. He may suspect me at first, but he won't long;

I'll be such a confounded good workman. I only wish I hadn't such pronounced features. They've stood awfully in my way, Mr. Gryce. I don't like to talk about my appearance, but I'm so confounded plain that people remember me. Why couldn't I have had one of those putty faces which don't mean anything? It would have been a deuced sight more convenient."

"You've done very well as it is."

"But I want to do better. I want to deceive him to his face. He's clever, this same Brotherson, and there's glory to be got in making a fool of him. Do you think it could be done with a beard? I've never worn a beard. While I'm settling back into my old trade, I can let the hair grow."

"Do. It'll make you look as weak as water. It'll be blonde, of course."

"And silky and straggling. Charming addition to my beauty. But it'll take half an inch off my nose, and it'll cover my mouth, which means a lot in my case. Then my complexion! It must be changed naturally. I'll consult a doctor about that. No sort of make-believe will go with this man. If my eyes look weak, they must really be so. If I walk slowly and speak huskily, it must be because I cannot help it. I can bear the slight inconvenience of temporary ill-health in a cause like this; and if necessary the cough will be real, and the headache positive.

"Sweetwater! We'd better give the task to another man—to someone Brotherson has never seen and won't be suspicious of?"

"He'll be suspicious of everybody who tries to make friends with him now; only a little more so with me; that's all. But I've got to meet that, and I'll do it by being, temporarily, of course, exactly the man I seem. My health will not be good for the next few weeks, I'm sure of that. But I'll be a model workman, neat and conscientious with just a suspicion of dash where dash is needed. He knows the real thing when he sees it, and there's not a fellow living more alive to shams. I won't be a sham. I'll be it. You'll see."

"But the doubt. Can you do all this in doubt of the issue?"

"No; I must have confidence in the end, and I must believe in his guilt. Nothing else will carry me through. I must believe in his guilt."

"Yes, that's essential."

"And I do. I never was surer of anything than I am of that. But I'll have the deuce of a time to get evidence enough for a grand jury. That's plainly to be seen, and that's why I'm so dead set on the business. It's such an even toss-up."

"I don't call it even. He's got the start of you every way. You can't go to his tenement; the janitor there would recognise you even if he didn't."

"Now I will give you a piece of good news. They're to have a new janitor next week. I learned that yesterday. The present one is too easy. He'll be out long before I'm ready to show myself there; and so will the woman who took care of the poor washerwoman's little child. I'd not have risked her curiosity. Luck isn't all against us. How does Mr. Challoner feel about it?"

"Not very confident; but willing to give you any amount of rope. Sweetwater, he let me have a batch of letters written by his daughter which he found in a secret drawer. They are not to be read, or even opened, unless a great necessity arises. They were written for Brotherson's eye—or so the father says—but she never sent them; too exuberant perhaps. If you ever want them—I cannot give them to you to-night, and wouldn't if I could,—don't go to Mr. Challorer—you must never be seen at his hotel—and don't come to me, but to the little house in West Twenty-ninth Street, where they will be kept for you, tied up in a package with your name on it. By the way, what name are you going to work under?"

"My mother's—Zugg."

"Good! I'll remember. You can always write or even telephone to Twenty-ninth Street. I'm in constant communication with them there, and it's quite safe."

"Thanks. You're sure the Superintendent is with me?"

"Yes, but not the Inspector. He sees nothing but the victim of a strange coincidence in Orlando Brotherson."

"Again the scales hang even. But they won't remain so. One side is bound to rise. Which? That's the question, Mr. Gryce."

CHAPTER XVI

OPPOSED

There was a new tenant in the Hicks Street tenement. He arrived late one afternoon and was shown two rooms, one in the rear building and another in the front one. Both were on the fourth floor. He demurred at the former, thought it gloomy but finally consented to try it. The other, he said, was too expensive. The janitor—new to the business—was not much taken with him and showed it, which seemed to offend the newcomer, who was evidently an irritable fellow owing to ill health.

However, they came to terms as I have said, and the man went away, promising to send in his belongings the next day. He smiled as he said this and the janitor who had rarely seen such a change take place in a human face, looked uncomfortable for a moment and seemed disposed to make some remark about the room they were leaving. But, thinking better of it, locked the door and led the way downstairs. As the prospective tenant followed, he may have noticed, probably did, that the door they had just left was a new one—the only new thing to be seen in the whole shabby place.

The next night that door was locked on the inside. The young man had taken possession. As he put away the remnants of a meal he had cooked for himself, he cast a look at his surroundings, and imperceptibly sighed. Then he brightened again, and sitting down or his solitary chair, he turned his eyes on the window which, uncurtained and without shade, stared open-mouthed, as it were, at the opposite wall rising high across the court.

In that wall, one window only seemed to interest him and that was on a level with his own. The shade of this window was up, but there was no light back of it and so nothing of the interior could be seen. But his eye remained fixed upon it, while his hand, stretched out towards the lamp burning near him, held itself in readiness to lower the light at a minute's notice.

Did he see only the opposite wall and that unillumined window? Was there no memory of the time when, in a previous contemplation of those dismal panes, he beheld stretching between them and himself, a long, low bench with a plain wooden tub upon it, from which a dripping cloth beat out upon the boards beneath a dismal note, monotonous as the ticking of a clock?

One might judge that such memories were indeed his, from the rapid glance he cast behind him at the place where the bed had stood in those days. It was placed differently now.

But if he saw, and if he heard these suggestions from the past, he was not less alive to the exactions of the present, for, as his glance flew back across the court, his finger suddenly moved and the flame it controlled sputtered and went out. At the same instant, the window opposite sprang into view as the lamp was lit within, and for several minutes the whole interior remained visible—the books, the work-table, the cluttered furniture, and, most interesting of all, its owner and occupant. It was upon the latter that the newcomer fixed his attention, and with an absorption equal to that he saw expressed in the countenance opposite.

But his was the absorption of watchfulness; that of the other of introspection. Mr. Brotherson—(we will no longer call him Dunn even here where he is known by no other name)—had entered the room clad in his heavy overcoat and, not having taken it off before lighting his lamp, still stood with it on, gazing eagerly down at the model occupying the place of honour on the large centre table. He was not touching it,—not at this moment—but that his thoughts were with it, that his whole mind was concentrated on it, was evident to the watcher across the court; and, as this watcher took in this fact and noticed the loving care with which the enthusiastic inventor finally put out his finger to re-arrange a thread or twirl a wheel, his disappointment found utterance in a sigh which echoed sadly through the dull and cheerless room. Had he expected this stern and self-contained man to show an open indifference to work and the hopes of a lifetime? If so, this was the first of the many surprises awaiting him.

He was gifted, however, with the patience of an automaton and continued to watch his fellow tenant as long as the latter's shade remained up. When it fell, he rose and took a few steps up and down, but not with the celerity and precision which usually accompanied his movements. Doubt disturbed his mind and impeded his activity. He had caught a fair glimpse of Brotherson's face as he approached the window, and though it continued to show abstraction, it equally displayed serenity and a complete satisfaction with the present if not with the future. Had he mistaken his man after all? Was his instinct, for the first time in his active career, wholly at fault?

He had succeeded in getting a glimpse of his quarry in the privacy of his own room, at home with his thoughts and unconscious of any espionage, and how had he found him? Cheerful, and natural in all his movements.

But the evening was young. Retrospect comes with later and more lonely hours. There will be opportunities yet for studying this impassive countenance under much more telling and productive circumstances than these. He would await these opportunities with cheerful anticipation. Meanwhile, he would keep up the routine watch he had planned for this night. Something might yet occur. At all events he would have exhausted the situation from this standpoint.

And so it came to pass that at an hour when all the other hard-working people in the building were asleep, or at least striving to sleep, these two men still sat at their work, one in the light, the other in the darkness, facing each other, consciously to the one, unconsciously to the other, across the hollow well of the now silent court. Eleven o'clock! Twelve! No change on Brotherson's part or in Brotherson's room; but a decided one in the place where Sweetwater sat. Objects which had been totally indistinguishable even to his penetrating eye could now be seen in ever brightening outline. The moon had reached the open space above the court, and he was getting the full benefit of it. But it was a benefit he would have been glad to dispense with. Darkness was like a shield to him. He did not feel quite sure that he wanted this shield removed. With no curtain to the window and no shade, and all this brilliance pouring into the room, he feared the disclosure of his presence there, or, if not that, some effect on his own mind of those memories he was more anxious to see mirrored in another's discomfiture than in his own.

Was it to escape any lack of concentration which these same memories might bring, that he rose and stepped to the window? Or was it under one of those involuntary impulses which move us in spite of ourselves to do the very thing our judgment disapproves?

No sooner had he approached the sill than Mr. Brotherson's shade flew way up and he, too, looked out. Their glances met, and for an instant the hardy detective experienced that involuntary stagnation of the blood which follows an inner shock. He felt that he had been recognised. The moonlight lay full upon his face, and the other had seen and known him. Else, why the constrained attitude and sudden rigidity observable in this confronting figure, with its partially lifted hand? A man like Brotherson makes no pause in any action however trivial, without a reason. Either he had been transfixed by this glimpse of his enemy on watch, or daring thought! had seen enough of sepulchral suggestion in the wan face looking forth from this fatal window to shake him from his composure and let loose the grinning devil of remorse from its iron prison-house? If so, the movement was a memorable one, and the hazard quite worth while. He had gained—no! he had gained nothing. He had been the fool of his own wishes. No one, let alone Brotherson, could have mistaken his face for that of a woman. He had forgotten his newly-grown beard. Some other cause must be found for the other's attitude. It savoured of shock, if not fear. If it were fear, then had he roused an emotion which might rebound upon himself in sharp reprisal. Death had been known to strike people standing where he stood; mysterious death of a species quite unrecognisable. What warranty had he that it would not strike him, and now? None.

Yet it was Brotherson who moved first. With a shrug of the shoulder plainly visible to the man opposite, he turned away from the window and without lowering the shade began gathering up his papers for the night, and later banking up his stove with ashes.

Sweetwater, with a breath of decided relief, stepped back and threw himself on the bed. It had really been a trial for him to stand there under the other's eye, though his mind refused to formulate his fear, or to give him any satisfaction when he asked himself what there was in the situation suggestive of death to the woman or harm to himself.

Nor did morning light bring counsel, as is usual in similar cases. He felt the mystery more in the hubbub and restless turmoil of the day than in the night's silence and inactivity. He was glad when the stroke of six gave him an excuse to leave the room, and gladder yet when in doing so, he ran upon an old woman from a neighbouring room, who no sooner saw him than she leered at him and eagerly remarked:

"Not much sleep, eh? We didn't think you'd like it. Did you see anything?"

Now this gave him the one excuse he wanted.

"See anything?" he repeated, apparently with all imaginable innocence. "What do you mean by that?"

"Don't you know what happened in that room?"

"Don't tell me!" he shouted out. "I don't want to hear any nonsense. I haven't time. I've got to be at the shop at seven and I don't feel very well. What did happen?" he mumbled in drawing off, just loud enough for the woman to hear. "Something unpleasant I'm sure." Then he ran downstairs.

At half past six he found the janitor. He was, to all appearance, in a state of great excitement and he spoke very fast.

"I won't stay another night in that room," he loudly declared, breaking in where the family were eating breakfast by lamplight. "I don't want to make any trouble and I don't want to give my reasons; but that room don't suit me. I'd rather take the dark one you talked about yesterday. There's the money. Have my things moved to-day, will ye?"

"But your moving out after one night's stay will give that room a bad name," stammered the janitor, rising awkwardly. "There'll be talk and I won't be able to let that room all winter."

"Nonsense! Every man hasn't the nerves I have. You'll let it in a week. But let or not let, I'm going front into the little dark room. I'll get the boss to let me off at half past four. So that's settled."

He waited for no reply and got none; but when he appeared promptly at a quarter to five, he found his few belongings moved into a middle room on the fourth floor of the front building, which, oddly perhaps, chanced to be next door to the one he had held under watch the night before.

The first page of his adventure in the Hicks Street tenement had been turned, and he was ready to start upon another.

CHAPTER XVII

IN WHICH A BOOK PLAYS A LEADING PART

When Mr. Brotherson came in that night, he noticed that the door of the room adjoining his own stood open. He did not hesitate. Making immediately for it, he took a glance inside, then spoke up with a ringing intonation:

"Halloo! coming to live in this hole?"

The occupant a young man, evidently a workman and somewhat sickly if one could judge from his complexion—turned around from some tinkering he was engaged in and met the intruder fairly, face to face. If his jaw fell, it seemed to be from admiration. No other emotion would have so lighted his eye as he took in the others proportions and commanding features. No dress—Brotherson was never seen in any other than the homeliest garb in these days—could make him look common or akin to his surroundings. Whether seen near or far, his presence always caused surprise, and surprise was what the young man showed, as he answered briskly:

"Yes, this is to be my castle. Are you the owner of the buildings? If so—"

"I am not the owner. I live next door. Haven't I seen you before, young man?"

Never was there a more penetrating eye than Orlando Brotherson's. As he asked this question it took some effort on the part of the other to hold his own and laugh with perfect naturalness as he replied:

"If you ever go up Henry Street it's likely enough that you've seen me not once, but many times. I'm the fellow who works at the bench next the window in Schuper's repairing shop. Everybody knows me."

Audacity often carries the day when subtler means would fa l. Brotherson stared at the youth, then ventured another question:

"A carpenter, eh?"

"Yes, and I'm an A1 man at my job. Excuse my brag. It's my one card o⁻ introduction."

"I've seen you. I've seen you somewhere else than in Schuper's shop. Do you remember me?"

"No, sir; I'm sorry to be imperlite but I don't remember you at all. Won't you sit down? It's not very cheerful, but I'm so glad to get out of the room I was in last night that this looks all right to me. Back there, other building," he whispered. "I didn't know, and took the room which had a window in it; but—" The stop was significant; so was his smile which had a touch of sickliness in it, as well as humour.

But Brotherson was not to be caught.

"You slept in the building last night? In the other half, I mean?"

"Yes, I—slept."

The strong lip of the other man curled disdainfully.

"I saw you," said he. "You were standing in the window overlooking the court. You were not sleeping then. I suppose you know that a woman died in that room?'

"Yes; they told me so this morning."

"Was that the first you'd heard of it?"

"Sure!" The word almost jumped at the questioner. "Do you suppose I'd have taken the room if—"

But here the intruder, with a disdainful grunt, turned and went out, disgust in every feature,—plain, unmistakable, downright disgust, and nothing more!

This was what gave Sweetwater his second bad night; this and a certain discovery he made. He had counted on hearing what went on in the neighbouring room through the partition running back of his own closet. But he could hear nothing, unless it was the shutting down of a window, a loud sneeze, or the rattling of coals as they were put on the fire. And these possessed no significance. What he wanted was to catch the secret sigh, the muttered word, the involuntary movement. He was too far removed from this man still.

How should he manage to get nearer him—at the door of his mind—of his heart? Sweetwater stared all night from his miserable cot into the darkness of that separating closet, and with no result. His task looked hopeless; no wonder that he could get no rest.

Next morning he felt ill, but he rose all the same, and tried to get his own breakfast. He had but partially succeeded and was sitting on the edge of his bed in wretched discomfort, when the very man he was thinking of appeared at his door.

"I've come to see how you are," said Brotherson. "I noticed that you did not look well last night. Won't you come in and share my pot of coffee?"

"I—I can't eat," mumbled Sweetwater, for once in his life thrown completely off his balance. "You're very kind, but I'll manage all right. I'd rather. I'm not quite dressed, you see, and I must get to the shop." Then he thought—"What an opportunity I'm losing. Have I any right to turn tail because he plays his game from the outset with trumps? No, I've a small trump somewhere about me to lay on this trick. It isn't an ace, but it'll show I'm not chicane." And smiling, though not with his usual cheerfulness, Sweetwater added, "Is the coffee all made? I might take a drop of that. But you mustn't ask me to eat—I just couldn't."

"Yes, the coffee is made and it isn't bad either. You'd better put on your coat; the hall's draughty." And waiting till Sweetwater did so, he led the way back to his own room. Brotherson's manner expressed perfect ease, Sweetwater's not. He knew himself changed in looks, in bearing, in feeling, even; but was he changed enough to deceive this man on the very spot where they had confronted each other a few days before in a keen moral struggle? The looking-glass he passed on his way to the table where the simple breakfast was spread out, showed him a figure so unlike the alert, business-like chap he had been that night, that he felt his old assurance revive in time to ease a situation which had no counterpart in his experience.

"I'm going out myself to-day, so we'll have to hurry a bit," was Brotherson's first remark as they seated themselves at table. "Do you like your coffee plain or with milk in it?"

"Plain. Gosh! what pictures! Where do you get 'em? You must have a lot of coin." Sweetwater was staring at the row of photographs, mostly of a very high order, tacked along the wall separating the two rooms. They were unframed, but they were mostly copies of great pictures, and the effect was rather imposing in contrast to the shabby furniture and the otherwise homely fittings.

"Yes, I've enough for that kind of thing," was his host's reply. But the tone was reserved, and Sweetwater did not presume again along this line. Instead, he looked well at the books piled upon the shelves under these photographs, and wondered aloud at their number and at the man who could waste such a lot of time in reading them. But he made no more direct remarks. Was he cowed by the penetrating eye he encountered whenever he yielded to the fascination exerted by Mr. Brotherson's personality and looked his way? He hated to think so, yet something held him in check and made him listen, open-mouthed, when the other chose to speak.

Yet there was one cheerful moment. It was when he noticed the careless way in which those books were arranged upon their shelves. An idea had come to him. He hid his relief in his cup, as he drained the last drops of the coffee which really tasted better than he had expected.

When he returned from work that afternoon it was with an auger under his coat and a conviction which led him to empty out the contents of a small phial which he took down from a shelf. He had told Mr. Gryce that he was eager for the business because of its difficulties, but that was when he was feeling fine and up to any game which might come his way. Now he felt weak and easily discouraged. This would not do. He must regain his health at all hazards, so he poured out the mixture which had given him such a sickly air. This done and a rude supper eaten, he took up his auger. He had heard Mr. Brotherson's step go by. But next minute he laid it down again in great haste and flung a newspaper over it. Mr. Brotherson was coming back, had stopped at his door, had knocked and must be let in.

"You're better this evening," he heard in those kindly tones which so confused and irritated him.

"Yes," was the surly admission. "But it's stifling here. If I have to live long in this hole I'll dry up from want of air. It's near the shop or I wouldn't stay out the week." Twice this day he had seen Brotherson's tall figure stop before the window of this shop and look in at him at his bench. But he said nothing about that.

"Yes," agreed the other, "it's no way to live. But you're alone. Upstairs there's a whole family huddled into a room just like this. Two of the kids sleep in the closet. It's things like that which have made me the friend of the poor, and the mortal enemy of men and women who spread themselves over a dozen big rooms and think themselves ill-used if the gas burns poorly or a fireplace smokes. I'm off for the evening; anything I can do for you?"

"Show me how I can win my way into such rooms as you've just talked about. Nothing less will make me look up. I'd like to sleep in one to-night. In the best bedroom, sir. 'm ambitious; I am."

A poor joke, though they both laughed. There Mr. Brotherson passed on, and Sweetwater listened till he was sure that his too attentive neighbour had really gone down the three flights between him and the street. Then he took up his auger again and shut himself up in his closet.

There was nothing peculiar about this closet. It was just an ordinary one with drawers and shelves on one side, and an open space on the other for the hanging up of clothes. Very few clothes hung there at present; but it was in this portion of the closet that he stopped and began to try the wall of Brotherson's room, with the butt end of the tool he carried

The sound seemed to satisfy him, for very soon he was boring a hole at a point exactly level with his ear; but not without frequent pauses and much attention given to the possible return of those departed foot-steps. He remembered that Mr. Brotherson had a way of coming back on unexpected errands after giving out his intention of being absent for hours.

Sweetwater did not want to be caught in any such trap as that; so he carefully followed every sound that reached him from the noisy halls. But he did not forsake his post; he did not have to. Mr. Brotherson had been sincere in his good-bye, and the auger finished its job and was withdrawn without any interruption from the man whose premises had been thus audaciously invaded.

"Neat as well as useful," was the gay comment with which Sweetwater surveyed his work, then laid his ear to the hole. Whereas previously he could barely hear the rattling of coals from the coal-scuttle, he was now able to catch the sound of an ash falling into the ash-pit.

His next move was to test the depth of the partition by inserting his finger in the hole he had made. He found it stopped by some obstacle before it had reached half its length, and anxious to satisfy himself of the nature of this obstacle, he gently moved the tip of his finger to and fro over what was certainly the edge of a book.

This proved that his calculations had been correct and that the opening so accessible on his side, was completely veiled on the other by the books he had seen packed on the shelves. As these shelves had no other backing than the wall, he had feared striking a spot not covered by a book. But he had not undertaken so risky a piece of work without first noting how nearly the tops of the books approached the line of the shelf above them, and the consequent unlikelihood of his striking the space between, at the height he planned the hole. He had even been careful to assure himself that all the volumes at this exact point stood far enough forward to afford room behind them for the chips and plaster he must necessarily push through with his auger, and also—important consideration—for the free passage of the sounds by which he hoped to profit.

As he listened for a moment longer, and then stooped to gather up the debris which had fallen on his own side of the partition, he muttered, in his old self-congratulatory way:

"If the devil don't interfere in some way best known to himself, this opportunity I have made for myself of listening to this arrogant fellow's very heartbeats should give me some clew to his secret. As soon as I can stand it, I'll spend my evenings at this hole."

But it was days before he could trust himself so far. Meanwhile their acquaintance ripened, though with no very satisfactory results. The detective found himself led into telling stories of his early home-life to keep pace with the man who always had something of moment and solid interest to impart. This was undesirable, for instead of calling out a corresponding confidence from Brotherson, it only seemed to make his conversation more coldly impersonal.

In consequence, Sweetwater suddenly found himself quite well and one evening, when he was sure that his neighbour was at home, he slid softly into his closet and laid his ear to the opening he had made there. The result was unexpected. Mr. Brotherson was pacing the floor, and talking softly to himself.

At first, the cadence and full music of the tones conveyed nothing to our far from literary detective. The victim of his secret machinations was expressing himself in words, words;—that was the point which counted with him. But as he listened longer and gradually took in the sense of these words, his heart went down lower and lower till it reached his boots. His inscrutable and ever disappointing neighbour was not indulging in self-communings of any kind. He was reciting poetry, and what was worse, poetry which he only half remembered and was trying to recall;—an incredible occupation for a man weighted with a criminal secret.

Sweetwater was disgusted, and was withdrawing in high indignation from his vantage-point when something occurred of a startling enough nature to hold him where he was in almost breathless expectation.

The hole which in the darkness of the closet was always faintly visible, even when the light was not very strong in the adjoining room, had suddenly become a bright and shining loop-hole, with a suggestion of movement in the space beyond. The book which had hid this hole on Brotherson's side had been taken down—the one book in all those hundreds whose removal threatened Sweetwater's schemes, if not himself.

For an instant the thwarted detective listened for the angry shout or the smothered oath which would naturally follow the discovery by Brotherson of this attempted interference with his privacy.

But all was still on his side of the wall. A rustling of leaves could be heard, as the inventor searched for the poem he wanted, but nothing more. In withdrawing the book, he had failed to notice the hole in the plaster back of it. But he could hardly fail to see it when he came to put the book back. Meantime, suspense for Sweetwater.

It was several minutes before he heard Mr. Brotherson's voice again, then it was in triumphant repetition of the lines which had escaped his memory. They were great words surely and Sweetwater never forgot them, but the impression which they made upon his mind, an impression so forcible that he was able to repeat them, months afterward to Mr. Gryce, did not prevent him from noting the tone in which they were uttered, nor the thud which followed as the book was thrown down upon the floor.

"Fool!" The word rang out in bitter irony from his irate neighbour's lips. "What does he know of woman! Woman! Let him court a rich one and see—but that's all over and done with. No more harping on that string, and no more reading of poetry. I'll never,—" The rest was lost in his throat and was quite unintelligible to the anxious listener.

Self-revealing words, which an instant before would have aroused Sweetwater's deepest interest! But they had suddenly lost all force for the unhappy listener. The sight of that hole still shining brightly before his eyes had distracted his thoughts and roused his liveliest apprehensions. If that book should be allowed to lie where it had fallen, then he was in for a period of uncertainty he shrank from contemplating. Any moment his neighbour might look up and catch sight of this hole bored in the backing of the shelves before him. Could the man who had been guilty of submitting him to this outrage stand the strain of waiting indefinitely for the moment of discovery? He doubted it, if the suspense lasted too long.

Shifting his position, he placed his eye where his ear had been. He could see very little. The space before him, limited as it was to the width of the one volume withdrawn, precluded his seeing aught but what lay directly before him. Happily, it was in this narrow line of vision that Mr. Brotherson stood. He had resumed work upon his model and was so placed that while his face was not visible, his hands were, and as Sweetwater watched these hands and noticed the delicacy of their manipulation, he was enough of a workman to realise that work so fine called for an undivided attention. He need not fear the gaze shifting, while those hands moved as warily as they did now.

Relieved for the moment, he left his post and, sitting down on the edge of his cot, gave himself up to thought.

He deserved this mischance. Had he profited properly by Mr. Gryce's teachings, he would not have been caught like this; he would have calculated not upon the nine hundred and ninety-nine chances of that book being left alone, but upon the thousandth one of its being the very one to be singled out and removed. Had he done this,—had he taken pains to so roughen and discolour the opening he had made, that it would look like an ancient rat hole instead of showing a clean bore, he would have some answer to give Brotherson when he came to question him in regard to it. But now the whole thing seemed up! He had shown himself a fool and by good rights ought to acknowledge his defeat and return to Headquarters. But he had too much spirit for that. He would rather—yes, he would rather face the pistol he had once seen in his enemy's hand. Yet it was hard to sit here waiting, waiting—Suddenly he started upright. He would go meet his fate—be present in the room itself when the discovery was made which threatened to upset all his plans. He was not ashamed of his calling, and Brotherson would think twice before attacking him when once convinced that he had the Department behind him.

"Excuse me, comrade," were the words with which he endeavoured to account for his presence at Brotherson's door. "My lamp smells so, and I've made such a mess of my work to-day that I've just stepped in for a chat. If I'm not wanted, say so. I don't want to bother you, but you do look pleasant here. I hope the thing I'm turning over in my head—every man has his schemes for making a fortune, you know—will be a success some day. I'd like a big room like this, and a lot of books, and—and pictures."

Craning his neck, he took a peep at the shelves, with an air of open admiration which effectually concealed his real purpose. What he wanted was to catch one glimpse of that empty space from his present standpoint, and he was both astonished and relieved to note how narrow and inconspicuous it looked. Certainly, he had less to fear than he supposed, and when, upon Mr. Brotherson's invitation, he stepped into the room, it was with a dash of his former audacity, which gave him, unfortunately, perhaps, a quick, strong and unexpected likeness to his old self.

But if Brotherson noticed this, nothing in his manner gave proof of the fact. Though usually averse to visitors, especially when employed as at present on his precious model, he quite warmed towards his unexpected guest, and even led the way to where it stood uncovered on the table.

"You find me at work," he remarked. "I don't suppose you understand any but your own?"

"If you mean to ask if I understand what you're trying to do there, I'm free to say that I don't. I couldn't tell now, off-hand, whether it's an air-ship you're planning, a hydraulic machine or—or—" He stopped, with a laugh and turned towards the book-shelves. "Now here's what I like. These books just take my eye."

"Look at them, then. I like to see a man interested in books. Only, I thought if you knew how to handle wire, I would get you to hold this end while I work with the other."

"I guess I know enough for that," was Sweetwater's gay rejoinder. But when he felt that communicating wire in his hand and experienced for the first time the full influence of the other's eye, it took all his hardihood to hide the hypnotic thrill it gave him. Though he smiled and chatted, he could not help asking himself between whiles, what had killed the poor washerwoman across the court, and what had killed Miss Challoner. Something visible or something invisible? Something which gave warning of attack, or something which struck in silence. He found himself gazing long and earnestly at this man's hand, and wondering if death lay under it. It was a strong hand, a deft, clean-cut member, formed to respond to the slightest hint from the powerful brain controlling it. But was this its whole story. Had he said all when he had said this?

Fascinated by the question, Sweetwater died a hundred deaths in his awakened fancy, as he followed the sharp short instructions which fell with cool precision from the other's lips. A hundred deaths, I say, but with no betrayal of his folly. The anxiety he showed was that of one eager to please, which may explain why on the conclusion of his task, Mr. Brotherson gave him one of his infrequent smiles and remarked, as he buried the model under its cover, "You're handy and you're quiet at your job. Who knows but that I shall want you again. Will you come if I call you?"

"Won't I?" was the gay retort, as the detective thus released, stooped for the book still lying on the floor. "Paolo and Francesca," he read, from the back, as he laid it on the table. "Poetry?" he queried.

"Rot," scornfully returned the other, as he moved to take down a bottle and some glasses from a cupboard let into another portion of the wall.

Sweetwater taking advantage of the moment, sidled towards the shelf where that empty space still gaped with the tell-tale hole at the back. He could easily have replaced the missing book before Mr.

Brotherson turned. But the issue was too doubtful. He was dealing with no absent-minded fool, and it behooved him to avoid above all things calling attention to the book or to the place on the shelf where it belonged.

But there was one thing he could do and did. Reaching out a finger as deft as Brotherson's own, he pushed a second volume into the place of the one that was gone. This veiled the auger-hole completely; a fact which so entirely relieved his mind that his old smile came back like sunshine to his lips, and it was only by a distinct effort that he kept the dancing humour from his eyes as he prepared to refuse the glass which Brotherson now brought forward:

"None of that!" said he. "You mustn't tempt me. The doctor has shut down on all kinds of spirits for two months more, at least. But don't let me hinder you. I can bear to smell the stuff. My turn will come again some day."

But Brotherson did not drink. Setting down the glass he carried, he took up the book lying near, weighed it in his hand and laid it down again, with an air of thoughtful inquiry. Then he suddenly pushed it towards Sweetwater. "Do you want it?" he asked.

Sweetwater was too taken aback to answer immediately. This was a move he did not understand. Want it, he? What he wanted was to see it put back in its place on the shelf. Did Brotherson suspect this? The supposition was incredible; yet who could read a mind so mysterious?

Sweetwater, debating the subject, decided that the risk of adding to any such possible suspicion was less to be dreaded than the continued threat offered by that unoccupied space so near the hole which testified so unmistakably of the means he had taken to spy upon this suspected man's privacy. So, after a moment of awkward silence, not out of keeping with the character he had assumed, he calmly refused the present as he had the glass.

Unhappily he was not rewarded by seeing the despised volume restored to its shelf. It still lay where its owner had pushed it, when, with some awkwardly muttered thanks, the discomfited detective withdrew to his own room.

CHAPTER XVIII

WHAT AM I TO DO NOW

Early morning saw Sweetwater peering into the depths of his closet. The hole was hardly visible. This meant that the book he had pushed across it from the other side had not been removed.

Greatly re-assured by the sight, he awaited his opportunity, and as soon as a suitable one presented itself, prepared the hole for inspection by breaking away its edges and begriming it well with plaster and old dirt. This done, he left matters to arrange themselves; which they did, after this manner.

Mr. Brotherson suddenly developed a great need of him, and it became a common thing for him to spend the half and, sometimes, the whole of the evening in the neighbouring room. This was just what he had worked for, and his constant intercourse with the man whose secret he sought to surprise should have borne fruit. But it did not. Nothing in the eager but painstaking inventor showed a distracted mind or a heavily-burdened soul. Indeed, he was so calm in all his ways, so precise and so self-contained, that Sweetwater often wondered what had become of the fiery agitator and eloquent propagandist of new and startling doctrines.

Then, he thought he understood the riddle. The model was reaching its completion, and Brotherson's extreme interest in it and the confidence he had in its success swallowed up all lesser emotions. Were the invention to prove a failure—but there was small hope of this. The man was of too well-poised a mind to over-estimate his work or miscalculate its place among modern improvements. Soon he would reach the goal of his desires, be praised, feted, made much of by the very people he now professedly scorned. There was no thoroughfare for Sweetwater here. Another road must be found; some secret, strange and unforeseen method of reaching a soul inaccessible to all ordinary or even extraordinary impressions.

Would a night of thought reveal such a method? Night! the very word brought inspiration. A man is not his full self at night. Secrets which, under the ordinary circumstances of everyday life, lie too deep for surprise, creep from their hiding-places in the dismal hours of universal quiet, and lips which are dumb to the most subtle of questioners break into strange and self-revealing mutterings when sleep lies heavy on ear and eye and the forces of life and death are released to play with the rudderless spirit.

It was in different words from these that Sweetwater reasoned, no doubt, but his conclusions were the same, and as he continued to brood over them, he saw a chance—a fool's chance, possibly, (but fools sometimes win where wise men fail) of reaching those depths he still believed in, notwithstanding his failure to sound them.

Addressing a letter to his friend in Twenty-ninth Street, he awaited reply in the shape of a small package he had ordered sent to the corner drug-store. When it came, he carried it home in a state of mingled hope and misgiving. Was he about to cap his fortnight of disappointment by another signal failure; end the matter by disclosing his hand; lose all, or win all by an experiment as daring and possibly as fanciful as were his continued suspicions of this seemingly upright and undoubtedly busy man?

He made no attempt to argue the question. The event called for the exercise of the most dogged elements in his character and upon these he must rely. He would make the effort he contemplated, simply because he was minded to do so. That was all there was to it. But any one noting him well that night, would have seen that he ate little and consulted his watch continually. Sweetwater had not yet passed the line where work becomes routine and the feelings remain totally under control.

Brotherson was unusually active and alert that evening. He was anxious to fit one delicate bit of mechanism into another, and he was continually interrupted by visitors. Some big event was on in the socialistic world, and his presence was eagerly demanded by one brotherhood after another. Sweetwater, posted at his loop-hole, heard the arguments advanced by each separate spokesman, followed by Brotherson's unvarying reply: that when his work was done and he had proved his right to approach them with a message, they might look to hear from him again; but not before. His patience was inexhaustible, but he showed himself relieved when the hour grew too late for further interruption. He began to whistle—a token that all was going well with him, and Sweetwater, who had come to understand some of his moods, looked forward to an hour or two of continuous work on Brotherson's part and of dreary and impatient waiting on his own. But, as so many times before, he misread the man. Earlier than common—much earlier, in fact, Mr. Brotherson laid down his tools and gave himself up to a restless pacing of the floor. This was not usual with him. Nor did he often indulge himself in playing on the piano as he did to-night, beginning with a few heavenly strains and ending with a bang that made the key-board jump. Certainly something was amiss in the quarter where peace had hitherto reigned undisturbed. Had the depths begun to heave, or were physical causes alone responsible for these unwonted ebullitions of feeling?

The question was immaterial. Either would form an excellent preparation for the coup planned by Sweetwater; and when, after another hour of uncertainty, perfect silence greeted him from his neighbour's room, hope had soared again on exultant wing, far above all former discouragements.

Mr. Brotherson's bed was in a remote corner from the loop-hole made by Sweetwater; but in the stillness now pervading the whole building, the latter could hear his even breathing very distinctly. He was in a deep sleep.

The young detective's moment had come.

Taking from his breast a small box, he placed it on a shelf close against the partition. An instant of quiet listening, then he touched a spring in the side of the box and laid his ear, in haste, to his loop-hole.

A strain of well-known music broke softly, from the box and sent its vibrations through the wall.

It was answered instantly by a stir within; then, as the noble air continued, awakening memories of that fatal instant when it crashed through the corridors of the Hotel Clermont, drowning Miss Challoner's cry if not the sound of her fall, a word burst from the sleeping man's lips which carried its own message to the listening detective.

It was Edith! Miss Challoner's first name, and the tone bespoke a shaken soul.

Sweetwater, gasping with excitement, caught the box from the shelf and silenced it. It had done its work and it was no part of Sweetwater's plan to have this strain located, or even to be thought real. But its echo still lingered in Brotherson's otherwise unconscious ears; for another "Edith!" escaped his lips, followed by a smothered but forceful utterance of these five words, "You know I promised you—"

Promised her what? He did not say. Would he have done so had the music lasted a trifle longer? Would he yet complete his sentence? Sweetwater trembled with eagerness and listened breathlessly for the next sound. Brotherson was awake. He was tossing in his bed. Now he has leaped to the floor. Sweetwater hears him groan, then comes another silence, broken at last by the sound of his body falling back upon the bed and the troubled ejaculation of "Good God!" wrung from lips no torture could have forced into complaint under any daytime conditions.

Sweetwater continued to listen, but he had heard all, and after some few minutes longer of fruitless waiting, he withdrew from his post. The episode was over. He would hear no more that night.

Was he satisfied? Certainly the event, puerile as it might seem to some, had opened up strange vistas to his aroused imagination. The words "Edith, you know I promised you—" were in themselves provocative of strange and doubtful conjectures. Had the sleeper under the influence of a strain of music indissolubly associated with the death of Miss Challoner, been so completely forced back into the circumstances and environment of that moment that his mind had taken up and his lips repeated the thoughts with which that moment of horror was charged? Sweetwater imagined the scene—saw the figure of Brotherson hesitating at the top of the stairs—saw hers advancing from the writing-room, with startled and uplifted hand—heard the music—the crash of that great finale—and decided, without hesitation, that the words he had just heard were indeed the thoughts of that moment. "Edith, you know I promised you—" What had he promised? What she received was death! Had this been in his mind? Would this have been the termination of the sentence had he wakened less soon to consciousness and caution?

Sweetwater dared to believe it. He was no nearer comprehending the mystery it involved than he had been before, but he felt sure that he had been given one true and positive glimpse into this harassed soul which showed its deeply hidden secret to be both deadly and fearsome; and happy to have won his way so far into the mystic labyrinth he had sworn to pierce, he rested in happy unconsciousness till morning when—

Could it be? Was it he who was dreaming now, or was the event of the night a mere farce of his own imagining? Mr. Brotherson was whistling in his room, gaily and with ever increasing verve, and the tune which filled the whole floor with music was the same grand finale from William Tell which had seemed to work such magic in the night. As Sweetwater caught the mellow but indifferent notes sounding from those lips of brass, he dragged forth the music-box he held hidden in his coat pocket, and flinging it on the floor stamped upon it.

"The man is too strong for me," he cried. "His heart is granite; he meets my every move. What am I to do now?"

CHAPTER XIX

THE DANGER MOMENT

For a day Sweetwater acknowledged himself to be mentally crushed, disillusioned and defeated. Then his spirits regained their poise. It would take a heavy weight indeed to keep them down permanently.

His opinion was not changed in regard to his neighbour's secret guilt. A demeanour of this sort suggested bravado rather than bravery to the ever suspicious detective. But he saw, very plainly by this time, that he would have to employ more subtle methods yet ere his hand would touch the goal which so tantalisingly eluded him.

His work at the bench suffered that week; he made two mistakes. But by Saturday night he had satisfied himself that he had reached the point where he would be justified in making use of Miss Challoner's letters. So he telephoned his wishes to New York, and awaited the promised developments with an anxiety we can only understand by realising how much greater were his chances of failure than of success. To ensure the latter, every factor in his scheme must work to perfection. The medium of communication (a young, untried girl) must do her part with all the skill of artist and author combined. Would she disappoint them? He did not think so. Women possess a marvellous adaptability for this kind of work and this one was French, which made the case still more hopeful.

But Brotherson! In what spirit would he meet the proposed advances? Would he even admit the girl, and, if he did, would the interview bear any such fruit as Sweetwater hoped for? The man who could mock the terrors of the night by a careless repetition of a strain instinct with the most sacred memories, was not to be depended upon to show much feeling at sight of a departed woman's writing. But no other hope remained, and Sweetwater faced the attempt with heroic determination.

The day was Sunday, which ensured Brotherson's being at home. Nothing would have lured Sweetwater out for a moment, though he had no reason to expect that the affair he was anticipating would come off till early evening.

But it did. Late in the afternoon he heard the expected steps go by his door—a woman's steps. But they were not alone. A man's accompanied them. What man? Sweetwater hastened to satisfy himself on this point by laying his ear to the partition.

Instantly the whole conversation became audible. "An errand? Oh, yes, I have an errand!" explained the evidently unwelcome intruder, in her broken English. "This is my brother Pierre. My name is Celeste; Celeste Ledru. I understand English ver well. I have worked much in families. But he understands nothing. He is all French. He accompanies me fo—for the—what you call it? les convenances. He knows nothing of the beesiness."

Sweetwater in the darkness of his closet laughed in his gleeful appreciation.

"Great!" was his comment. "Just great! She has thought of everything—or Mr. Gryce has."

Meanwhile, the girl was proceeding with increased volubility

"What is this beesiness, monsieur? I have something to sell—so you Americans speak. Something you will want much—ver sacred, ver precious. A souvenir from the tomb, monsieur. Will you give ten—no, that is too leetle—fifteen dollars for it? It is worth—Oh, more, much more to the true lover. Pierre, tu es bete. Teins-tu droit sur ta chaise. M. Brotherson est un monsieur comme il faut."

This adjuration, uttered in sharp reprimand and with but little of the French grace, may or may not have been understood by the unsympathetic man they were meant to impress. But the name which accompanied them—his own name, never heard but once before in this house, undoubtedly caused the silence which almost reached the point of embarrassment, before he broke it with the harsh remark:

"Your French may be good, but it does not go with me. Yet is it more intelligible than your English. What do you want here? What have you in that bag you wish to open; and what do you mean by the sentimental trash with which you offer it?"

"Ah, monsieur has not memory of me," came in the sweetest tones of a really seductive voice. "You astonish me, monsieur. I thought you knew—everybody else does—Oh, tout le monde, monsieur, that I was Miss Challoner's maid—near her when other people were not—near her the very day she died."

A pause; then an angry exclamation from some one. Sweetwater thought from the brother, who may have misinterpreted some look or gesture on Brotherson's part. Brotherson himself would not be apt to show surprise in any such noisy way.

"I saw many things—Oh many things—" the girl proceeded with an admirable mixture of suggestion and reserve. "That day and other days too. She did not talk—Oh, no, she did not talk, but I saw—Oh, yes, I saw that she—that you—I'll have to say it, monsieur, that you were tres bons amis after that week in Lenox."

"Well?" His utterance of this word was vigorous, but not tender. "What are you coming to? What can you have to show me in this connection that I will believe in for a moment?"

"I have these—is monsieur certaine that no one can hear? I wouldn't have anybody hear what I have to tell you, for the world—for all the world."

"No one can overhear."

For the first time that day Sweetwater breathed a full, deep breath. This assurance had sounded heartfelt. "Blessings on her cunning young head. She thinks of everything."

"You are unhappy. You have thought Miss Challoner cold;—that she had no response for your ver ardent passion. But—" these words were uttered sotto voce and with telling pauses "—but—I—know—ver much better than that. She was ver proud. She had a right; she was no poor girl like me—but she spend hours—hours in writing letters she—nevaire send. I saw one, just once, for a leetle minute; while you could breathe so short as that; and began with Cheri, or your English for that, and ended with words—Oh, ver much like these: You may nevaire see these lines, which was ver interesting, veree so, and made one want to see what she did with letters she wrote and nevaire mail; so I watch and look, and one day I see them. She had a leetle ivory box—Oh, ver nice, ver pretty. I thought it was jewels she kept locked up so tight. But, non, non, non. It was letters—these letters. I heard them rattle, rattle, not once but many times. You believe me, monsieur?"

"I believe you to have taken every advantage possible to spy upon your mistress. I believe that, yes."

"From interest, monsieur, from great interest."

"Self-interest."

"As monsieur pleases. But it was strange, ver strange for a grande dame like that to write letters—sheets on sheets—and then not send them, nevaire. I dreamed of those letters—I could not help it, no; and when she died so quick—with no word for any one, no word at all, I thought of those writings so secret, so of the heart, and when no one noticed—or thought about this box, or—or the key she kept shut tight, oh, always tight in her leetle gold purse, I—Monsieur, do you want to see those letters?" asked the girl, with a gulp. Evidently his appearance frightened her—or had her acting reached this point of extreme finish? "I had nevaire the chance to put them back. And—and they belong to monsieur. They are his—all his—and so beautiful! Ah, just like poetry."

"I don't consider them mine. I haven't a particle of confidence in you or in your story. You are a thief—self-convicted; or you're an agent of the police whose motives I neither understand nor care to investigate. Take up your bag and go. I haven't a cent's worth of interest in its contents."

She started to her feet. Sweetwater heard her chair grate on the painted floor, as she pushed it back in rising. The brother rose too, but more calmly. Brotherson did not stir. Sweetwater felt his hopes rapidly dying down—down into ashes, when suddenly her voice broke forth in pants:

"And Marie said—everybody said—that you loved our great lady; that you, of the people, common, common, working with the hands, living with men and women working with the hands, that you had soul, sentiment—what you will of the good and the great, and that you would give your eyes for her words, si fines, si spirituelles, so like des vers de poete. False! false! all false! She was an angel. You are—read that!" she vehemently broke in, opening her bag and whisking a paper down before him. "Read and understand my proud and lovely lady. She did right to die. You are hard—hard. You would have killed her if she had not—"

"Silence, woman! I will read nothing!" came hissing from the strong man's teeth, set in almost ungovernable anger. "Take back this letter, as you call it, and leave my room."

"Nevaire! You will not read? But you shall, you shall. Behold another! One, two, three, four!" Madly they flew from her hand. Madly she continued her vituperative attack. "Beast! beast! That she should pour out her innocent heart to you, you! I do not want your money, Monsieur of the common street, of the common house. It would be dirt. Pierre, it would be dirt. Ah, bah! je m'oublie tout a fait. Pierre, il est bete. Il refuse de les toucher. Mais il faut qu'il les touche, si je les laisse sur le plancher. Va-t'en! Je me moque de lui. Canaille! L'homme du peuple, tout a fait du peuple!"

A loud slam—the skurrying of feet through the hall, accompanied by the slower and heavier tread of the so-called brother, then silence, and such silence that Sweetwater fancied he could catch the sound of Brotherson's heavy breathing. His own was silenced to a gasp. What a treasure of a girl! How natural her indignation! What an instinct she showed and what comprehension! This high and mighty handling of a most difficult situation and a most difficult man, had imposed on Brotherson, had almost imposed upon himself. Those letters so beautiful, so spirituelle! Yet, the odds were that she had never read them, much less abstracted them. The minx! the ready, resourceful, wily, daring minx!

But had she imposed on Brotherson? As the silence continued, Sweetwater began to doubt. He understood quite well the importance of his neighbour's first movement. Were he to tear those letters into shreds! He might be thus tempted. All depended on the strength of his present mood and the real nature of the secret which lay buried in his heart.

Was that heart as flinty as it seemed? Was there no place for doubt or even for curiosity, in its impenetrable depths? Seemingly, he had not moved foot or hand since his unwelcome visitors had left. He was doubtless still staring at the scattered sheets lying before him; possibly battling with unaccustomed impulses; possibly weighing deeds and consequences in those slow moving scales of his in which no man could cast a weight with any certainty how far its even balance would be disturbed.

There was a sound as of settling coal. Only at night would one expect to hear so slight a sound as that in a tenement full of noisy children. But the moment chanced to be propitious, and it not only attracted the attention of Sweetwater on his side of the wall, but it struck the ear of Brotherson also. With an ejaculation as bitter as it was impatient, he roused himself and gathered up the letters. Sweetwater could hear the successive rustlings as he bundled them up in his hand. Then came another silence—then the lifting of a stove lid.

Sweetwater had not been wrong in his secret apprehension. His identification with his unimpressionable neighbour's mood had shown him what to expect. These letters—these innocent and precious outpourings of a rare and womanly soul—the only conceivable open sesame to the hard-locked nature he found himself pitted against, would soon be resolved into a vanishing puff of smoke.

But the lid was thrust back, and the letters remained in hard. Mortal strength has its limits. Even Brotherson could not shut down that lid on words which might have been meant for him, harshly as he had repelled the idea.

The pause which followed told little; but when Sweetwater heard the man within move with characteristic energy to the door, turn the key and step back again to his place at the table, he knew that the danger moment had passed and that those letters were about to be read, not casually, but seriously, as indeed their contents merited.

This caused Sweetwater to feel serious himself. Upon what result might he calculate? What would happen to this hardy soul, when the fact he so scornfully repudiated, was borne in upon him, and he saw that the disdain which had antagonised him was a mere device—a cloak to hide the secret heart of love and eager womanly devotion? Her death—little as Brotherson would believe it up till now—had been his personal loss the greatest which can befall a man. When he came to see this—when the modest fervour of her unusual nature began to dawn upon him in these self-revelations, would the result be remorse, or just the deadening and final extinction of whatever tenderness he may have retained for her memory?

Impossible to tell. The balance of probability hung even. Sweetwater recognised this, and clung, breathless, to his loop-hole. Fain would he have seen, as well as heard.

Mr. Brotherson read the first letter, standing. As it soon became public property, I will give it here, just as it afterwards appeared in the columns of the greedy journals:

"Beloved:

"When I sit, as I often do, in perfect quiet under the stars, and dream that you are looking at them too, not for hours as I do, but for one full moment in which your thoughts are with me as wholly as mine are with you, I feel that the bond between us, unseen by the world, and possibly not wholly recognised by ourselves, is instinct with the same power which links together the eternities.

"It seems to have always been; to have known no beginning, only a budding, an efflorescence, the visible product of a hidden but always present reality. A month ago and I was ignorant, even, of your name. Now, you seem the best known to me, the best understood, of God's creatures. One afternoon of perfect companionship—one flash of strong emotion, with its deep, true insight into each other's soul, and the miracle was wrought. We had met, and henceforth, parting would mean separation only, and not the severing of a mutual bond. One hand, and one only, could do that now. I will not name that hand. For us there is nought ahead but life.

"Thus do I ease my heart in the silence which conditions impose upon us. Some day I shall hear your voice again, and then-"

The paper dropped from the reader's hand. It was several minutes before he took up another.

This one, as it happened, antedated the other, as will appear on reading it:

"My friend:

"I said that I could not write to you—that we must wait. You were willing; but there is much to be accomplished, and the silence may be long. My father is not an easy man to please, but he desires my happiness and will listen to my plea when the right hour comes. When you have won your place—when you have shown yourself to be the man I feel you to be, then my father will recognise your worth, and the way will be cleared, despite the obstacles which now intervene.

"But meantime! Ah, you will not know it, but words will rise —the heart must find utterance. What the lip cannot utter, nor the looks reveal, these pages shall hold in sacred trust for you till the day when my father will place my hand in yours, with heart-felt approval.

"Is it a folly? A woman's weak evasion of the strong silence of man? You may say so some day; but somehow, I doubt it—I doubt it."

The creaking of a chair;—the man within had seated himself. There was no other sound; a soul in turmoil wakens no echoes. Sweetwater envied the walls surrounding the unsympathetic reader. They could see. He could only listen.

A little while; then that slight rustling again of the unfolding sheet. The following was read, and then the fourth and last:

"Dearest:

"Did you think I had never seen you till that day we met in Lenox? I am going to tell you a secret—a great, great secret—such a one as a woman hardly whispers to her own heart.

"One day, in early summer, I was sitting in St. Bartholomew's Church on Fifth Avenue, waiting for the services to begin. It was early and the congregation was assembling. While idly watching the people coming in, I saw a gentleman pass by me up the aisle, who made me forget all the others. He had not the air of a New Yorker; he was not even dressed in city style, but as I noted his face and expression, I said way down in my heart, 'That is the kind of man I could love; the only man I have ever seen who could make me forget my own world and my own people.' It was a passing thought, soon forgotten. But when in that hour of embarrassment and peril on Greylock Mountain, I looked up into the face of my rescuer and saw again that countenance which so short a time before had called into life impulses till then utterly unknown, I knew that my hour was come. And that was why my confidence was so spontaneous and my belief in the future so absolute

"I trust your love which will work wonders; and I trust my own, which sprang at a look but only gathered strength and permanence when I found that the soul of the man I loved bettered his outward attractions, making the ideal of my foolish girlhood seem as unsubstantial and evanescent as a dream in the glowing noontide."

"My Own:

"I can say so now; for you have written to me, and I have the dancing words with which to silence any unsought doubt which might subdue the exuberance of these secret outpourings.

"I did not expect this. I thought that you would remain as silent as myself. But men's ways are not our ways. They cannot exhaust longing in purposeless words on scraps of soulless paper, and I am glad that they cannot. I love you for your impatience; for your purpose, and for the manliness which will win for you yet all that you covet of fame, accomplishment and love. You expect no reply, but there are ways in which one can keep silent and yet speak. Won't you be surprised when your answer comes in a manner you have never thought of?"

CHAPTER XX

CONFUSION

In his interest in what was going on on the other side of the wall, Sweetwater had forgotten himself. Daylight had declined, but in the darkness of the closet this change had passed unheeded. Night itself might come, but that should not force him to leave his post so long as his neighbour remained behind his locked door, brooding over the words of love and devotion which had come to him, as it were from the other world.

But was he brooding? That sound of iron clattering upon iron! That smothered exclamation and the laugh which ended it! Anger and determination rang in that laugh. It had a hideous sound which prepared Sweetwater for the smell which now reached his nostrils. The letters were burning; this time the lid had been lifted from the stove with unrelenting purpose. Poor Edith Challoner's touching words had met, a different fate from any which she, in her ignorance of this man's nature,—a nature to which she had ascribed untold perfections—could possibly have conceived.

As Sweetwater thought of this, he stirred nervously in the darkness, and broke into silent invective against the man who could so insult the memory of one who had perished under the blight of his own coldness and misunderstanding. Then he suddenly started back surprised and apprehensive. Brotherson had unlocked his door, and was coming rapidly his way. Sweetwater heard his step in the hall and had hardly time to bound from his closet, when he saw his own door burst in and found himself face to face with his redoubtable neighbour, in a state of such rage as few men could meet without quailing, even were they of his own stature, physical vigour and prowess; and Sweetwater was a small man.

However, disappointment such as he had just experienced brings with it a desperation which often outdoes courage, and the detective, smiling with an air of gay surprise, shouted out:

"Well, what's the matter now? Has the machine busted, or tumbled into the fire or sailed away to lands unknown out of your open window?"

"You were coming out of that closet," was the fierce rejoinder. "What have you got there? Something which concerns me, or why should your face go pale at my presence and your forehead drip with sweat? Don't think that you've deceived me for a moment as to your business here. I recognised you immediately. You've played the stranger well, but you've a nose and an eye nobody could forget. I have known all along that I had a police spy for a neighbour; but it didn't faze me. I've nothing to conceal, and wouldn't mind a regiment of you fellows if you'd only play a straight game. But when it comes to foisting upon me a parcel of letters to which I have no right, and then setting a fellow like you to count my groans or whatever else they expected to hear, I have a right to defend myself, and defend myself I will, by God! But first, let me be sure that my accusations will stand. Come into this closet with me. It abuts on the wall of my room and has its own secret, I know. What is it? I have you at an advantage now, and you shall tell."

He did have Sweetwater at an advantage, and the detective knew it and disdained a struggle which would have only called up a crowd, friendly to the other but inimical to himself. Allowing Brotherson to drag him into the closet, he stood quiescent, while the determined man who held him with one hand, felt about with the other over the shelves and along the partitions till he came to the hole which had offered such a happy means of communication between the two rooms. Then, with a laugh almost as bitter in tone as that which rang from Brotherson's lips, he acknowledged that business had its necessities and that apologies from him were in order; adding, as they both stepped out into the rapidly darkening room:

"We've played a bout, we two; and you've come out ahead. Allow me to congratulate you, Mr. Brotherson. You've cleared yourself so far as I am concerned. I leave this ranch to-night."

The frown had come back to the forehead of the indignant man who confronted him.

"So you listened," he cried; "listened when you weren't sneaking under my eye! A fine occupation for a man who can dove-tail a corner like an adept. I wish I had let you join the brotherhood you were good enough to mention. They would know how to appreciate your double gifts and how to reward your excellence in the one, if not in the other. What did the police expect to learn about me that they should consider it necessary to call into exercise such extraordinary talents?"

"I'm not good at conundrums. I was given a task to perform, and I performed it," was Sweetwater's sturdy reply. Then slowly, with his eye fixed directly upon his antagonist, "I guess they thought you a man. And so did I until I heard you burn those letters. Fortunately we have copies."

"Letters!" Fury thickened the speaker's voice, and lent a savage gleam to his eye. "Forgeries! Make believes! Miss Challoner never wrote the drivel you dare to designate as letters. It was concocted at Police Headquarters. They made me tell my story and then they found some one who could wield the poetic pen. I'm obliged to them for the confidence they show in my credulity. I credit Miss Challoner with such words as have been given me to read here to-day? I knew the lady, and I know myself. Nothing that passed between us, not an event in which we were both concerned, has been forgotten by me, and no feature of our intercourse fits the language you have ascribed to her. On the contrary, there is a lamentable contradiction between facts as they were and the fancies you have made her indulge in. And this, as you must acknowledge, not only proves their falsity, but exonerates Miss Challoner from all possible charge of sentimentality."

"Yet she certainly wrote those letters. We had them from Mr. Challoner. The woman who brought them was really her maid. We have not deceived you in this.'

"I do not believe you."

It was not offensively said; but the conviction it expressed was absolute. Sweetwater recognised the tone, as one of truth, and inwardly laid down his arms. He could never like the man; there was too much iron in his fibre; but he had to acknowledge that as a foe he was invulnerable and therefore admirable to one who had the good sense to appreciate him.

"I do not want to believe you." Thus did Brotherson supplement his former sentence. "For if I were to attribute those letters to her, I should have to acknowledge that they were written to another man than myself. And this would be anything but agreeable to me. Now I am going to my room and to my work. You may spend the rest of the evening or the whole night, if you will, listening at that hole. As heretofore, the labour will be all yours, and the indifference mine."

With a satirical play of feature which could hardly be called a smile, he nodded and left the room.

CHAPTER XXI

A CHANGE

"It's all up. I'm beaten on my own ground." Thus confessed Sweetwater, in great dejection, to himself. "But I'm going to take advantage of the permission he's just given me and continue the listening act. Just because he told me to and just because he thinks I won't. I'm sure it's no worse than to spend hours of restless tossing in bed, trying to sleep."

But our young detective did neither.

As he was putting his supper dishes away, a messenger boy knocked at his door and handed him a note. It was from Mr. Gryce and ran thus:

"Steal off, if you can, and as soon as you can, and meet me in Twenty-ninth Street. A discovery has been made which alters the whole situation."

CHAPTER XXII

O. B. AGAIN

"What's happened? Something very important. I ought to hope so after this confounded failure."

"Failure? Didn't he read the letters?"

"Yes, he read them. Had to, but—"

"Didn't weaken? Eh?"

"No, he didn't weaken. You can't get water out of a millstone. You may squeeze and squeeze; but it's your fingers which suffer, not it. He thinks we manufactured those letters ourselves on purpose to draw him."

"Humph! I knew we had a reputation for finesse, but I didn't know that it ran that high."

"He denies everything. Said she would never have written such letters to him; even goes so far to declare that if she did write them—(he must be strangely ignorant of her handwriting) they were meant for some other man than himself. All rot, but—" A hitch of the shoulder conveyed Sweetwater's disgust. His uniform good nature was strangely disturbed.

But Mr. Gryce's was not. The faint smile with which he smoothed with an easy, circling movement, the already polished top of his ever present cane conveyed a secret complacency which called up a flash of discomfiture to his greatly irritated companion.

"He says that, does he? You found him on the whole tolerably straightforward, eh? A hard nut; but hard nuts are usually sound ones. Come, now! prejudice aside, what's your honest opinion of the man you've had under your eye and ear for three solid weeks? Hasn't there been the best of reasons for your failure? Speak up, my boy. Squarely, now."

"I can't. I hate the fellow. I hate any one who makes me look ridiculous. He—well, well, if you'll have it, sir, I will say this much. If it weren't for that blasted coincidence of the two deaths equally mysterious, equally under his eye, I'd stake my life on his honesty. But that coincidence stumps me and—and a sort of feeling I have here."

It is to be hoped that the slap he gave his breast, at this point, carried off some of his superfluous emotion. "You can't account for a feeling, Mr. Gryce. The man has no heart. He's as hard as rocks."

"A not uncommon lack where the head plays so big a part. We can't hang him on any such argument as that. You've found no evidence against him?"

"N—no." The hesitating admission was only a proof of Sweetwater's obstinacy.

"Then listen to this. The test with the letters failed, because what he said about them was true. They were not meant for him. Miss Challoner had another lover."

"Only another? I thought there were a half-dozen, at least."

"Another whom she favoured. The letters found in her possession—not the ones she wrote herself, but those which were written to her over the signature O. B. were not all from the same hand. Experts have been busy with them for a week, and their reports are unanimous. The O. B. who wrote the threatening lines acknowledged to by Orlando Brotherson, was not the O. B. who penned all of those love letters. The similarity in the writing misled us at first, but once the doubt was raised by Mr. Challoner's discovery of an allusion in one of them which pointed to another writer than Mr. Brotherson, and experts had no difficulty in reaching the decision I have mentioned."

"Two O. B.s! Isn't that incredible, Mr. Gryce?"

"Yes, it is incredible; but the incredible is not the impossible The man you've been shadowing denies that these expressive effusions of Miss Challoner were meant for him Let us see, then, if we can find the man they were meant for."

"The second O. B.?"

"Yes."

Sweetwater's face instantly lit up.

"Do you mean that I—after my egregious failure—am not to be kept on the dunce's seat? That you will give me this new job?"

"Yes. We don't know of a better man. It isn't your fault, you said it yourself, that water couldn't be squeezed out of a millstone."

"The Superintendent—how does he feel about it?"

"He was the first one to mention you."

"And the Inspector?"

"Is glad to see us on a new tack."

A pause, during which the eager light in the young detective's eye clouded over. Presently he remarked:

"How will the finding of another O. B. alter Mr. Brotherson's position? He still will be the one person on the spot, known to have cherished a grievance against the victim of this mysterious killing. To my mind, this discovery of a more favoured rival, brings in an element of motive which may rob our self-reliant friend of some of his complacency. We may further, rather than destroy, our case against Brotherson by locating a second O.B."

Mr. Gryce's eyes twinkled.

"That won't make your task any more irksome," he smiled. "The loop we thus throw out is as likely to catch Brotherson as his rival. It all depends upon the sort of man we find in this second O. B.; and whether, in some way unknown to us, he gave her cause for the sudden and overwhelming rush of despair which alone supports this general theory of suicide."

"The prospect grows pleasing. Where am I to look for my man?"

"Your ticket is bought to Derby, Pennsylvania. If he is not employed in the great factories there, we do not know where to find him. We have no other clew."

"I see. It's a short journey I have before me."

"It'll bring the colour to your cheeks."

"Oh, I'm not kicking."

"You will start to-morrow."

"Wish it were to-day."

"And you will first inquire, not for O. B., that's too indefinite; but for a young girl by the name of Doris Scott. She holds the clew; or rather she is the clew to this second O. B."

"Another woman!"

"No, a child;—well, I won't say child exactly; she must be sixteen."

"Doris Scott."

"She lives in Derby. Derby is a small place. You will have no trouble in finding this child. It was to her Miss Challoner's last letter was addressed. The one—"

"I begin to see."

"No, you don't, Sweetwater. The affair is as blind as your hat; nobody sees. We're just feeling along a thread. O. B.'s letters—the real O. B., I mean, are the manliest effusions possible. He's no more of a milksop than this Brotherson; and unlike your indomitable friend he seems to have some heart. I only wish he'd given us some facts; they would have been serviceable. But the letters reveal nothing except that he knew Doris. He writes in one of them: 'Doris is learning to embroider. It's like a fairy weaving a cobweb!' Doris isn't a very common name. She must be the same little girl to whom Miss Challoner wrote from time to time."

"Was this letter signed O. B.?"

"Yes; they all are. The only difference between his letters and Brotherson's is this: Brotherson's retain the date and address; the second O. B.'s do not."

"How not? Torn off, do you mean?"

"Yes, or rather, neatly cut away; and as none of the envelopes were kept, the only means by which we can locate the writer is through this girl Doris."

"If I remember rightly Miss Challoner's letter to this child was free from all mystery."

"Quite so. It is as open as the day. That is why it has been mentioned as showing the freedom of Miss Challoner's mind five minutes before that fatal thrust."

Sweetwater took up the sheet Mr. Gryce pushed towards him and re-read these lines:

"Dear Little Doris:

"It is a snowy night, but it is all bright inside and I feel no chill in mind or body. I hope it is so in the little cottage in Derby; that my little friend is as happy with harsh winds blowing from the mountains as she was on the summer day she came to see me at this hotel. I like to think of her as cheerful and beaming, rejoicing in tasks which make her so womanly and sweet. She is often, often in my mind.

"Affectionately your friend, "EDITH A. CHALLONER."

"That to a child of sixteen!"

"Just so."

"D-o-r-i-s spells something besides Doris."

"Yet there is a Doris. Remember that O. B. says in one of his letters, 'Doris is learning to embroider.'"

"Yes, I remember that."

"So you must first find Doris."

"Very good, sir."

"And as Miss Challoner's letter was directed to Derby, Pennsylvania, you will go to Derby."

"Yes, sir."

"Anything more?"

"I've been reading this letter again."

"It's worth it."

"The last sentence expresses a hope."

"That has been noted."

Sweetwater's eyes slowly rose till they rested on Mr. Gryce's face: "I'll cling to the thread you've given me. I'll work myself through the labyrinth before us till I reach HIM."

Mr. Gryce smiled; but there was more age, wisdom and sympathy for youthful enthusiasm in that smile than there was confidence or hope.

BOOK III

THE HEART OF MAN

CHAPTER XXIII

DORIS

"A young girl named Doris Scott?"

The station-master looked somewhat sharply at the man he was addressing, and decided to give the direction asked.

"There is but one young girl in town of that name," he declared, "and she lives in that little house you see just beyond the works. But let me tell you, stranger," he went on with some precipitation—

But here he was called off, and Sweetwater lost the conclusion of his warning, if warning it was meant to be. This did not trouble the detective. He stood a moment, taking in the prospect; decided that the Works and the Works alone made the town, and started for the house which had been pointed out to him. His way lay through the chief business street, and greatly preoccupied by his errand, he gave but a passing glance to the rows on rows of workmen's dwellings stretching away to the left in seemingly endless perspective. Yet in that glance he certainly took in the fact that the sidewalks were blocked with people and wondered if it were a holiday. If so, it must be an enforced one, for the faces showed little joy. Possibly a strike was on. The anxiety he everywhere saw pictured on young faces and old, argued some trouble; but if the trouble was that, why were all heads turned indifferently from the Works, and why were the Works themselves in full blast?

These questions he may have asked himself and he may not. His attention was entirely centred on the house he saw before him and on the possible developments awaiting him there. Nothing else mattered. Briskly he stepped out along the sandy road, and after a turn or two which led him quite away from the Works and its surrounding buildings, he came out upon the highway and this house.

It was a low and unpretentious one, and had but one distinguishing feature. The porch which hung well over the doorstep was unique in shape and gave an air of picturesqueness to an otherwise simple exterior; a picturesqueness which was much enhanced in its effect by the background of illimitable forest, which united the foreground of this pleasing picture with the great chain of hills which held the Works and town in its ample basin.

As he approached the doorstep, his mind involuntarily formed an anticipatory image of the child whose first stitches in embroidery were like a fairy's weaving to the strong man who worked in ore and possibly figured out bridges. That she would prove to be of the anemic type, common among working girls gifted with an imagination they have but scant opportunity to exercise, he had little doubt.

He was therefore greatly taken aback, when at his first step upon the porch, the door before him flew open and he beheld in the dark recess beyond a young woman of such bright and blooming beauty that he hardly noticed her expression of extreme anxiety, till she lifted her hand and laid an admonitory finger softly on her lip:

"Hush!" she whispered, with an earnestness which roused him from his absorption and restored him to the full meaning of this encounter. "There is sickness in the house and we are very anxious. Is your errand an important one? If not—" The faltering break in the fresh, young voice, the look she cast behind her into the darkened interior, were eloquent with the hope that he would recognise her impatience and pass on.

And so he might have done,—so he would have done under all ordinary circumstances. But if this was Doris—and he did not doubt the fact after the first moment of startled surprise—how dare he forego this opportunity of settling the question which had brought him here.

With a slight stammer but otherwise giving no evidence of the effect made upon him by the passionate intensity with which she had urged this plea, he assured her that his errand was important, but one so quickly told that it would delay her but a moment. "But first," said he, with very natural caution, "let me make sure that it is to Miss Doris Scott I am speaking. My errand is to her and her only."

Without showing any surprise, perhaps too engrossed in her own thoughts to feel any, she answered with simple directness, "Yes, I am Doris Scott." Whereupon he became his most persuasive self, and pulling out a folded paper from his pocket, opened it and held it before her, with these words:

"Then will you be so good as to glance at this letter and tell me if the person whose initials you will find at the bottom happens to be in town at the present moment?"

In some astonishment now, she glanced down at the sheet thus boldly thrust before her, and recognising the O and the B of a well-known signature, she flashed a look back at Sweetwater in which he read a confusion of emotions for which he was hardly prepared.

"Ah," thought he, "it's coming. In another moment I shall hear what will repay me for the trials and disappointments of all these months."

But the moment passed and he had heard nothing. Instead, she dropped her hands from the door-jamb and gave such unmistakable evidences of intended flight, that but one alternative remained to him; he became abrupt.

Thrusting the paper still nearer, he said, with an emphasis which could not fail of making an impression, "Read it. Read the whole letter. You will find your name there. This communication was addressed to Miss Challoner, but—"

Oh, now she found words! With a low cry, she put out her hand in quick entreaty, begging him to desist and not speak that name on any pretext or for any purpose. "He may rouse and hear," she explained, with another quick look behind her. "The doctor says that this is the critical day. He may become conscious any minute. If he should and were to hear that name, it might kill him."

"He!" Sweetwater perked up his ears. "Who do you mean by he?"

"Mr. Brotherson, my patient, he whose letter—" But here her impatience rose above every other consideration. Without attempting to finish her sentence, or yielding in the least to her curiosity or interest in this man's errand, she cried out with smothered intensity, "Go! go! I cannot stay another moment from his bedside."

But a thunderbolt could not have moved Sweetwater after the hearing of that name. "Mr. Brotherson!" he echoed. "Brotherson! Not Orlando?"

"No, no; his name is Oswald. He's the manager of these Works. He's sick with typhoid. We are caring for him. If you belonged here you would know that much. There! that's his voice you hear. Go, if you have any mercy." And she began to push to the door.

But Sweetwater was impervious to all hint. With eager eyes straining into the shadowy depths just visible over her shoulder, he listened eagerly for the disjointed words now plainly to be heard in some near-by but unseen chamber.

"The second O. B.!" he inwardly declared. "And he's a Brotherson also, and—sick! Miss Scott," he whisperingly entreated as her hand fell in manifest despair from the door, "don't send me away yet. I've a question of the greatest importance to put you, and one minute more cannot make any difference to him. Listen! those cries are the cries of delirium; he cannot miss you; he's not even conscious."

"He's calling out in his sleep. He's calling her, just as he has called for the last two weeks. But he will wake conscious—or he will not wake at all."

The anguish trembling in that latter phrase would have attracted Sweetwater's earnest, if not pitiful, attention at any other time, but now he had ears only for the cry which at that moment came ringing shrilly from within—

"Edith! Edith!"

The living shouting for the dead! A heart still warm sending forth its longing to the pierced and pulseless one, hidden in a far-off tomb! To Sweetwater, who had seen Miss Challoner buried, this summons of distracted love came with weird force.

Then the present regained its sway. He heard her name again, and this time it sounded less like a call and more like the welcoming cry of meeting spirits. Was death to end this separation? Had he found the true O. B., only to behold another and final seal fall upon this closely folded mystery? In his fear of this possibility, he caught at Doris' hand as she was about to bound away, and eagerly asked:

"When was Mr. Brotherson taken ill? Tell me, I entreat you; the exact day and, if you can, the exact hour. More depends upon this than you can readily realise."

She wrenched her hand from his, panting with impatience and a vague alarm. But she answered him distinctly:

"On the Twenty-fifth of last month, just an hour after he was made manager. He fell in a faint at the Works."

The day—the very day of Miss Challoner's death!

"Had he heard—did you tell him then or afterwards what happened in New York on that very date?"

"No, no, we have not told him. It would have killed him—and may yet."

"Edith! Edith!" came again through the hush, a hush so deep that Sweetwater received the impression that the house was empty save for patient and nurse.

This discovery had its effects upon him. Why should he subject this young and loving girl to further pain? He had already learned more than he had expected to. The rest would come with time. But at the first intimation he gave of leaving, she lost her abstracted air and turned with absolute eagerness towards him.

"One moment," said she. "You are a stranger and I do not know your name or your purpose here. But I cannot let you go without begging you not to mention to any one in this town that Mr. Brotherson has any interest in the lady whose name we must not speak. Do not repeat that delirious cry you have heard or betray in any way our intense and fearful interest in this young lady's strange death. You have shown me a letter. Do not speak of that letter, I entreat you. Help us to retain our secret a little longer. Only the doctor and myself know what awaits Mr. Brotherson if he lives. I had to tell the doctor, but a doctor reveals nothing. Promise that you will not either, at least till this crisis is passed. It will help my father and it will help me; and we need all the help we can get."

Sweetwater allowed himself one minute of thought, then he earnestly replied:

"I will keep your secret for to-day, and longer, if possible."

"Thank you," she cried; "thank you. I thought I saw kindness in your face." And she again prepared to close the door.

But Sweetwater had one more question to ask. "Pardon me," said he, as he stepped down on the walk, "you say that this is a critical day with your patient. Is that why every one whom I have seen so far wears such a look of anxiety?"

"Yes, yes," she cried, giving him one other glimpse of her lovely, agitated face. "There's but one feeling in town to-day, but one hope, and, as I believe, but one prayer. That the man whom every one loves and every one trusts may live to run these Works."

"Edith! Edith!" rose in ceaseless reiteration from within.

But it rang but faintly now in the ears of our detective. The door had fallen to, and Sweetwater's share in the anxieties of that household was over.

Slowly he moved away. He was in a confused yet elated condition of mind. Here was food for a thousand new thoughts and conjectures. An Orlando Brotherson and an Oswald Brotherson— relatives possibly, strangers possibly; but whether relatives or strangers, both given to signing their letters with their initials simply; and both the acknowledged admirers of the deceased Miss Challoner. But she had loved only one, and that one, Oswald. It not difficult to recognise the object of this high hearted woman's affections in this man whose struggle with the master-destroyer had awakened the solicitude of a whole town.

CHAPTER XXIV

SUSPENSE

Ten minutes after Sweetwater's arrival in the village streets, he was at home with the people he found there. His conversation with Doris in the doorway of her home had been observed by the curious and far-sighted, and the questions asked and answered had made him friends at once. Of course, he could tell them nothing, but that did not matter, he had seen and talked with Doris and their idolised young manager was no worse and might possibly soon be better.

Of his own affairs—of his business with Doris and the manager, they asked nothing. All ordinary interests were lost in the stress of their great suspense.

It was the same in the bar-room of the one hotel. Without resorting to more than a question or two, he readily learned all that was generally known of Oswald Brotherson. Every one was talking about him, and each had some story to tell illustrative of his kindness, his courage and his quick mind. The Works had never produced a man of such varied capabilities and all round sympathies. To have him for manager meant the greatest good which could befall this little community.

His rise had been rapid. He had come from the east three years before, new to the work. Now, he was the one man there. Of his relationships east, family or otherwise, nothing was said. For them his life began and ended in Derby, and Sweetwater could see, though no actual expression was given to the feeling, that there was but one expectation in regard to him and Doris, to whose uncommon beauty and sweetness they all seemed fully alive. And Sweetwater wondered, as many of us have wondered, at the gulf frequently existing between fancy and fact.

Later there came a small excitement. The doctor was seen riding by on his way to the sick man. From the window where he sat, Sweetwater watched him pass up the street and take the road he had himself so lately traversed. It was so straight a one and led so directly northward that he could follow with his eye the doctor's whole course, and even get a glimpse of his figure as he stepped from the buggy and proceeded to tie up the horse. There was an energy about him pleasing to Sweetwater. He might have much to do with this doctor. If Oswald Brotherson died—but he was not willing to consider this possibility—yet. His personal sympathies, to say nothing of his professional interest in the mystery to which this man—and this man only—possibly held the key, alike forbade. He would hope, as these others were hoping, and if he did not count the minutes, he at least saw every move of the old horse waiting with drooping head and the resignation of long custom for the re-appearance of his master with his news of life or death.

And so an hour—two hours passed. Others were watching the old horse now. The street showed many an eager figure with head turned northward. From the open door-ways women stepped, looked in the direction of their anxiety and retreated to their work again. Suspense was everywhere; the moments dragged like hours; it became so keen at last that some impatient hearts could no longer stand it. A woman put her baby into another woman's arms and hurried up the road; another followed, then another; then an old man, bowed with years and of tottering steps, began to go that way, halting a dozen times before he reached the group now collected in the dusty highway, near but not too near that house. As Sweetwater's own enthusiasm swelled at this sight, he thought of the other Brotherson with his theories and active advocacy for reform, and wondered if men and women would forego their meals and stand for hours in the keen spring wind just to be the first to hear if he were to live or die. He knew that he himself would not. But he had suffered much both in his pride and his purse at the hands of the Brooklyn inventor; and such despoliation is not a reliable basis for sympathy. He was questioning his own judgment in this matter and losing himself in the mazes of past doubts and conjectures when a sudden change took place in the aspect of the street; he saw people running, and in another moment saw why. The doctor had shown himself on the porch which all were watching. Was he coming out? No, he stands quite still, runs his eye over the people waiting quietly in the road, and beckons to one of the smaller boys. The child, with upturned face, stands listening to what he has to say, then starts on a run for the village. He is stopped, pulled about, questioned, and allowed to run on. Many rush forth to meet him. He is panting, but gleeful. Mr. Brotherson has waked up conscious, and the doctor says, HE WILL LIVE.

CHAPTER XXV

THE OVAL HUT

That night Dr. Fenton had a visitor. We know that visitor and we almost know what his questions were, if not the answers of the good doctor. Nevertheless, it may be better to listen to a part at least of their conversation. Sweetwater, who knew when to be frank and open, as well as when to be reserved and ambiguous, made no effort to disguise the nature of his business or his chief cause of interest in Oswald Brotherson. The eye which met his was too penetrating not to detect the smallest attempt at subterfuge; besides, Sweetwater had no need to hide his errand; it was one of peace, and it threatened nobody—"the more's the pity," thought he in uneasy comment to himself, as he realised the hopelessness of the whole situation.

His first word, therefore, was a plain announcement.

"Dr. Fenton, my name is Sweetwater. I am from New York, and represent for the nonce, Mr. Challoner, whose name I have simply to mention, for you to understand that my business is with Mr. Brotherson whom I am sorry to find seriously, if not dangerously, ill. Will you tell me how long you think it will be before I can have a talk with him on a subject which I will not disguise from you may prove a very exciting one?"

"Weeks, weeks," returned the doctor. "Mr. Brotherson has been a very sick man and the only hope I have of his recovery is the fact that he is ignorant of his trouble or that he has any cause for doubt or dread. Were this happy condition of things to be disturbed —were the faintest rumour of sorrow or disaster to reach him in his present weakened state, I should fear a relapse, with all its attendant dangers. What then, if any intimation should be given him of the horrible tragedy suggested by the name you have mentioned? The man would die before your eyes. Mr. Challoner's business will have to wait."

"That I see; but if I knew when I might speak—"

"I can give you no date. Typhoid is a treacherous complaint; he has the best of nurses and the chances are in favour of a quick recovery; but we never can be sure. You had better return to New York. Later, you can write me if you wish, or Mr. Challoner can. You may have confidence in my reply; it will not mislead you."

Sweetwater muttered his thanks and rose. Then he slowly sat down again.

"Dr. Fenton," he began, "you are a man to be trusted. I'm in a devil of a fix, and there is just a possibility that you may be able to help me out. It is the general opinion in New York, as you may know, that Miss Challoner committed suicide. But the circumstances do not fully bear out this theory, nor can Mr. Challoner be made to accept it. Indeed, he is so convinced of its falsehood, that he stands ready to do anything, pay anything, suffer anything, to have this distressing blight removed from his daughter's good name. Mr. Brotherson was her dearest friend, and as such may have the clew to this mystery, but Mr. Brotherson may not be in a condition to speak for several weeks. Meanwhile, Mr. Challoner must suffer from great suspense unless—" a pause during which he searched the doctor's face with a perfectly frank and inquiring expression—"unless some one else can help us out. Dr. Fenton, can you?"

The doctor did not need to speak; his expression conveyed his answer.

"No more than another," said he. "Except for what Doris felt compelled to tell me, I know as little as yourself. Mr. Brotherson's delirium took the form of calling continually upon one name. I did not know this name, but Doris did, also the danger lurking in the fact that he had yet to hear of the tragedy which had robbed him of this woman to whom he was so deeply attached. So she told me just this much. That the Edith whose name rung so continuously in our ears was no other than the Miss Challoner of New York of whose death and its tragic circumstances the papers have been full; that their engagement was a secret one unshared so far as she knew by any one but herself. That she begged me to preserve this secret and to give her all the help I could when the time came for him to ask questions. Especially did she entreat me to be with her at the crisis. I was, but his waking was quite natural. He did not ask for Miss Challoner; he only inquired how long he had been ill and whether Doris had received a letter during that time. She had not received one, a fact which seemed to disappoint him; but she carried it off so gaily (she is a wonderful girl, Mr. Sweetwater—the darling of all our hearts), saying that he must not be so egotistical as to think that the news of his illness had gone beyond Derby, that he soon recovered his spirits and became a very promising convalescent. That is all I know about the matter; little more, I take it, than you know yourself."

Sweetwater nodded; he had expected nothing from the doctor, and was not disappointed at his failure. There were two strings to his bow, and the one proving valueless, he proceeded to test the other.

"You have mentioned Miss Scott, as the confidante—and only confidante of this unhappy pair," said he. "Would it be possible—can you make it possible for me to see her?"

It was a daring proposition; he understood this at once from the doctor's expression; and, fearing a hasty rebuff, he proceeded to supplement his request with a few added arguments, urged with such unexpected address and show of reason that Dr. Fenton's aspect visibly softened and in the end he found himself ready to promise that he would do what he could to secure his visitor the interview he desired if he would come to the house the next day at the time of his own morning visit.

This was as much as the young detective could expect, and having expressed his thanks, he took his leave in anything but a discontented frame of mind. With so powerful an advocate as the doctor, he felt confident that he should soon be able to conquer this young girl's reticence and learn all that was to be learned from any one but Mr. Brotherson himself. In the time which must elapse between that happy hour and the present, he would circulate and learn what he could about the prospective manager. But he soon found that he could not enter the Works without a permit, and this he was hardly in a position to demand; so he strolled about the village instead, and later wandered away into the forest.

Struck by the inviting aspect of a narrow and little used road opening from the highway shortly above the house where his interests were just then centred, he strolled into the heart of the spring woods till he came to a depression where a surprise awaited him, in the shape of a peculiar structure rising from its midst where it just fitted, or so nearly fitted that one could hardly walk about it without brushing the surrounding tree trunks. Of an oval shape, with its door facing the approach, it nestled there, a wonder to the eye and the occasion of considerable speculation to his inquiring mind. It had not been long built, as was shown very plainly by the fresh appearance of the unpainted boards of which it was constructed; and while it boasted of a door, as I've already said, there were no evidences visible of any other break in the smooth, neatly finished walls. A wooden ellipse with a roof but no windows; such it appeared and such it proved to be. A mystery to Sweetwater's eyes, and like all mysteries, interesting. For what purpose had it been built and why this isolation? It was too flimsy for a reservoir and too expensive for the wild freak of a crank.

A nearer view increased his curiosity. In the projection of the roof over the curving sides he found fresh food for inquiry. As he examined it in the walk he made around the whole structure, he came to a place where something like a hinge became visible and further on another. The roof was not simply a roof; it was also a lid capable of being raised for the air and light which the lack of windows necessitated. This was an odd discovery indeed, giving to the uncanny structure the appearance of a huge box, the cover of which could be raised or lowered at p easure. And again he asked himself for what it could be intended? What enterprise, even of the great Works, could demand a secrecy so absolute that such pains as these should be taken to shut out all possibility of a prying eye. Nothing in his experience supplied him with an answer.

He was still looking up at these hinges, with a glance which took in at the same time the nearness and extreme height of the trees by which this sylvan mystery was surrounded, when a sound from the road on the opposite side of the hollow brought his conjectures to a standstill and sent him hurrying on to the nearest point from which that road became visible.

A team was approaching. He could hear the heavy tread of horses working their laborious way through trees whose obstructing branches swished before and behind them. They were bringing in a load for this shed, whose uses he would consequently soon understand. Grateful for his good luck— for his was a curiosity which could not stand defeat—he took a few steps into the wood, and from the vantage point of a concealing cluster of bushes, fixed his eyes upon the spot where the road opened into the hollow.

Something blue moved there, and in another moment, to his great amazement, there stepped into view the spirited form of Doris Scott, who if he had given the matter a thought he would have supposed to be sitting just then by the bedside of her patient, a half mile back on the road.

She was dressed for the woods in a blue skirt and jacket and moved like a leader in front of a heavily laden wagon now coming to a standstill before the closely shut shed—if such we may call it.

"I have a key," so she called out to the driver who had paused for orders. "When I swing the doors wide, drive straight in."

Sweetwater took a look at the wagon. It was piled high with large wooden boxes on more than one of which he could see scrawled the words: O. Brotherson, Derby, Pa.

This explained her presence, but the boxes told nothing. They were of all sizes and shapes, and some of them so large that the assistance of another man was needed to handle them. Sweetwater was about to offer his services when a second man appeared from somewhere in the rear, and the detective's attention being thus released from the load out of which he could make nothing, he allowed it to concentrate upon the young girl who had it in charge and who, for many reasons, was the one person of supreme importance to him.

She had swung open the two wide doors, and now stood waiting for horse and wagon to enter. With locks flying free—she wore no bonnet—she presented a picture of ever increasing interest to Sweetwater. Truly she was a very beautiful girl, buoyant, healthy and sweet; as unlike as possible his preconceived notions of Miss Challoner's humble little protegee. Her brown hair of a rich chestnut hue, was in itself a wonder. On no head, even in the great city he had just left, had he seen such abundance, held in such modest restraint. Nature had been partial to this little working girl and given her the chevelure of a queen.

But this was nothing. No one saw this aureole when once the eye had rested on her features and caught the full nobility of their expression and the lurking sweetness underlying her every look. She herself made the charm and whether placed high or placed low, must ever attract the eye and afterwards lure the heart, by an individuality which hardly needed perfect features in which to express itself.

Young yet, but gifted, as girls of her class often are, with the nicest instincts and purest aspirations, she showed the elevation of her thoughts both in her glance and the poise with which she awaited events. Sweetwater watched her with admiration as she superintended the unloading of the wagon and the disposal of the various boxes on the floor within; but as nothing she said during the process was calculated to afford the least enlightenment in regard to their contents, he presently wearied of his inaction and turned back towards the highway, comforting himself with the reflection that in a few short hours he would have her to himself when nothing but a blunder on his part should hinder him from sounding her young mind and getting such answers to his questions as the affair in which he was so deeply interested, demanded.

CHAPTER XXVI

SWEETWATER RETURNS

"You see me again, Miss Scott. I hope that yesterday's intrusion has not prejudiced you against me."

"I have no prejudices," was her simple but firm reply. "I am only hurried and very anxious. The doctor is with Mr. Brotherson just now; but he has several other equally sick patients to visit and I dare not keep him here too long."

"Then you will welcome my abruptness. Miss Scott, here is a letter from Mr. Challoner. It will explain my position. As you will see, his only desire is to establish the fact that his daughter did not commit suicide. She was all he had in the world, and the thought that she could, for any reason, take her own life is unbearable to him. Indeed, he will not believe she did so, evidence or no evidence. May I ask if you agree with him? You have seen Miss Challoner, I believe. Do you think she was the woman to plunge a dagger in her heart in a place as public as a hotel reception room?"

"No, Mr. Sweetwater. I'm a poor working girl, with very little education and almost no knowledge of the world and such ladies as she. But something tells me for all that, that she was too nice to do this. I saw her once and it made me want to be quiet and kind and beautiful like her. I never shall think she did anything so horrible. Nor will Mr. Brotherson ever believe it. He could not and live. You see, I am talking to you as if you knew him,—the kind of man he is and just how he feels towards Miss Challoner. He is—" Her voice trailed off and a look, uncommon and almost elevated, illumined her face. "I will not tell you what he is; you will know, if you ever see him."

"If the favourable opinion of a whole town makes a good fellow, he ought to be of the best," returned Sweetwater, with his most honest smile. "I hear but one story of him wherever I turn."

"There is but one story to tell," she smiled, and her head drooped softly, but with no air of self-consciousness.

Sweetwater watched her for a moment, and then remarked "I'm going to take one thing for granted; that you are as anxious as we are to clear Miss Challoner's memory."

"O yes, O yes."

"More than that, that you are ready and eager to help us. Your very looks show that."

"You are right; I would do anything to help you. But what can a girl like me do? Nothing; nothing. I know too little. Mr. Challoner must see that when you tell him I'm only the daughter of a foreman."

"And a friend of Mr. Brotherson," supplemented Sweetwater.

"Yes," she smiled, "he would want me to say so. But that's his goodness. I don't deserve the honour."

"His friend and therefore his confidante," Sweetwater continued. "He has talked to you about Miss Challoner?"

"He had to. There was nobody else to whom he could talk; and then, I had seen her and could understand."

"Where did you see her?"

"In New York. I was there once with father, who took me to see her. I think she had asked Mr. Brotherson to send his little friend to her hotel if ever we came to New York."

"That was some time ago?"

"We were there in June."

"And you have corresponded ever since with Miss Challoner?"

"She has been good enough to write, and I have ventured at times to answer her."

The suspicion which might have come to some men found no harbour in Sweetwater's mind. This young girl was beautiful, there was no denying that, beautiful in a somewhat startling and quite unusual way; but there was nothing in her bearing, nothing in Miss Challoner's letters to indicate that she had been a cause for jealousy in the New York lady's mind. He, therefore, ignored this possibility, pursuing his inquiry along the direct lines he had already laid out for himself. Smiling a little, but in a very earnest fashion, he pointed to the letter she still held and quietly said:

"Remember that I'm not speaking for myself, Miss Scott, when I seem a little too persistent and inquiring. You have corresponded with Miss Challoner; you have been told the fact of her secret engagement to Mr. Brotherson and you have been witness to his conduct and manner for the whole time he has been separated from her. Do you, when you think of it carefully, recall anything in the whole story of this romance which would throw light upon the cruel tragedy which has so unexpectedly ended it? Anything, Miss Scott? Straws show which way the stream flows."

She was vehement, instantly vehement, in her disclaimer.

"I can answer at once," said she, "because I have thought of nothing else for all these weeks. Here all was well. Mr. Brotherson was hopeful and happy and believed in her happiness and willingness to wait for his success. And this success was coming so fast! Oh, how can we ever tell him! How can we ever answer his questions even, or keep him satisfied and calm until he is strong enough to hear the truth. I've had to acknowledge already that I have had no letter from her for weeks. She never wrote to him directly, you know, and she never sent him messages, but he knew that a letter to me, was also a letter to him and I can see that he is troubled by this long silence, though he says I was right not to let her know of his illness and that I must continue to keep her in ignorance of it till he is quite well again and can write to her himself. It is hard to hear him talk like this and not look sad or frightened."

Sweetwater remembered Miss Challoner's last letter, and wished he had it here to give her. In default of this, he said:

"Perhaps this not hearing may act in the way of a preparation for the shock which must come to him sooner or later. Let us hope so, Miss Scott."

Her eyes filled.

"Nothing can prepare him," said she. Then added, with a yearning accent, "I wish I were older or had more experience. I should not feel so helpless. But the gratitude I owe him will give me strength when I need it most. Only I wish the suffering might be mine rather than his."

Unconscious of any self-betrayal, she lifted her eyes, startling Sweetwater by the beauty of her look. "I don't think I'm so sorry for Oswald Brotherson," he murmured to himself as he left her. "He's a more fortunate man than he knows, however deeply he may feel the loss of his first sweetheart."

That evening the disappointed Sweetwater took the train for New York. He had failed to advance the case in hand one whit, yet the countenance he showed Mr. Gryce at their first interview was not a wholly gloomy one.

"Fifty dollars to the bad!" was his first laconic greeting. "All I have learned is comprised in these two statements. The second O. B. is a fine fellow; and not intentionally the cause of our tragedy. He does not even know about it. He's down with the fever at present and they haven't told him. When he's better we may hear something; but I doubt even that."

"Tell me about it."

Sweetwater complied; and such is the unconsciousness with which we often encounter the pivotal circumstance upon which our future or the future of our most cherished undertaking hangs, he omitted from his story, the sole discovery which was of any real importance in the unravelling of the mystery in which they were so deeply concerned. He said ncthing of his walk in the woods or of what he saw there.

"A meagre haul," he remarked at the close.

"But that's as it should be, if you and I are right in our impressions anc the clew to this mystery lies here in the character and daring of Orlando Brotherson. That's why I'm not down in the mouth. Which goes to show what a grip my prejudices have on me.'

"As prejudiced as a bulldog."

"Exactly. By the way, what news of the gentleman I've just mentioned? Is he as serene in my absence as when under my eye?"

"More so; he looks like a man on the verge of triumph. But I fear the triumph he anticipates has nothing to do with our affairs. All his time and thought is taken up with his invention."

"You discourage me, sir. And now to see Mr. Challoner. Small comfort can I carry him."

CHAPTER XXVII

THE IMAGE OF DREAD

In the comfortable little sitting-room of the Scott cottage Doris stood. looking eagerly from the window which gave upon the road. Behind her on the other side of the room, could be seen through a partly opened door, a neatly spread bed, with a hand lying quietly on the patched coverlet. It was a strong looking hand which, even when quiescent, conveyec the idea of purpose and vitality. As Doris said, the fingers never curled up languidly, but always with the hint of a clench. Several weeks had passed since the departure of Sweetwater and the invalid was fast gaining strength. To-morrow, he would be up.

Was Doris thinking of him? Undoubtedly, for her eyes often flashed his way; but her main attention was fixed upon the road, though no one was in sight at the moment. Some one had passed for whose return she looked; some one whom, if she had beer asked to describe, she would have called a tall, fine-looking man of middle age, of a cultivated appearance seldom seen in this small manufacturing town; seldom seen, possibly, in any town. He had glanced up at the window as he went by, in a manner too marked not to excite her curiosity. Would he look up again when he came back? She was waiting there to see. Why, she did not know. She was not used to indulging in petty suppositions of this kind; her life was too busy, her anxieties too keen. The great dread looming ever before her,—the dread of that hour when she must speak,—left her very little heart for anything dissociated with this coming event. For a girl of seventeen she was unusually thoughtful. Life had been hard in this little cottage since her mother died, or rather she had felt its responsibilities keenly.

Life itself could not be hard where Oswald Brotherson lived; neither to man, nor woman. The cheer of some natures possesses a divine faculty. If it can help no other way, it does so by the aid of its own light. Such was the character of this man's temperament. The cottage was a happy place; only— she never fathomed the depths of that only. If in these days she essayed at times to do so, she gave full credit to the Dread which rose ever before her—rose like a ghost! She, Doris, led by inscrutable Fate, was waiting to hurt him who hurt nobody; whose mere presence was a blessing.

But her interest had been caught to-day, caught by this stranger, and when during her eager watch the small messenger from the Works came to the door with the usual daily supply of books and magazines for the patient, she stepped out on the porch to speak to him and to point out the gentleman who was now rapidly returning from his stroll up the road.

"Who is that, Johnny?" she asked. "You know everybody who comes to town. What is the name of the gentleman you see coming?"

The boy looked, searched his memory, not without some show of misgiving.

"A queer name," he admitted at last. "I never heard the likes of it here before. Shally something. Shally—Shally—"

"Challoner?"

"Yes, that's it. How could you guess? He's from New York. Nobody knows why he's here. Don't seem to have no business."

"Well, never mind. Run on, Johnny. And don't forget to come earlier to-morrow; Mr. Brotherson gets tired waiting."

"Does he? I'll come quick then; quick as I can run." And he sped off at a pace which promised well for the morrow.

Challoner! There was but one Challoner in the world for Doris Scott,—Edith's father. Was this he? It must be, or why this haunting sense of something half remembered as she caught a glimpse of his face. Edith's father! and he was approaching, approaching rapidly, on his way back to town. Would he stop this time? As the possibility struck her, she trembled and drew back, entering the house, but pausing in the hall with her ear turned to the road. She had not closed the door; something within— a hope or a dread—had prevented that. Would he take it as an invitation to come in? No, no; she was not ready for such an encounter yet. He might speak Edith's name; Oswald might hear and— with a gasp she recognised the closeness of his step; heard it lag, almost halt just where the path to the house ran into the roadside. But it passed on. He was not going to force an interview yet. She could hear him retreating further and further away. The event was not for this day, thank God! She would have one night at least in which to prepare herself.

With a sense of relief so great that she realised, for one shocked moment, the full extent of her fears, she hastened back into the sitting-room, with her collection of books and pamphlets. A low voice greeted her. It came from the adjoining room.

"Doris, come here, sweet child. I want you."

How she would have bounded joyously at the summons, had not that Dread raised its bony finger in every call from that dearly loved voice. As it was, her feet moved slowly, lingering at the sound. But they carried her to his side at last, and once there, she smiled.

"See what an armful," she cried in joyous greeting, as she held out the bundle she had brought. "You will be amused all day. Only, do not tire yourself."

"I do not want the papers, Doris; not yet. There's something else which must come first. Doris, I have decided to let you write to her. I'm so much better now, she will not feel alarmed. I must—must get a word from her. I'm starving for it. I lie here and can think of nothing else. A message—one little message of six short words would set me on my feet again. So get your paper and pen, dear child, and write her one of your prettiest letters."

Had he loved her, he would have perceived the chill which shook her whole body, as he spoke. But his first thought, his penetrating thought, was not for her and he saw only the answering glance, the patient smile. She had not expected him to see more. She knew that she was quite safe from the divining look; otherwise, he would have known her secret long ago.

"I'm ready," said she. But she did not lay down her bundle. She was not ready for her task, poor child. She quailed before it. She quailed so much that she feared to stir lest he should see that she had no command over her movements.

The man who watched without seeing wondered that she stood so still and spoke so briefly. But only for a moment. He thought he understood her hesitation, and a look of great earnestness replaced his former one of grave decision.

"I know that in doing this I am going beyond my sacred compact with Miss Challoner," he said. "I never thought of illness,—at least, of illness on my part. I never dreamt that I, always so well, always so full of life, could know such feebleness as this, feebleness which is all of the body, Doris, leaving the mind free to dream and long. Talk of her, child. Tell me all over again just how she looked and spoke that day you saw her in New York."

"Would it not be better for me to write my letter first? Papa will be coming soon and Truda can never cook your bird as you like it."

Surprised now by something not quite natural in her manner, he caught at her hand and held her as she was moving away.

"You are tired," said he. "I've wearied you with my commission and complaints. Forgive me, dear child, and—"

"You are mistaken," she interrupted softly. "I am not tired; I only wished to do the important thing first. Shall I get my desk? Do you really wish me to write?"

"Yes," said he, softly dropping her hand. "I wish you to write. It will ensure me good sleep, and sleep will make me strong. A few words, Doris; just a few words."

She nodded; turning quickly away to hide her tears. His smile had gone to her very soul. It was always a beautiful one, his chief personal attraction, but at this moment it seemed to concentrate within it the unspoken fervours and the boundless expectations of a great love, and she who was the aim and cause of all this sweetness lay in unresponsive silence in a distant tomb!

But Doris' own smile was not lacking in encouragement and beauty when she came back a few minutes later and sat down by his side to write. His melted before it, leaving his eyes very earnest as he watched her bending figure and the hard-worked little hand at its unaccustomed task.

"I must give her daily exercises," he decided within himself. "That look of pain shows how difficult this work is for her. It must be made easy at any cost to my time. Such beauty calls for accomplishment. I must not neglect so plain a duty."

Meantime, she was struggling to find words in face of that great Dread. She had written Dear Miss Challoner and was staring in horror at the soulless words. Only her sense of duty upheld her. Gladly would she have torn the sheet in two and rushed away. How could she add sentences to this hollow phrase, the mere employment of which seemed a sacrilege. Dear Miss Challoner. Oh, she was dear, but—

Unconsciously the young head drooped, and the pen slid from her hand.

"I cannot," she murmured, "I cannot think what to say."

"Shall I help you?" came softly from the bed. "I'll try and not forget that it is Doris writing."

"If you will be so good," she answered, with renewed courage. "I can put the words down if you will only find them for me."

"Write then. 'Dear Miss Challoner!'"

"I have already written that."

"Why do you shudder?"

"I'm cold. I've been cold all day. But never mind that, Mr. Brotherson. Tell me how to begin my letter."

"This way. 'I've not been able to answer your kind letter, because I have had to play nurse for some three or four weeks to a very fretful and exacting patient.' Have you written that?"

"No," said Doris, bending over her desk till her curls fell in a tangle over her white cheeks. "I do not like to," she protested at last, with an attempt at naivete which seemed real enough to him.

"Well, leave out the fretful if you must, but keep in the exacting. I have been exacting, you know."

Silence, broken only by the scratching of the stubborn, illy-directed pen.

"It's down," she whispered. She said, afterward, that it was like writing with a ghost looking over one's shoulder.

"Then add, 'Mr. Brotherson has had a slight attack of fever, but he is getting well fast, and will soon—, Do I run on too quickly?"

"No, no, I can follow."

"But not without losing breath; eh, Doris?"

As he laughed, she smiled. There was a heroism in that smile, Oswald Brotherson, of which you knew nothing.

"You might speak a little more slowly," she admitted.

Quietly he repeated the last phrase. "'But he is getting well fast and will soon be ready to take up the management of the Works which was given him just before he was taken ill.' That will show her that I am working up," he brightly remarked as Doris carefully penned the last word. "Of myself you need say nothing more, unless—" he paused and his face took on a wistful look which Doris dared not meet; "unless—but no, no, she must think it has been only a passing indisposition. If she knew I had been really ill, she would suffer, and perhaps act imprudently or suffer and not dare to act at all, which might be sadder for her still. Leave it where it is and begin about yourself. Write a good deal about yourself, so that she will see that you are not worried and that all is well with us here. Cannot you do that without assistance? Surely you can tell her about that last piece of embroidery you showed me. She will be glad to hear—why, Doris!"

"Oh, Mr. Brotherson," the poor child burst out, "you must let me cry! I'm so glad to see you better and interested in all sorts of things. These are not tears of grief. I—I—but I'm forgetting what the doctor told me. You are growing excited, and I was to see that you were calm, always calm. I will take my desk away. I will write the rest in the other room, while you look at the magazines."

"But bring your letter back for me to seal. I want to see it in its envelope. Oh, Doris, you are a good little girl!"

She shook her head, and hastened to hide herself from him in the other room; and it was a long time before she came back with the letter folded and in its envelope. When she did, her face was composed and her manner natural. She had quite made up her mind what her duty was and how she was going to perform it.

"Here is the letter," said she, laying it in his outstretched hand. Then she turned her back. She knew, with a woman's unerring instinct why he wished to handle it before it went. She felt that kiss he folded away in it, in every fibre of her aroused and sympathetic heart. but the hardest part of the ordeal was over and her eyes beamed softly when she turned again to take it from his hand and affix the stamp.

"You will mail it yourself?" he asked. "I should like to have you put it into the box with your own hand."

"I will put it in to-night, after supper," she promised him.

His smile of contentment assured her that this trial of her courage and self-control was not without one blessed result. He would rest for several days in the pleasure of what he had done or thought he had done. She need not cringe before that image of Dread for two, three days at least. Meanwhile, he would grow strong in body, and she, perhaps, in spirit. Only one precaution she must take. No hint of Mr. Challoner's presence in town must reach him. He must be guarded from a knowledge of that fact as certainly as from the more serious one which lay behind it.

CHAPTER XXVIII

I HOPE NEVER TO SEE THAT MAN

That this would be a difficult thing to do, Doris was soon to realise. Mr. Challoner continued to pass the house twice a day and the time finally came when he ventured up the walk.

Doris was in the window and saw him coming. She slipped softly out and intercepted him before he had stepped upon the porch. She had caught up her hat as she passed through the hall, and was fitting it to her head as he looked up and saw her.

"Miss Scott?" he asked.

"Yes, Mr. Challoner."

"You know me?" he went on, one foot on the step and one still on the walk.

Before replying she closed the door behind her. Then as she noted his surprise she carefully explained:

"Mr. Brotherson, our boarder, is just recovering from typhoid. He is still weak and acutely susceptible to the least noise. I was afraid that our voices might disturb him. Do you mind walking a little way up the road? That is, if your visit was intended for me."

Her flush, the beauty which must have struck even him, but more than all else her youth, seemed to reconcile him to this unconventional request. Bowing, he took his foot from the step, saying, as she joined him:

"Yes, you are the one I wanted to see; that is, to-day. Later, I hope to have the privilege of a conversation with Mr. Brotherson."

She gave him one quick look, trembling so that he offered her his arm with a fatherly air.

"I see that you understand my errand here," he proceeded, with a grave smile, meant as she knew for her encouragement. "I am glad, because we can go at once to the point. Miss Scott," he continued in a voice from which he no longer strove to keep back the evidences of deep feeling, "I have the strongest interest in your patient that one man can have in another, where there is no personal acquaintanceship. You who have every reason to understand my reasons for this, will accept the statement, I hope, as frankly as it is made."

She nodded. Her eyes were full of tears, but she did not hesitate to raise them. She had the greatest desire to see the face of the man who could speak like this to-day, and yet of whose pride and sense of superiority his daughter had stood in such awe, that she had laid a seal upon the impulses of her heart, and imposed such tasks and weary waiting upon her lover. Doris forgot, in meeting his softened glance and tender, almost wistful, expression, the changes which can be made by a great grief, and only wondered why her sweet benefactress had not taken him into her confidence and thus, possibly, averted the doom which Doris felt had in some way grown out of this secrecy.

"Why should she have feared the disapproval of this man?" she inwardly queried, as she cast him a confiding look which pleased him greatly, as his tone now showed.

"When I lost my daughter, I lost everything," he declared, as they walked slowly up the road. "Nothing excites my interest, save that which once excited hers. I am told that the deepest interest of her life lay here. I am also told that it was an interest quite worthy of her. I expect to find it so. I hope with all my heart to find it so, and that is why I have come to this town and expect to linger till

Mr. Brotherson has recovered sufficiently to see me. I hope that this will be agreeable to him. I hope that I am not presuming too much in cherishing these expectations."

Doris turned her candid eyes upon him.

"I cannot tell; I do not know," said she. "Nobody knows, not even the doctor, what effect the news we so dread to give him will have upon Mr. Brotherson. You will have to wait—we all shall have to wait the results of that revelation. It cannot be kept from him much longer. When I return, I shall shrink from his first look, in the fear of seeing it betray this dreadful knowledge. Yet I have a faithful woman there to keep every one out of his room."

"You have had much to carry for one so young," was Mr. Challoner's sympathetic remark. "You must let me help you when that awful moment comes. I am at the hotel and shall stay there till Mr. Brotherson is pronounced quite well. I have no other duty now in life but to sustain him through his trouble and then, with what aid he can give, search out and find the cause of my daughter's death which I will never admit without the fullest proof, to have been one of suicide."

Doris trembled.

"It was not suicide," she declared, vehemently. "I have always felt sure that it was not; but to-day I KNOW."

Her hand fell clenched on her breast and her eyes gleamed strangely. Mr. Challoner was himself greatly startled. What had happened—what could have happened since yesterday that she should emphasise that now?

"I've not told any one," she went on, as he stopped short in the road, in his anxiety to understand her. "But I will tell you. Only, not here, not with all these people driving past; most of whom know me. Come to the house later—this evening, after Mr. Brotherson's room is closed for the night. I have a little sitting-room on the other side of the hall where we can talk without being heard. Would you object to doing that? Am I asking too much of you?"

"No, not at all," he assured her. "Expect me at eight. Will that be too early?"

"No, no. Oh, how those people stared! Let us hasten back or they may connect your name with what we want kept secret."

He smiled at her fears, but gave in to her humour; he would see her soon again and possibly learn something which would amply repay him, both for his trouble and his patience.

But when evening came and she turned to face him in that little sitting-room where he had quietly followed her, he was conscious of a change in her manner which forbade these high hopes. The gleam was gone from her eyes; the tremulous eagerness from her mobile and sensitive mouth. She had been thinking in the hours which had passed, and had lost the confidence of that one impetuous moment. Her greeting betrayed embarrassment and she hesitated painfully before she spoke.

"I don't know what you will think of me," she ventured at last, motioning to a chair but not sitting herself. "You have had time to think over what I said and probably expect something real,—something you could tell people. But it isn't like that. It's a feeling—a belief. I'm so sure—"

"Sure of what, Miss Scott?"

She gave a glance at the door before stepping up nearer. He had not taken the chair she preferred.

"Sure that I have seen the face of the man who murdered her. It was in a dream," she whisperingly completed, her great eyes misty with awe.

"A dream, Miss Scott?" He tried to hide his disappointment.

"Yes; I knew that it would sound foolish to you; it sounds foolish to me. But listen, sir. Listen to what I have to tell and then you can judge. I was very much agitated yesterday. I had to write a letter at Mr. Brotherson's dictation—a letter to her. You can understand my horror and the effort I made to hide my emotion. I was quite unnerved. I could not sleep till morning, and then—and then—I saw—I hope I can describe it."

Grasping at a near-by chair, she leaned on it for support, closing her eyes to all but that inner vision. A breathless moment followed, then she murmured in strained monotonous tones:

"I see it again—just as I saw it in the early morning—but even more plainly, if that is possible. A hall—(I should call it a hall, though I don't remember seeing any place like it before), with a little staircase at the side, up which there comes a man, who stops just at the top and looks intently my way. There is fierceness in his face—a look which means no good to anybody—and as his hand goes to his overcoat pocket, drawing out something which I cannot describe, but which he handles as if it were a pistol, I feel a horrible fear, and—and—" The child was staggering, and the hand which was free had sought her heart where it lay clenched, the knuckles showing white in the dim light.

Mr. Challoner watched her with dilated eyes, the spell under which she spoke falling in some degree upon him. Had she finished? Was this all? No; she is speaking again, but very low, almost in a whisper.

"There is music—a crash—but I plainly see his other hand approach the object he is holding. He takes something from the end—the object is pointed my way—I am looking into—into—what? I do not know. I cannot even see him now. The space where he stood is empty. Everything fades, and I wake with a loud cry in my ears and a sense of death here." She had lifted her hand and struck at her heart, opening her eyes as she did so. "Yet it was not I who had been shot," she added softly.

Mr. Challoner shuddered. This was like the reopening of his daughter's grave. But he had entered upon the scene with a full appreciation of the ordeal awaiting him and he did not lose his calmness, or the control of his judgment.

"Be seated, Miss Scott," he entreated, taking a chair himself. "You have described the spot and some of the circumstances of my daughter's death as accurately as if you had been there. But you have doubtless read a full account of those details in the papers; possibly seen pictures which would make the place quite real to you. The mind is a strange storehouse. We do not always know what lies hidden within it."

"That's true," she admitted. "But the man! I had never seen the man, or any picture of him, and his face was clearest of all. I should know it if I saw it anywhere. It is imprinted on my memory as plainly as yours. Oh, I hope never to see that man!"

Mr. Challoner sighed; he had really anticipated something from the interview. The disappointment was keen. A moment of expectation; the thrill which comes to us all under the shadow of the supernatural, and then—this! a young and imaginative girl's dream, convincing to herself but supplying nothing which had not already been supplied both by the facts and his own imagination! A man had stood at the staircase, and this man had raised his arm. She said that she had seen something like a pistol in his hand, but his daughter had not been shot. This he thought it well to point out to her.

Leaning toward her that he might get her full attention, he waited till her eyes met his, then quietly asked:

"Have you ever named this man to yourself?"

She started and dropped her eyes.

"I do not dare to," said she.

"Why?"

"Because I've read in the papers that the man who stood there had the same name as—"

"Tell me, Miss Scott."

"As Mr. Brotherson's brother."

"But you do not think it was his brother?"

"I do not know."

"You've never seen his brother?"

"Never."

"Nor his picture?"

"No, Mr. Brotherson has none."

"Aren't they friends? Does he never mention Orlando?"

"Very, very rarely. But I've no reason to think they are not on good terms. I know they correspond."

"Miss Scott?"

"Yes, Mr. Challoner."

"You must not rely too much upon your dream."

Her eyes flashed to his and then fell again.

"Dreams are not revelations; they are the reproduction of what already lies hidden in the mind. I can prove that your dream is such."

"How?" She looked startled.

"You speak of seeing something being leveled at you which made you think of a pistol."

"Yes, I was looking directly into it."

"But my daughter was not shot. She died from a stab."

Doris' lovely face, with its tender lines and girlish curves, took on a strange look of conviction which deepened, rather than melted under his indulgent, but penetrating gaze.

"I know that you think so;—but my dream says no. I saw this object. It was pointed directly towards me—above all, I saw his face. It was the face of one whose finger is on the trigger and who means death; and I believe my dream."

Well, it was useless to reason further. Gentle in all else, she was immovable so far as this idea was concerned and, seeing this, he let the matter go and prepared to take his leave.

She seemed to be quite ready for this. Anxiety about her patient had regained its place in her mind and her glance sped constantly toward the door. Taking her hand in his, he said some kind words, then crossed to the door and opened it. Instantly her finger flew to her lips and, obedient to its silent injunction, he took up his hat in silence, and was proceeding down the hall, when the bell rang, startling them both and causing him to step quickly back.

"Who is it?" she asked. "Father's in and visitors seldom come so late."

"Shall I see?"

She nodded, looking strangely troubled as the door swung open, revealing the tall, strong figure of a man facing them from the porch.

"A stranger," formed itself upon her lips, and she was moving forward, when the man suddenly stepped into the glare of the light, and she stopped, with a murmur of dismay which pierced Mr. Challoner's heart and prepared him for the words which now fell shudderingly from her lips:

"It is he! it is he! I said that I should know him wherever I saw him." Then with a quiet turn towards the intruder, "Oh, why, why, did you come here!"

CHAPTER XXIX

DO YOU KNOW MY BROTHER

Her hands were thrust out to repel, her features were fixed; her beauty something wonderful. Orlando Brotherson, thus met, stared for a moment at the vision before him, then slowly and with effort withdrawing his gaze, he sought the face of Mr. Challoner with the first sign of open disturbance that gentleman had ever seen in him.

"Ah," said he, "my welcome is readily understood. I see you far from home, sir." And with an ironical bow he turned again to Doris, who had dropped her hands, but in whose cheeks the pallor still lingered in a way to check the easy flow of words with which he might have sought to carry off the situation. "Am I in Oswald Brotherson's house?" he asked. "I was directed here. But possibly there may be some mistake."

"It is here he lives," said she; moving back automatically till she stood again by the threshold of the small room in which she had received Mr. Challoner. "Do you wish to see him to-night? If so, I fear it is impossible. He has been very ill and is not allowed to receive visits from strangers."

"I am not a stranger," announced the newcomer, with a smile few could see unmoved, it offered such a contrast to his stern and dominating figure. "I thought I heard some words of recognition which would prove your knowledge of that fact."

She did not answer. Her lips had parted, but her thought or at least the expression of her thought hung suspended in the terror of this meeting for which she was not at all prepared. He seemed to note this terror, whether or not he understood its cause, and smiled again, as he added:

"Mr. Brotherson must have spoken of his brother Orlando. I am he, Miss Scott. Will you let me come in now?"

Her eyes sought those of Mr. Challoner, who quietly nodded. Immediately she stepped from before the door which her figure had guarded and, motioning him to enter, she begged Mr. Challoner, with an imploring look, to sustain her in the interview she saw before her. He had no desire for this encounter, especially as Mr. Brotherson's glance in his direction had been anything but conciliatory. He was quite convinced that nothing was to be gained by it, but he could not resist her appeal, and followed them into the little room whose limited dimensions made the tall Orlando look bigger and stronger and more lordly in his self-confidence than ever.

"I am sorry it is so late," she began, contemplating his intrusive figure with forced composure. "We have to be very quiet in the evenings so as not to disturb your brother's first sleep which is of great importance to him."

"Then I'm not to see him to-night?"

"I pray you to wait. He's—he's been a very sick man."

"Dangerously so?"

"Yes."

Orlando continued to regard her with a peculiar awakening gaze, showing, Mr. Challoner thought, more interest in her than in his brother, and when he spoke it was mechanically and as if in sole obedience to the proprieties of the occasion.

"I did not know he was ill till very lately. His last letter was a cheerful one, and I supposed that all was right till chance revealed the truth. I came on at once. I was intending to come anyway. I have business here, as you probably know, Miss Scott."

She shook her head. "I know very little about business," said she.

"My brother has not told you why he expected me?"

"He has not even told me that he expected you."

"No?" The word was highly expressive; there was surprise in it and a touch of wonder, but more than all, satisfaction. "Oswald was always close-mouthed," he declared. "It's a good fault; I'm obliged to the boy."

These last words were uttered with a lightness which imposed upon his two highly agitated hearers, causing Mr. Challoner to frown and Doris to shrink back in indignation at the man who could indulge in a sportive suggestion in presence of such fears, if not of such memories, as the situation evoked. But to one who knew the strong and self-contained man—to Sweetwater possibly, had he been present,—there was in this very attempt—in his quiet manner and in the strange and fitful flash of his ordinarily quick eye, that which showed he was labouring—and had been labouring almost from his first entrance, under an excitement of thought and feeling which in one of his powerfully organised nature must end and that soon in an outburst of mysterious passion which would carry everything before it. But he did not mean that it should happen here. He was too accustomed to self-command to forget himself in this presence. He would hold these rampant dogs in leash till the hour of solitude; then—a glittering smile twisted his lips as he continued to gaze, first at the girl who had just entered his life, and then at the man he had every reason to distrust, and with that firm restraint upon himself still in full force, remarked, with a courteous inclination:

"The hour is late for further conversation. I have a room at the hotel and will return to it at once. In the morning I hope to see my brother."

He was going, Doris not knowing what to say, Mr. Challoner not desirous of detaining him, when there came the sound of a little tinkle from the other side of the hall, blanching the young girl's cheeks and causing Orlando Brotherson's brows to rise in peculiar satisfaction.

"My brother?" he asked.

"Yes," came in faltering reply. "He has heard our voices; I must go to him."

"Say that Orlando wishes him a good night," smiled her heart's enemy, with a bow of infinite grace.

She shuddered, and was hastening from the room when her glance fell on Mr. Challoner. He was pale and looked greatly disturbed. The prospect of being left alone with a man whom she had herself denounced to him as his daughter's murderer, might prove a tax to his strength to which she had no right to subject him. Pausing with an appealing air, she made him a slight gesture which he at once understood.

"I will accompany you into the hall," said he. "Then if anything is wrong, you have but to speak my name."

But Orlando Brotherson, displeased by this move, took a step which brought him between the two.

"You can hear her from here if she chooses to speak. There's a point to be settled between us before either of us leaves this house, and this opportunity is as good as another. Go to my brother, Miss Scott; we will await your return."

A flash from the proud banker's eye; but no demur, rather a gesture of consent. Doris, with a look of deep anxiety, sped away, and the two men stood face to face.

It was one of those moments which men recognise as memorable. What had the one to say or the other to hear, worthy of this preamble and the more than doubtful re ation in which they stood each to each? Mr. Challoner had more time than he expected in which to wonder and gird himself for whatever suffering or shock awaited him. For, Orlando Brotherson, ur like his usual self, kept him waiting while he collected his own wits, which, strange to say, seemed to have vanished with the girl.

But the question finally came.

"Mr. Challoner, do you know my brother?"

"I have never seen him."

"Do you know him? Does he know you?"

"Not at all. We are strangers."

It was said honestly. They did not know each other. Mr. Challoner was quite correct in his statement.

But the other had his doubts. Why shouldn't he have? The coincidence of finding this mourner if not avenger of Edith Challoner, in his own direct radius again, at a spot so distant, so obscure and so disconnected with any apparent business reason, was certainly startl ng enough unless the tie could be found in his brother's name and close relationship to himself.

He, therefore, allowed himself to press the question:

"Men sometimes correspond who do not know each other. You knew that a Brotherson lived here?"

"Yes."

"And hoped to learn something about me?"

"No; my interest was solely with your brother."

"With my brother? With Oswald? What interest can you have in him apart from me? Oswald is—"

Suddenly a thought came—an unimaginable one; one with power to blanch even his hardy cheek and shake a soul unassailable by all small emotions.

"Oswald Brotherson!" he repeated; adding in unintelligible tones to himself—"O. B. The same initials! They are following up these initials. Poor Oswald." Then aloud: "It hardly becomes me, perhaps, to question your motives in this attempt at making my brother's acquaintance. I think I can guess them; but your labour will be wasted. Oswald's interests do not extend beyond this town; they hardly extend to me. We are strangers, almost. You will learn nothing from him on the subject which naturally engrosses you."

Mr. Challoner simply bowed. "I do not feel called upon," said he, "to explain my reasons for wishing to know your brother. I will simply satisfy you upon a point which may well rouse your curiosity. You remember that—that my daughter's last act was the writing of a letter to a little protegee of hers. Miss Scott was that protegee. In seeking her, I came upon him. Do you require me to say more on this subject? Wait till I have seen Mr. Oswald Brotherson and then perhaps I can do so."

Receiving no answer to this, Mr. Challoner turned again to the man who was the object of his deepest suspicions, to find him still in the daze of that unimaginable thought, battling with it, scoffing at it, succumbing to it and all without a word. Mr. Challoner was without clew to this struggle, but the might of it and the mystery of it, drove him in extreme agitation from the room. Though proof was lacking, though proof might never come, nothing could ever alter his belief from this moment on that Doris was right in her estimate of this man's guilt, however unsubstantial her reasoning might appear.

How far he might have been carried by this new conviction; whether he would have left the house without seeing Doris again or exchanging another word with the man whose very presence stifled him, he had no opportunity to show, for before he had taken another step, he encountered the hurrying figure of Doris, who was returning to her guests with an air of marked relief.

"He does not know that you are here," she whispered to Mr. Challoner, as she passed him. Then, as she again confronted Orlando who hastened to dismiss his trouble at her approach, she said quite gaily, "Mr. Brotherson heard your voice, and is glad to know that you're here. He bade me give you this key and say that you would have found things in better shape if he had been in condition to superintend the removal of the boxes to the place he had prepared for you before he became ill. I was the one to do that," she added, controlling her aversion with manifest effort. "When Mr. Brotherson came to himself he asked if I had heard about any large boxes having arrived at the station shipped to his name. I said that several notices of such had come to the house. At which he requested me to see that they were carried at once to the strange looking shed he had had put up for him in the woods. I thought that they were for him, and I saw to the thing myself. Two or three others have come since and been taken to the same place. I think you will find nothing broken or disturbed; Mr. Brotherson's wishes are usually respected."

"That is fortunate for me," was the courteous reply.

But Orlando Brotherson was not himself, not at all himself as he bowed a formal adieu and withdrew past the drawn-up sentinel-like figure of Mr. Challoner, without a motion on his part or on the part of that gentleman to lighten an exit which had something in it of doom and dread presage.

CHAPTER XXX

CHAOS

It is not difficult to understand Mr. Challoner's feelings or even those of Doris at the moment of Mr. Brotherson's departure. But why this change in Brotherson himself? Why this sense of something new and terrible rising between him and the suddenly beclouded future? Let us follow him to his lonely hotel-room and see if we can solve the puzzle.

But first, does he understand his own trouble? He does not seem to. For when, his hat thrown aside, he stops, erect and frowning under the flaring gas-jet he had no recollection of lighting, his first act was to lift his hand to his head in a gesture of surprising helplessness for him, while snatches of broken sentences fell from his lips among which could be heard:

"What has come to me? Undone in an hour! Doubly undone! First by a face and then by this thought which surely the devils have whispered to me. Mr. Challoner and Oswald! What is the link between them? Great God! what is the link? Not myself? Who then or what?"

Flinging himself into a chair, he buried his face in his hands. There were two demons to fight—the first in the guise of an angel. Doris! Unknown yesterday, unknown an hour ago; but now! Had there ever been a day—an hour—when she had not been as the very throb of his heart, the light of his eyes, and the crown of all imaginable blisses?

He was startled at his own emotion as he contemplated her image in his fancy and listened for the lost echo of the few words she had spoken—words so full of music when they referred to his brother, so hard and cold when she simply addressed himself.

This was no passing admiration of youth for a captivating woman. This was not even the love he had given to Edith Challoner. This was something springing full-born out of nothing! a force which, for the first time in his life, made him complaisant to the natural weaknesses of man! a dream and yet a reality strong enough to blot out the past, remake the present, change the aspect of all his hopes, and outline a new fate. He did not know himself. There was nothing in his whole history to give him an understanding of such feelings as these.

Can a man be seized as it were by the hair, and swung up on the slopes of paradise or down the steeps of hell—without a forewarning, without the chance even to say whether he wished such a cataclysm in his life or no?

He, Orlando Brotherson, had never thought much of love. Science had been his mistress; ambition his lode-star. Such feeling as he had acknowledged to had been for men—struggling men, men who were down-trodden and gasping in the narrow bounds of poverty and helplessness. Miss Challoner had roused—well, his pride. He could see that now. The might of this new emotion made plain many things he had passed by as useless, puerile, unworthy of a man of mental calibre and might. He had never loved Edith Challoner at any moment of their acquaintanceship though he had been sincere in thinking that he did. Doris' beauty, the hour he had just passed with her, had undeceived him.

Did he hail the experience? It was not likely to bring him joy. This young girl whose image floated in light before his eyes, would never love him. She loved his brother. He had heard their names mentioned together before he had been in town an hour. Oswald, the cleverest man, Doris, the most beautiful girl in Western Pennsylvania.

He had accepted the gossip then; he had not seen her and it all seemed very natural;—hardly worth a moment's thought. But now!

And here, the other Demon sprang erect and grappled with him before the first one had let go his hold. Oswald and Challoner! The secret, unknown something which had softened that hard man's eye when his brother's name was mentioned! He had noted it and realised the mystery; a mystery before which sleep and rest must fly; a mystery to which he must now give his thought, whatever the cost, whatever the loss to those heavenly dreams the magic of which was so new it seemed to envelope him in the balm of Paradise. Away, then, image of light! Let the faculties thou hast dazed, act again. There is more than Fate's caprice in Challoner's interest in a man he never saw. Ghosts of old memories rise and demand a hearing. Facts, trivial and commonplace enough to have been lost in oblivion with the day which gave them birth, throng again from the past, proving that nought dies without a possibility of resurrection. Their power over this brooding man is shown by the force with which his fingers crush against his bowed forehead. Oswald and Challoner! Had he found the connecting link? Had it been—could it have been Edith? The preposterous is sometimes true; could it be true in this case?

He recalled the letters read to him as hers in that room of his in Brooklyn. He had hardly noted them then, he was so sure of their being forgeries, gotten up by the police to mislead him. Could they have been real, the effusions of her mind, the breathings of her heart, directed to an actual O. B., and that O. B., his brother? They had not been meant for him. He had read enough of the mawkish lines to be sure of that. None of the allusions fitted in with the facts of their mutual intercourse. But they might with those of another man; they might with the possible acts and affections of Oswald whose temperament was wholly different from his and who might have loved her, should it ever be shown that they had met and known each other. And this was not an impossibility. Oswald had been east, Oswald had even been in the Berkshires before himself. Oswald—Why it was Oswald who had suggested that he should go there—go where she still was. Why this second coincidence, if there were no tie—if the Challoners and Oswald were as far apart as they seemed and as conventionalities would naturally place them. Oswald was a sentimentalist, but very reserved about his sentimentalities. If these suppositions were true, he had had a sentimentalist's motive for what he did. As Orlando realised this, he rose from his seat, aghast at the possibilities confronting him from this line of thought. Should he contemplate them? Risk his reason by dwelling on a supposition which might have no foundation in fact? No. His brain was too full—his purposes too important for any unnecessary strain to be put upon his faculties. No thinking! investigation first. Mr. Challoner should be able to settle this question. He would see him. Even at this late hour he ought to be able to find him in one of the rooms below; and, by the force of an irresistible demand, learn in a moment whether he had to do with a mere chimera of his own overwrought fancy, or with a fact which would call into play all the resources of an hitherto unconquered and undaunted nature.

There was a wood-fire burning in the sitting-room that night, and around it was grouped a number of men with their papers and pipes. Mr. Brotherson, entering, naturally looked that way for the man he was in search of, and was disappointed not to find him there; but on casting his glances elsewhere, he was relieved to see him standing in one of the windows overlooking the street. His back was to the room and he seemed to be lost in a fit of abstraction.

As Orlando crossed to him, he had time to observe how much whiter was this man's head than in the last interview he had held with him in the coroner's office in New York. But this evidence of grief in one with whom he had little, if anything, in common, neither touched his feelings nor deterred his step. The awakening of his heart to new and profound emotions had not softened him towards the sufferings of others if those others stood without the pale he had previously raised as the legitimate boundary of a just man's sympathies.

He was, as I have said, an extraordinary specimen of manly vigour in body and in mind, and his presence in any company always attracted attention and roused, if it never satisfied, curiosity. Conversation accordingly ceased as he strode up to Mr. Challoner's side, so that his words were quite audible as he addressed that gentleman with a somewhat curt:

"You see me again, Mr. Challoner. May I beg of you a few minutes' further conversation? I will not detain you long."

The grey head turned, and the many eyes watching showed surprise at the expression of dislike and repulsion with which this New York gentleman met the request thus emphatically urged. But his answer was courteous enough. If Mr. Brotherson knew a place where they would be left undisturbed, he would listen to him if he would be very brief.

For reply, the other pointed to a small room quite unoccupied which opened out of the one in which they then stood. Mr. Challoner bowed and in an other moment the door closed upon them, to the infinite disappointment of the men about the hearth.

"What do you wish to ask?" was Mr. Challoner's immediate inquiry.

"This; I make no apologies and expect in answer nothing more than an unequivocal yes or no. You tell me that you have never met my brother. Can that be said of the other members of your family— of your deceased daughter, in fact?"

"No."

"She was acquainted with Oswald Brotherson?"

"She was."

"Without your knowledge?"

"Entirely so."

"Corresponded with him?"

"Not exactly."

"How, not exactly?"

"He wrote to her—occasionally. She wrote to him frequently—but she never sent her letters."

"Ah!"

The exclamation was sharp, short and conveyed little. Yet with its escape, the whole scaffolding of this man's hold upon life and his own fate went down in indistinguishable chaos. Mr. Challoner realised a sense of havoc, though the eyes bent upon his countenance had not wavered, nor the stalwart figure moved.

"I have read some of those letters," the inventor finally acknowledged. "The police took great pains to place them under my eye, supposing them to have been meant for me because of the initials written on the wrapper. But they were meant for Oswald. You believe that now?"

"I know it."

"And that is why I found you in the same house with him."

"It is. Providence has robbed me of my daughter; if this brother of yours should prove to be the man I am led to expect, I shall ask him to take that place in my heart and life which was once hers."

A quick recoil, a smothered exclamation on the part of the man he addressed. A barb had been hidden in this simple statement which had reached some deeply-hidden but vulnerable spot in Brotherson's breast, which had never been pierced before. His eye which alone seemed alive, still rested piercingly upon that of Mr. Challoner, but its light was fast fading, and speedily became lost in a dimness in which the other seemed to see extinguished the last upflaring embers of those inner fires which feed the aspiring soul. It was a sight no man could see unmoved. Mr. Challoner turned sharply away, in dread of the abyss which the next word he uttered might open between them.

But Orlando Brotherson possessed resources of strength of which, possibly, he was not aware himself. When Mr. Challoner, still more affected by the silence than by the dread I have mentioned, turned to confront him again, it was to find his features composed and his glance clear. He had conquered all outward manifestation of the mysterious emotion which for an instant had laid his proud spirit low.

"You are considerate of my brother," were the words with which he re-opened this painful conversation. "You will not find your confidence misplaced. Oswald is a straightforward fellow, of few faults."

"I believe it. No man can be so universally beloved without some very substantial claims to regard. I am glad to see that your opinion, though given somewhat coldly, coincides with that of his friends."

"I am not given to exaggeration," was the even reply.

The flush which had come into Mr. Challoner's cheek under the effort he had made to sustain with unflinching heroism this interview with the man he looked upon as his mortal enemy, slowly faded out till he looked the wraith of himself even to the unsympathetic eyes of Orlando Brotherson. A duty lay before him which would tax to its utmost extent his already greatly weakened self-control. Nothing which had yet passed showed that this man realised the fact that Oswald had been kept in ignorance of Miss Challoner's death. If these brothers were to meet on the morrow, it must be with the full understanding that this especial topic was to be completely avoided. But in what words could he urge such a request upon this man? None suggested themselves, yet he had promised Miss Scott that he would ensure his silence in this regard, and it was with this difficulty and no other he had been struggling when Mr. Brotherson came upon him in the other room.

"You have still something to say," suggested the latter, as an oppressive silence swallowed up that icy sentence I have already recorded.

"I have," returned Mr. Challoner, regaining his courage under the exigencies of the moment. "Miss Scott is very anxious to have your promise that you will avoid all disagreeable topics with your brother till the doctor pronounces him strong enough to meet the trouble which awaits him."

"You mean—"

"He is not as unhappy as we. He knows nothing of the affliction which has befallen him. He was taken ill—" The rest was almost inaudible.

But Orlando Brotherson had no difficulty in understanding him, and for the second time in this extraordinary interview, he gave evidences of agitation and of a mind shaken from its equipoise. But only for an instant. He did not shun the other's gaze or even maintain more than a momentary silence. Indeed, he found strength to smile, in a curious, sardonic way, as he said:

"Do you think I should be apt to broach this subject with any one, let alone with him, whose connection with it I shall need days to realise? I'm not so given to gossip. Besides, he and I have other topics of interest. I have an invention ready with which I propose to experiment in a place he has already prepared for me. We can talk about that."

The irony, the hardy self-possession with which this was said struck Mr. Challoner to the heart. Without a word he wheeled about towards the door. Without a word, Brotherson stood, watching him go till he saw his hand fall on the knob when he quietly prevented his exit by saying:

"Unhappy truths cannot be long concealed. How soon does the doctor think my brother can bear these inevitable revelations?"

"He said this morning that if his patient were as well to-morrow as his present condition gives promise of, he might be told in another week."

Orlando bowed his appreciation of this fact, but added quickly:

"Who is to do the telling?"

"Doris. Nobody else could be trusted with so delicate a task."

"I wish to be present."

Mr. Challoner looked up, surprised at the feeling with which this request was charged.

"As his brother—his only remaining relative, I have that right. Do you think that Dor—that Miss Scott, can be trusted not to forestall that moment by any previous hint of what awaits him?"

"If she so promises. But will you exact this from her? It surely cannot be necessary for me to say that your presence will add infinitely to the difficulty of her task."

"Yet it is a duty I cannot shirk. I will consult the doctor about it. I will make him see that I both understand and shall insist upon my rights in this matter. But you may tell Miss Doris that I will sit out of sight, and that I shall not obtrude myself unless my name is brought up in an undesirable way."

The hand on the door-knob made a sudden movement.

"Mr. Brotherson, I can bear no more to-night. With your permission, I will leave this question to be settled by others." And with a repetition of his former bow, the bereaved father withdrew.

Orlando watched him till the door closed, then he too dropped his mask.

But it was on again, when in a little while he passed through the sitting-room on his way upstairs.

No other day in his whole life had been like this to the hardy inventor; for in it both his heart and his conscience had been awakened, and up to this hour he had not really known that he possessed either.

CHAPTER XXXI

WHAT IS HE MAKING

Other boxes addressed to O. Brotherson had been received at the station, and carried to the mysterious shed in the woods; and now, with locked door and lifted top, the elder brother contemplated his stores and prepared himself for work.

He had been allowed a short interview with Oswald, and he had indulged himself in a few words with Doris. But he had left those memories behind with other and more serious matters. Nothing that could unnerve his hand or weaken his insight should enter this spot sacred to his great hope. Here genius reigned. Here he was himself wholly and without flaw;—a Titan with his grasp on a mechanical idea by means of which he would soon rule the world.

Not so happy were the other characters in this drama. Oswald's thoughts, disturbed for a short time by the somewhat constrained interview he had held with his brother, had flown eastward again, in silent love and longing; while Doris, with a double dread now in her heart, went about her daily tasks, praying for strength to endure the horrors of this week, without betraying the anxieties secretly devouring her. And she was only seventeen and quite alone in her trouble. She must bear it all unassisted and smile, which she did with heavenly sweetness, when the magic threshold was passed and she stood in her invalid's presence, overshadowed though it ever was by the great Dread.

And Mr. Challoner? Let those endless walks of his through the woods and over the hills tell his story if they can; or his rapidly whitening hair, and lagging step. He had been a strong man before his trouble, and had the stroke which laid him low been limited to one quick, sharp blow he might have risen above it after a while and been ready to encounter life again. But this long drawn out misery was proving too much for him. The sight of Brotherson, though they never really met, acted like acid upon a wound, and it was not till six days had passed and the dreaded Sunday was at hand, that he slept with any sense of rest or went his way about the town without that halting at the corners which betrayed his perpetual apprehension of a most undesirable encounter.

The reason for this change will be apparent in the short conversation he held with a man he had come upon one evening in the small park just beyond the workmen's dwellings.

"You see I am here," was the stranger's low greeting.

"Thank God," was Mr. Challoner's reply. "I could not have faced to-morrow alone and I doubt if Miss Scott could have found the requisite courage. Does she know that you are here?"

"I stopped at her door."

"Was that safe?"

"I think so. Mr. Brotherson—the Brooklyn one,—is up in his shed. He sleeps there now, I am told, and soundly too I've no doubt."

"What is he making?"

"What half the inventors on both sides of the water are engaged upon just now. A monoplane, or a biplane, or some machine for carrying men through the air. I know, for I helped him with it. But you'll find that if he succeeds in this undertaking, and I believe he will, nothing short of fame awaits him. His invention has startling points. But I'm not going to give them away. I'll be true enough to him for that. As an inventor he has my sympathy; but—Well, we will see what we shall see, to-morrow. You say that he is bound to be present when Miss Scott relates her tragic story. He won't be the only unseen listener. I've made my own arrangements with Miss Scott. If he feels the need of watching her and his brother Oswald, I feel the need of watching him."

"You take a burden of intolerable weight from my shoulders. Now I shall feel easier about that interview. But I should like to ask you this: Do you feel justified in this continued surveillance of a man who has so frequently, and with such evident sincerity, declared his innocence?"

"I do that. If he's as guiltless as he says he is, my watchfulness won't hurt him. If he's not, then, Mr. Challoner, I've but one duty; to match his strength with my patience. That man is the one great mystery of the day, and mysteries call for solution. At least, that's the way a detective looks at it."

"May Heaven help your efforts!"

"I shall need its assistance," was the dry rejoinder. Sweetwater was by no means blind to the difficulties awaiting him.

CHAPTER XXXII

TELL ME, TELL IT ALL

The day was a grey one, the first of the kind in weeks. As Doris stepped into the room where Oswald sat, she felt how much a ray of sunshine would have encouraged her and yet how truly these leaden skies and this dismal atmosphere expressed the gloom which soon must fall upon this hopeful, smiling man.

He smiled because any man must smile at the entrance of so lovely a woman, but it was an abstracted smile, and Doris, seeing it, felt her courage falter for a moment, though her steps did not, nor her steady compassionate gaze. Advancing slowly, and not answering because she did not hear some casual remark of his, she took her stand by his side and then slowly and with her eyes on his face, sank down upon her knees, still without speaking, almost without breathing.

His astonishment was evident, for her air was strange and full of presage,—as, indeed, she had meant it to be. But he remained as silent as she, only reached out his emaciated hand and, laying it on her head, smiled again but this time far from abstractedly. Then, as he saw her cheeks pale in terror of the task before her, he ventured to ask gently:

"What is the matter, child? So weary, eh? Nothing worse than that, I hope."

"Are you quite strong this morning? Strong enough to listen to my troubles; strong enough to bear your own if God sees fit to send them?" came hesitatingly from her lips as she watched the effect of each word, in breathless anxiety.

"Troubles? There can be but one trouble for me," was his unexpected reply. "That I do not fear—will not fear in my hour of happy recovery. So long as Edith is well—Doris! Doris! You alarm me. Edith is not ill;—not ill?"

The poor child could not answer save with her sympathetic look and halting, tremulous breath; and these signs, he would not, could not read, his own words had made such an echo in his ears.

"Ill! I cannot imagine Edith ill. I always see her in my thoughts, as I saw her on that day of our first meeting; a perfect, animated woman with the joyous look of a glad, harmonious nature. Nothing has ever clouded that vision. If she were ill I would have known it. We are so truly one that—Doris, Doris, you do not speak. You know the depth of my love, the terror of my thoughts. Is Edith ill?"

The eyes gazing wildly into his, slowly left his face and raised themselves aloft, with a sublime look. Would he understand? Yes, he understood, and the cry which rang from his lips stopped for a moment the beating of more than one heart in that little cottage.

"Dead!" he shrieked out, and fell back fainting in his chair, his lips still murmuring in semi-unconsciousness, "Dead! dead!"

Doris sprang to her feet, thinking of nothing but his wavering, slipping life till she saw his breath return, his eyes refill with light. Then the horror of what was yet to come—the answer which must be given to the how she saw trembling on his lips, caused her to sink again upon her knees in an unconscious appeal for strength. If that one sad revelation had been all!

But the rest must be told; his brother exacted it and so did the situation. Further waiting, further hiding of the truth would be insupportable after this. But oh, the bitterness of it! No wonder that she turned away from those frenzied, wildly-demanding eyes.

"Doris?"

She trembled and looked behind her. She had not recognised his voice. Had another entered? Had his brother dared—No, they were alone; seemingly so, that is. She knew,—no one better—that they were not really alone, that witnesses were within hearing, if not within sight.

"Doris," he urged again, and this time she turned in his direction and gazed, aghast. If the voice were strange, what of the face which now confronted her. The ravages of sickness had been marked, but they were nothing to those made in an instant by a blasting grief. She was startled, although expecting much, and could only press his hands while she waited for the question he was gathering strength to utter. It was simple when it came; just two words:

"How long?"

She answered them as simply.

"Just as long as you have been ill," said she; then, with no attempt to break the inevitable shock, she went on: "Miss Challoner was struck dead and you were taken down with typhoid on the self-same day."

"Struck dead! Why do you use that word, struck? Struck dead! she, a young woman. Oh, Doris, an accident! My darling has been killed in an accident!"

"They do not call it accident. They call it what it never was. What it never was," she insisted, pressing him back with frightened hands, as he strove to rise. "Miss Challoner was—" How nearly the word shot had left her lips. How fiercely above all else, in that harrowing moment had risen the desire to fling the accusation of that word into the ears of him who listened from his secret hiding-place. But she refrained out of compassion for the man she loved, and declared instead, "Miss Challoner died from a wound; how given, why given, no one knows. I had rather have died myself than have to tell you this. Oh, Mr. Brotherson, speak, sob, do anything but—"

She started back, dropping his hands as she did so. With quick intuition she saw that he must be left to himself if he were to meet this blow without succumbing. The body must have freedom if the spirit would not go mad. Conscious, or perhaps not conscious, of his release from her restraining hand, albeit profiting by it, he staggered to his feet, murmuring that word of doom: "Wound! wound! my darling died of a wound! What kind of a wound?" he suddenly thundered out. "I cannot understand what you mean by wound. Make it clear to me. Make it clear to me at once. If I must bear this grief, let me know its whole depth. Leave nothing to my imagination or I cannot answer for myself. Tell it all, Doris."

And Doris told him:

"She was on the mezzanine floor of the hotel where she lives. She was seemingly happy and had been writing a letter—a letter to me which they never forwarded. There was no one else by but some strangers—good people whom one must believe. She was crossing the floor when suddenly she threw up her hands and fell. A thin, narrow paper-cutter was in her grasp; and it flew into the lobby. Some say she struck herself with that cutter; for when they picked her up they found a wound in her breast which that cutter might have made."

"Edith? never!"

The words were chokingly said; he was swaying, almost falling, but he steadied himself.

"Who says that?" he asked.

"It was the coroner's verdict."

"And she died that way—died?"

"Immediately."

"After writing to you?"

"Yes."

"What was in that letter?"

"Nothing of threat, they say. Only just cheer and expressions of hope. Just like the others, Mr. Brotherson."

"And they accuse her of taking her own life? Their verdict is a lie. They did not know her."

Then, after some moments of wild and confused feeling, he declared, with a desperate effort at self-control: "You said that some believe this. Then there must be others who do not. What do they say?"

"Nothing. They simply feel as you do. They see no reason for the act and no evidence of her having meditated it. Her father and her friend insist besides, that she was incapable of such a horror. The mystery of it is killing us all; me above others, for I've had to show you a cheerful face, with my brain reeling and my heart like lead in my bosom."

She held out her hands. She tried to draw his attention to herself; not from any sentiment of egotism, but to break, if she could, the strain of these insupportable horrors where so short a time before Hope sang and Life revelled in re-awakened joys.

Perhaps some faint realisation of this reached him, for presently he caught her by the hands and bowed his head upon her shoulder and finally let her seat him again, before he said:

"Do they know of—of my interest in this?"

"Yes; they know about the two O. B.s."

"The two—" He was on his feet again, but only for a moment; his weakness was greater than his will power.

"Orlando and Oswald Brotherson," she explained, in answer to his broken appeal. "Your brother wrote letters to her as well as you, and signed them just as you did, with his initials only. These letters were found in her desk, and he was supposed, for a time, to have been the author of all that were so signed. But they found out the difference after awhile. Yours were easily recognised after they learned there was another O. B. who loved her."

The words were plain enough, but the stricken listener did not take them in. They carried no meaning to him. How should they? The very idea she sought to impress upon him by this seemingly careless allusion was an incredible one. She found it her dreadful task to tell him the hard, bare truth.

"Your brother," said she, "was devoted to Miss Challoner, too. He even wanted to marry her. I cannot keep back this fact. It is known everywhere, and by everybody but you."

"Orlando?" His lips took an ironical curve, as he uttered the word. This was a young girl's imaginative fancy to him. "Why Orlando never knew her, never saw her, never—"

"He met her at Lenox."

The name produced its effect. He stared, made an effort to think, repeated Lenox over to himself; then suddenly lost his hold upon the idea which that word suggested, struggled again for it, seized it in an instant of madness and shouted out:

"Yes, yes, I remember. I sent him there—" and paused, his mind blank again.

Poor Doris, frightened to her very soul, looked blindly about for help; but she did not quit his side; she did not dare to, for his lips had reopened; the continuity of his thoughts had returned; he was going to speak.

"I sent him there." The words came in a sort of shout. "I was so hungry to hear of her and I thought he might mention her in his letter. Insane! Insane! He saw her and—What's that you said about his loving her? He couldn't have loved her; he's not of the loving sort. They've deceived you with strange tales. They've deceived the whole world with fancies and mad dreams. He may have admired her, but loved her,—no! or if he had, he would have respected my claims."

"He did not know them."

A laugh; a laugh which paled Doris' cheek; then his tones grew even again, memory came back and he muttered faintly:

"That is true. I said nothing to him. He had the right to court her—and he did, you say; wrote to her; imposed himself upon her, drove her mad with importunities she was forced to rebuke; and—and what else? There is something else. Tell me; I will know it all."

He was standing now, his feebleness all gone, passion in every lineament and his eye alive and feverish, with emotion. "Tell me," he repeated, with unrestrained vehemence. "Tell me all. Kill me with sorrow but save me from being unjust."

"He wrote her a letter; it frightened her. He followed it up by a visit— '

Doris paused; the sentence hung suspended. She had heard a step—a hand on the door.

Orlando had entered the room.

CHAPTER XXXIII

ALONE

Oswald had heard nothing, seen nothing. But he took note of Doris' silence, and turning towards her in frenzy saw what had happened, and so was in a measure prepared for the stern, short sentence which now rang through the room:

"Wait, Miss Scott! you tell the story badly. Let him listen to me. From my mouth only shall he hear the stern and seemingly unnatural part I played in this family tragedy."

The face of Oswald hardened. Those pliant features—beloved for their gracious kindliness—set themselves in lines which altered them almost beyond recognition; but his voice was not without some of its natural sweetness, as, after a long and hollow look at the other's composed countenance, he abruptly exclaimed:

"Speak! I am bound to listen; you are my brother."

Orlando turned towards Doris. She was slipping away.

"Don't go," said he.

But she was gone.

Slowly he turned back.

Oswald raised his hand and checked the words with which he would have begun his story.

"Never mind the beginnings," said he. "Doris has told all that. You saw Miss Challoner in Lenox—admired her—offered yourself to her and afterwards wrote her a threatening letter because she rejected you."

"It is true. Other men have followed just such unworthy impulses—and been ashamed and sorry afterwards. I was sorry and I was ashamed, and as soon as my first anger was over went to tell her so. But she mistook my purpose and—"

"And what?"

Orlando hesitated. Even his iron nature trembled before the misery he saw—a misery he was destined to augment rather than soothe. With pains altogether out of keeping with his character, he sought in the recesses of his darkened mind for words less bitter and less abrupt than those which sprang involuntarily to his lips. But he did not find them. Though he pitied his brother and wished to show that he did, nothing but the stern language suitable to the stern fact he wished to impart, would leave his lips.

"And ended the pitiful struggle of the moment with one quick, unpremeditated blow," was what he said. "There is no other explanation possible for this act, Oswald. Bitter as it is for me to acknowledge it, I am thus far guilty of this beloved woman's death. But, as God hears me, from the moment I first saw her, to the moment I saw her last, I did not know, nor did I for a moment dream that she was anything to you or to any other man of my stamp and station. I thought she despised my country birth, my mechanical attempts, my lack of aristocratic pretensions and traditions."

"Edith?"

"Now that I know she had other reasons for her contempt—that the words she wrote were in rebuke to the brother rather than to the man, I feel my guilt and deplore my anger. I cannot say more. I should but insult your grief by any lengthy expressions of regret and sorrow."

A groan of intolerable anguish from the sick man's lips, and then the quick thrust of his re-awakened intelligence rising superior to the overthrow of all his hopes.

"For a woman of Edith's principle to seek death in a moment of desperation, the provocation must have been very great. Tell me if I'm to hate you through life—yea through all eternity—or if I must seek in some unimaginable failure of my own character or conduct the cause of her intolerable despair."

"Oswald!" The tone was controlling, and yet that of one strong man to another. "Is it for us to read the heart of any woman, least of all of a woman of her susceptibilities and keen inner life? The wish to end all comes to some natures like a lightning flash from a clear sky. It comes, it goes, often without leaving a sign. But if a weapon chances to be near—(here it was in hand)—then death follows the impulse which, given an instant of thought, would have vanished in a back sweep of other emotions. Chance was the real accessory to this death by suicide. Oswald, let us realise it as such and accept our sorrow as a mutual burden and turn to what remains to us of life and labour. Work is grief's only consolation. Then let us work."

But of all this Oswald had caught but the one word.

"Chance?" he repeated. "Orlando, I believe in God."

"Then seek your comfort there. I find it in harnessing the winds; in forcing the powers of nature to do my bidding."

The other did not speak, and the silence grew heavy. It was broken, when it was broken, by a cry from Oswald:

"No more," said he, "no more." Then, in a yearning accent, "Send Doris to me."

Orlando started. This name coming so close upon that word comfort produced a strange effect upon him. But another look at Oswald and he was ready to do his bidding. The bitter ordeal was over; let him have his solace if it was in her power to give it to him.

Orlando, upon leaving his brother's room, did not stop to deliver that brother's message directly to Doris; he left this for Truda to do, and retired immediately to his hanger in the woods. Locking himself in, he slightly raised the roof and then sat down before the car which was rapidly taking on shape and assuming that individuality and appearance of sentient life which hitherto he had only seen in dreams. But his eye, which had never failed to kindle at this sight before, shone dully in the semi-gloom. The air-car could wait; he would first have his hour in this solitude of his own making. The gaze he dreaded, the words from which he shrank could not penetrate here. He might even shout her name aloud, and only these windowless walls would respond. He was alone with his past, his present and his future.

Alone!

He needed to be. The strongest must pause when the precipice yawns before him. The gulf can be spanned; he feels himself forceful enough for that; but his eyes must take their measurement of it first; he must know its depths and possible dangers. Only a fool would ignore these steeps of jagged rock; and he was no fool, only a man to whom the unexpected had happened, a man who had seen his way clear to the horizon and then had come up against this! Love, when he thought such folly dead! Remorse, when Glory called for the quiet mind and heart!

He recognised its mordant fang, and knew that its ravages, though only just begun, would last his lifetime. Nothing could stop them now, nothing, nothing. And he laughed, as the thought went home; laughed at the irony of fate and its inexorableness; laughed at his own defeat and his nearness to a barred Paradise. Oswald loved Edith, loved her yet, with a flame time would take long to quench. Doris loved Oswald and he Doris; and not one of them would ever attain the delights each was so fitted to enjoy. Why shouldn't he laugh? What s left to man but mockery when all props fall? Disappointment was the universal lot; and it should go merrily with him if he must take his turn at it. But here the strong spirit of the man re-asserted itself; it should be but a turn. A man's joys are not bounded by his loves or even by the satisfaction of a perfectly untrammelled mind. Performance makes a world of its own for the capable and the strong, and this was still left to him. He, Orlando Brotherson, despair while his great work lay unfinished! That would be to lay stress on the inevitable pains and fears of commonplace humanity. He was not of that ilk. Intellect was his god; ambition his motive power. What would this casual blight upon his supreme contentment be to him, when with the wings of his air-car spread, he should spurn the earth and soar into the heaven of fame simultaneously with his flight into the open.

He could wait for that hour. He had measured the gulf before him and found it passable. Henceforth no looking back.

Rising, he stood for a moment gazing, with an alert eye now, upon such sections of his car as had not yet been fitted into their places; then he bent forward to his work, and soon the lips which had uttered that sardonic laugh a few minutes before, parted in gentler fashion, and song took the place of curses—a ballad of love and fondest truth. But Orlando never knew what he sang. He had the gift and used it.

Would his tones, however, have rung out with quite so mellow a sweetness had he seen the restless figure even then circling his retreat with eyes darting accusation and arms lifted towards him in wild but impotent threat?

Yes, I think they would; for he knew that the man who thus expressed his helplessness along with his convictions, was no nearer the end he had set himself to attain than on the day he first betrayed his suspicions.

CHAPTER XXXIV

THE HUT CHANGES ITS NAME

That night Oswald was taken very ill. For three days his life hung in the balance, then youth and healthy living triumphed over shock and bereavement, and he came slowly back to his sad and crippled existence.

He had been conscious for a week or more of his surroundings, and of his bitter sorrows as well, when one morning he asked Doris whose face it was he had seen bending over him so often during the last week: "Have you a new doctor? A man with white hair and a comforting smile? Or have I dreamed this face? I have had so many fancies this might easily be one of them."

"No, it is not a fancy," was the quiet reply. "Nor is it the face of a doctor. It is that of friend. One whose heart is bound up in your recovery; one for whom you must live, Mr. Brotherson."

"I don't know him, Doris. It's a strange face to me. And yet, it's not altogether strange. Who is this man and why should he care for me so deeply?"

"Because you share one love and one grief. It is Edith's father whom you see at your bedside. He has helped to nurse you ever since you came down this second time."

"Edith's father! Doris, it cannot be. Edith's father!"

"Yes, Mr. Challoner has been in Derby for the last two weeks. He has only one interest now; to see you well again."

"Why?"

Doris caught the note of pain, if not suspicion, in this query, and smiled as she asked in turn:

"Shall he answer that question himself? He is waiting to come in. Not to talk. You need not fear his talking. He's as quiet as any man I ever saw."

The sick man closed his eyes, and Doris watching, saw the flush rise to his emaciated cheek, then slowly fade away again to a pallor that frightened her. Had she injured where she would heal? Had she pressed too suddenly and too hard on the ever gaping wound in her invalid's breast? She gasped in terror at the thought, then she faintly smiled, for his eyes had opened again and showed a calm determination as he said:

"I should like to see him. I should like him to answer the question I have just put you. I should rest easier and get well faster—or not get well at all."

This latter he half whispered, and Doris, tripping from the room may not have heard it, for her face showed no further shadow as she ushered in Mr. Challoner, and closed the door behind him. She had looked forward to this moment for days. To Oswald, however, it was an unexpected excitement and his voice trembled with something more than physical weakness as he greeted his visitor and thanked him for his attentions.

"Doris says that you have shown me this kindness from the desire you have to see me well again Mr. Challoner. Is this true?"

"Very true. I cannot emphasise the fact too strongly."

Oswald's eyes met his again, this time with great earnestness.

"You must have serious reasons for feeling so—reasons which I do not quite understand. May I ask why you place such value upon a life which, if ever useful to itself or others, has lost and lost forever, the one delight which gave it meaning?"

It was for Mr. Challoner's voice to tremble now, as reaching out his hand, he declared, with unmistakable feeling:

"I have no son. I have no interest left in life, outside this room and the possibilities it contains for me. Your attachment to my daughter has created a bond between us, Mr. Brotherson, which I sincerely hope to see recognised by you."

Startled and deeply moved, the young man stretched out a shaking hand towards his visitor, with the feeble but exulting cry:

"Then you do not blame me for her wretched and mysterious death. You hold me guiltless of the misery which nerved her despairing arm?"

"Quite guiltless."

Oswald's wan and pinched features took on a beautiful expression and Mr. Challoner no longer wondered at his daughter's choice.

"Thank God!" fell from the sick man's lips, and then there was a silence during which their two hands met.

It was some minutes before either spoke and then it was Oswald who said:

"I must confide to you certain facts. I honoured your daughter and realised her position fully. Our plight was never made in words, nor should I have presumed to advance any claim to her hand if I had not made good my expectations, Mr. Challoner. I meant to win both her regard and yours by acts, not words. I felt that I had a great deal to do and I was prepared to work and wait. I loved her—

" He turned away his head and the silence which filled up the gap, united those two hearts, as the old and young are seldom united.

But when a little later, Mr. Challoner rejoined Doris, in her little sitting-room, he nevertheless showed a perplexity she had hoped to see removed by this understanding with the younger Brotherson.

The cause became apparent as soon as he spoke.

"These brothers hold by each other," said he. "Oswald will hear nothing against Orlando. He says that he has redeemed his fault. He does not even protest that his brother's word is to be believed in this matter. He does not seem to think that necessary. He evidently regards Orlando's personality as speaking as truly and satisfactorily for itself, as his own does. And I dared not undeceive him."

"He does not know all our reasons for distrust. He has heard nothing about the poor washerwoman."

"No, and he must not,—not for weeks. He has borne all that he can."

"His confidence in his older brother is sublime. I do not share it; but I cannot help but respect him for it."

It was warmly said, and Mr. Challoner could not forbear casting an anxious look at her upturned face. What he saw there made him turn away with a sigh.

"This confidence has for me a very unhappy side," he remarked. "It shows me Oswald's thought. He who loved her best, accepts the cruel verdict of an unreasoning public."

Doris' large eyes burned with a weird light upon his face.

"He has not had my dream," she murmured, with all the quiet of an unmoved conviction.

Yet as the days went by, even her manner changed towards the busy inventor. It was hardly possible for it not to. The high stand he took; the regard accorded him on every side; his talent; his conversation, which was an education in itself, and, above all, his absorption in a work daily advancing towards completion, removed him so insensibly and yet so decidedly, from the hideous past of tragedy with which his name, if not his honour, was associated, that, unconsciously to herself, she gradually lost her icy air of repulsion and lent him a more or less attentive ear, when he chose to join their small company of an evening. The result was that he turned so bright a side upon her that toleration merged from day to day into admiration and memory lost itself in anticipation of the event which was to prove him a man of men, if not one of the world's greatest mechanical geniuses.

Meantime, Oswald was steadily improving in health, if not in spirits. He had taken his first walk without any unfavourable results, and Orlando decided from this that the time had come for an explanation of his device and his requirements in regard to it. Seated together in Oswald's room, he broached the subject thus:

"Oswald, what is your idea about what I'm making up there?"

"That it will be a success."

"I know; but its character, its use? What do you think it is?"

"I've an idea; but my idea don't fit the conditions."

"How's that?"

"The shed is too closely hemmed in. You haven't room—"

"For what?"

"To start an aeroplane."

"Yet it is certainly a device for flying."

"I supposed so; but—"

"It is an air-car with a new and valuable idea—the idea for which the whole world has been seeking ever since the first aeroplane found its way up from the earth. My car needs no room to start in save that which it occupies. If it did, it would be but the modification of a hundred others."

"Orlando!"

As Oswald thus gave expression to his surprise, their two faces were a study: the fire of genius in the one; the light of sympathetic understanding in the other.

"If this car, now within three days of its completion," Orlando proceeded, "does not rise from the oval of my hangar like a bird from its nest, and after a wide and circling flight descend again into the self same spot without any swerving from its direct course, then have I failed in my endeavour and must take a back seat with the rest. But it will not fail. I'm certain of success, Oswald. All I want just now is a sympathetic helper—you, for instance; someone who will aid me with the final fittings and hold his peace to all eternity if the impossible occurs and the thing proves a failure."

"Have you such pride as that?"

"Precisely."

"So much that you cannot face failure?"

"Not when attached to my name. You can see how I feel about that by the secrecy I have worked under. No other person living knows what I have just communicated to you. Every part shipped here came from different manufacturing firms; sometimes a part of a part was all I allowed to be made in any one place. My fame, like my ship, must rise with one bound into the air, or it must never rise at all. It was not made for petty accomplishment, or the slow plodding of commonplace minds. I must startle, or remain obscure. That is why I chose this place for my venture, and you for my helper and associate."

"You want me to ascend with you?"

"Exactly."

"At the end of three days?"

"Yes."

"Orlando, I cannot."

"You cannot? Not strong enough yet? I'll wait then,—three days more."

"The time's too short. A month is scarcely sufficient. It would be folly, such as you never show, to trust a nerve so undermined as mine till time has restored its power. For an enterprise like this you need a man of ready strength and resources; not one whose condition you might be obliged to consider at a very critical moment."

Orlando, balked thus at the outset, showed his displeasure.

"You do not do justice to your will. It is strong enough to carry you through anything."

"It was."

"You can force it to act for you."

"I fear not, Orlando."

"I counted on you and you thwart me at the most critical moment of my life."

Oswald smiled; his whole candid and generous nature bursting into view, in one quick flash.

"Perhaps," he assented; "but you will thank me when you realise my weakness. Another man must be found—quick, deft, secret, yet honourably alive to the importance of the occasion and your rights as a great original thinker and mechanician."

"Do you know such a man?"

"I don't; but there must be many such among our workmen."

"There isn't one; and I haven't time to send to Brooklyn. I reckoned on you."

"Can you wait a month?"

"No."

"A fortnight, then?"

"No, not ten days."

Oswald looked surprised. He would like to have asked why such precipitation was necessary, but the tone in which this ultimatum was given was of that decisive character which admits of no argument. He, therefore, merely looked his query. But Orlando was not one to answer looks; besides, he had no reply for the same importunate question urged by his own good sense. He knew that he must make the attempt upon which his future rested soon, and without risk of the sapping influence of lengthened suspense and weeks of waiting. He could hold on to those two demons leagued in attack against him, for a definite seven days, but not for an indeterminate time. If he were to be saved from folly,—from himself—events must rush.

He, therefore, repeated his no, with increased vehemence, adding, as he marked the reproach in his brother's eye, "I cannot wait. The test must be made on Saturday evening next, whatever the conditions; whatever the weather. An air-car to be serviceable must be ready to meet lightning and tempest, and what is worse, perhaps, an insufficient crew." Then rising, he exclaimed, with a determination which rendered him majestic, "If help is not forthcoming, I'll do it all myself. Nothing shall hold me back; nothing shall stop me; and when you see me and my car rise above the treetops, you'll feel that I have done what I could to make you forget—"

He did not need to continue. Oswald understood and flashed a grateful look his way before saying:

"You will make the attempt at night?"

"Certainly."

"And on Saturday?"

"I've said it."

"I will run over in my mind the qualifications of such men as I know and acquaint you with the result to-morrow."

"There are adjustments to be made. A man of accuracy is necessary."

"I will remember."

"And he must be likable. I can do nothing with a man with whom I'm not perfectly in accord."

"I understand that."

"Good-night then." A moment of hesitancy, then, "I wish not only yourself but Miss Scott to be present at this test. Prepare her for the spectacle; but not yet, not till within an hour or two of the occasion."

And with a proud smile in which flashed a significance which startled Oswald, he gave a hurried nod and turned away.

When in an hour afterwards, Doris looked in through the open door, she found Oswald sitting with face buried in his hands, thinking so deeply that he did not hear her. He had sat like this, immovable and absorbed, ever since his brother had left him.

CHAPTER XXXV

SILENCE—AND A KNOCK

Oswald did not succeed in finding a man to please Orlando. He suggested one person after another to the exacting inventor, but none were satisfactory to him and each in turn was turned down. It is not every one we want to have share a world-wide triumph or an ignominious defeat. And the days were passing.

He had said in a moment of elation, "I will do it alone;" but he knew even then that he could not. Two hands were necessary to start the car; afterwards, he might manage it alone. Descent was even possible, but to give the contrivance its first lift required a second mechanician. Where was he to find one to please him? And what was he to do if he did not? Conquer his prejudices against such men as he had seen, or delay the attempt, as Oswald had suggested, till he could get one of his old cronies on from New York. He could do neither. The obstinacy of his nature was such as to offer an invincible barrier against either suggestion. One alternative remained. He had heard of women aviators. If Doris could be induced to accompany him into the air, instead of clinging sodden-like to the weight of Oswald's woe, then would the world behold a triumph which would dwarf the ecstasy of the bird's flight and rob the eagle of his kingly pride. But Doris barely endured him as yet, and the thought was not one to be considered for a moment. Yet what other course remained? He was brooding deeply on the subject, in his hangar one evening—(it was Thursday and Saturday was but two days off) when there came a light knock at the door.

This had never occurred before. He had given strict orders, backed by his brother's authority, that he was never to be intruded upon when in this place; and though he had sometimes encountered the prying eyes of the curious flashing from behind the trees encircling the hangar, his door had never been approached before, or his privacy encroached upon. He started then, when this low but penetrating sound struck across the turmoil of his thoughts, and cast one look in the direction from which it came; but he did not rise, or even change his position on his workman's stool.

Then it came again, still low but with an insistence which drew his brows together and made his hand fall from the wire he had been unconsciously holding through the mental debate which was absorbing him. Still he made no response, and the knocking continued. Should he ignore it entirely, start up his motor and render himself oblivious to all other sounds? At every other point in his career he would have done this, but an unknown, and as yet unnamed, something had entered his heart during this fatal month, which made old ways impossible and oblivion a thing he dared not court too recklessly. Should this be a summons from Doris! Should (inconceivable idea, yet it seized upon him relentlessly and would not yield for the asking) should it be Doris herself!

Taking advantage of a momentary cessation of the ceaseless tap tap, he listened. Silence was never profounder than in this forest on that windless night. Earth and air seemed, to his strained ear, emptied of all sound. The clatter of his own steady, unhastened heart-beat was all that broke upon the stillness. He might be alone in the Universe for all token of life beyond these walls, or so he was saying to himself, when sharp, quick, sinister, the knocking recommenced, demanding admission, insisting upon attention, drawing him against his own will to his feet, and finally, though he made more than one stand against it, to the very door.

"Who's there?" he asked, imperiously and with some show of anger.

No answer, but another quiet knock.

"Speak! or go from my door. No one has the right to intrude here. What is your name and business?"

Continued knocking—nothing more.

With an outburst of wrath, which made the hangar ring, Orlando lifted his fist to answer this appeal in his own fierce fashion from his own side of the door, but the impulse paused at fulfilment, and he let his arm fall again in a rush of self-hatred which it would have pained his worst enemy, even little Doris, to witness. As it reached his side, the knock came again.

It was too much. With an oath, Orlando reached for his key. But before fitting it into the lock, he cast a look behind him. The car was in plain sight, filling the central space from floor to roof. A single glance from a stranger's eye, and its principal secret would be a secret no longer. He must not run such a risk. Before he answered this call, he must drop the curtain he had rigged up against such emergencies as these. He had but to pull a cord and a veil would fall before his treasure, concealing it as effectually as an Eastern bride is concealed behind her yashmak.

Stepping to the wall, he drew that cord, then with an impatient sigh, returned to the door.

Another quiet but insistent knock greeted him. In no fury now, but with a vague sense of portent which gave an aspect of farewell to the one quick glance he cast about the well-known spot, he fitted the key in the lock, and stood ready to turn it.

"I ask again your name and your business," he shouted out in loud command. "Tell them or—" He meant to say, "or I do not turn this key." But something withheld the threat. He knew that it would perish in the utterance; that he could not carry it out. He would have to open the door now, response or no response. "Speak!" was the word with which he finished his demand.

A final knock.

Pulling a pistol from his pocket, with his left hand, he turned the key with his right.

The door remained unopened.

Stepping slowly back, he stared at its unpainted boards for a moment, then he spoke up quietly, almost courteously:

"Enter."

But the command passed unheeded; the latch was not raised, and only the slightest tap was heard.

With a bound he reached forward and pulled the door open. Then a great silence fell upon him and a rigidity as of the grave seized and stiffened his powerful frame.

The man confronting him from the darkness was Sweetwater.

CHAPTER XXXVI

THE MAN WITHIN AND THE MAN WITHOUT

An instant of silence, during which the two men eyed each other; then, Sweetwater, with an ironical smile directed towards the pistol lightly remarked:

"Mr. Challoner and other men at the hotel are acquainted with my purpose and await my return. I have come—" here he cast a glowing look at the huge curtain cutting off the greater portion of the illy-lit interior—"to offer you my services, Mr. Brotherson. I have no other motive for this intrusion than to be of use. I am deeply interested in your invention, to the development of which I have already lent some aid, and can bring to the test you propose a sympathetic help which you could hardly find in any other person living."

The silence which settled down at the completion of these words had a weight which made that of the previous moment seem light and all athrob with sound. The man within had not yet caught his breath; the man without held his, in an anxiety which had little to do with the direction of the weapon, into which he looked. Then an owl hooted far away in the forest, and Orlando, slowly lowering his arm, asked in an oddly constrained tone:

"How long have you been in town?"

The answer cut clean through any lingering hope he may have had.

"Ever since the day your brother was told the story of his great misfortune."

"Ah! still at your old tricks! I thought you had quit that business as unprofitable."

"I don't know. I never expect quick returns. He who holds on for a rise sometimes reaps unlooked-for profits."

The arm and fist of Orlando Brotherson ached to hurl this fellow back into the heart of the midnight woods.

But they remained quiescent and he spoke instead. "I have buried the business. You will never resuscitate it through me."

Sweetwater smiled. There was no mirth in his smile though there was lightness in his tone as said:

"Then let us go back to the matter in hand. You need a helper; where are you going to find one if you don't take me?"

A growl from Brotherson's set lips. Never had he looked more dangerous than in the one burning instant following this daring repetition of the detective's outrageous request. But as he noted how slight was the figure opposing him from the other side of the threshold, he was swayed by his natural admiration of pluck in the physically weak, and lost his threatening attitude, only to assume one which Sweetwater secretly found it even harder to meet.

"You are a fool," was the stinging remark he heard flung at him. "Do you want to play the police-officer here and arrest me in mid air?"

"Mr. Brotherson, you understand me as little as I am supposed to understand you. Humble as my place is in society and, I may add, in the Department whose interests I serve, there are in me two men. One you know passably well—the detective whose methods, only indifferently clever show that he has very much to learn. Of the other—the workman acquainted with hammer and saw, but with some knowledge too of higher mathematics and the principles upon which great mechanical inventions depend, you know little, and must imagine much. I was playing the gawky when I helped you in the old house in Brooklyn. I was interested in your air-ship—Oh, I recognised it for what it was, notwithstanding its oddity and lack of ostensible means for flying—but I was not caught in the whirl of its idea; the idea by which you doubtless expect, and with very good reason too, to revolutionise the science of aviation. But since then I've been thinking it over, and am so filled with your own hopes that either I must have a hand in the finishing and sailing of the one you have yourself constructed, or go to work myself on the hints you have unconsciously given me, and make a car of my own."

Audacity often succeeds where subtler means fail. Orlando, with a curious twist of his strong lip, took hold of the detective's arm and drew him in, shutting and locking the door carefully behind him.

"Now," said he, "you shall tell me what you think you have discovered, to make any ideas of your own available in the manufacture of a superior self-propelling air-ship."

Sweetwater who had been so violently wheeled about in entering that he stood with his back to the curtain concealing the car, answered without hesitation.

"You have a device, entirely new so far as I can judge, by which this car can leap at once into space, hold its own in any direction, and alight again upon any given spot without shock to the machine or danger to the people controlling it."

"Explain the device."

"I will draw it."

"You can?"

"As I see it."

"As you see it!"

"Yes. It's a brilliant idea; I could never have conceived it."

"You believe—"

"I know."

"Sit here. Let's see what you know."

Sweetwater sat down at the table the other pointed out, and drawing forward a piece of paper, took up a pencil with an easy air. Brotherson approached and stood at his shoulder. He had taken up his pistol again, why he hardly knew, and as Sweetwater began his marks, his fingers tightened on its butt till they turned white in the murky lamplight.

"You see," came in easy tones from the stooping draughtsman, "I have an imagination which only needs a slight fillip from a mind like yours to send it in the desired direction. I shall not draw an exact reproduction of your idea, but I think you will see that I understand it very well. How's that for a start?"

Brotherson looked and hastily drew back. He did not want the other to note his surprise.

"But that is a portion you never saw," he loudly declared.

"No, but I saw this," returned Sweetwater, working busily on some curves; "and these gave me the fillip I mentioned. The rest came easily."

Brotherson, in dread of his own anger, threw his pistol to the other end of the shed:

"You knave! You thief!" he furiously cried.

"How so?" asked Sweetwater smilingly, rising and looking him calmly in the face. "A thief is one who appropriates another man's goods, or, let us say, another man's ideas. I have appropriated nothing yet. I've only shown you how easily I could do so. Mr. Brotherson, take me in as your assistant. I will be faithful to you, I swear it. I want to see that machine go up."

"For how many people have you drawn those lines?" thundered the inexorable voice.

"For nobody; not for myself even. This is the first time they have left their hiding-place in my brain."

"Can you swear to that?"

"I can and will, if you require it. But you ought to believe my word, sir. I am square as a die in all matters not connected—well, not connected with my profession," he smiled in a burst of that whimsical humour, which not even the seriousness of the moment could quite suppress.

"And what surety have I that you do not consider this very matter of mine as coming within the bounds you speak of?"

"None. But you must trust me that far."

Brotherson surveyed him with an irony which conveyed a very different message to the detective than any he had intended. Then quickly:

"To how many have you spoken, dilating upon this device, and publishing abroad my secret?"

"I have spoken to no one, not even to Mr. Gryce. That shows my honesty as nothing else can."

"You have kept my secret intact?"

"Entirely so, sir."

"So that no one, here or elsewhere, shares our knowledge of the new points in this mechanism?"

"I say so, sir."

"Then if I should kill you," came in ferocious accents, "now—here—"

"You would be the only one to own that knowledge. But you won't kill me."

"Why?"

"Need I go into reasons?"

"Why? I say."

"Because your conscience is already too heavily laden to bear the burden of another unprovoked crime."

Brotherson, starting back, glared with open ferocity upon the man who dared to face him with such an accusation.

"God! why didn't I shoot you on entrance!" he cried. "Your courage is certainly colossal."

A fine smile, without even the hint of humour now, touched the daring detective's lip. Brotherson's anger seemed to grow under it, and he loudly repeated:

"It's more than colossal; it's abnormal and—" A moment's pause, then with ironic pauses—"and quite unnecessary save as a matter of display, unless you think you need it to sustain you through the ordeal you are courting. You wish to help me finish and prepare for flight?"

"I sincerely do."

"You consider yourself competent?"

"I do."

Brotherson's eyes fell and he walked once to the extremity of the oval flooring and back.

"Well, we will grant that. But that's not all that is necessary. My requirements demand a companion in my first flight. Will you go up in the car with me on Saturday night?"

A quick affirmative was on Sweetwater's lips but the glimpse which he got of the speaker's face glowering upon him from the shadows into which Brotherson had withdrawn, stopped its utterance, and the silence grew heavy. Though it may not have lasted long by the clock, the instant of breathless contemplation of each other's features across the intervening space was of incalculable moment to Sweetwater, and, possibly, to Brotherson. As drowning men are said to live over their whole history between their first plunge and their final rise to light and air, so through the mind of the detective rushed the memories of his past and the fast fading glories of his future; and rebelling at the subtle peril he saw in that sardonic eye, he vociferated an impulsive:

"No! I'll not—" and paused, caught by a new and irresistible sensation.

A breath of wind—the first he had felt that night—had swept in through some crevice in the curving wall, flapping the canvas enveloping the great car. It acted like a peal to battle. After all, a man must take some risks in his life, and his heart was in this trial of a redoubtable mechanism in which he had full faith. He could not say no to the prospect of being the first to share a triumph which would send his name to the ends of the earth; and, changing the trend of his sentence, he repeated with a calmness which had the force of a great decision.

"I will not fail you in anything. If she rises—" here his trembling hand fell on the curtain shutting off his view of the ship, "she shall take me with her, so that when she descends I may be the first to congratulate the proud inventor of such a marvel."

"So be it!" shot from the other's lips, his eyes losing their threatening look, and his whole countenance suddenly aglow with the enthusiasm of awakened genius.

Coming from the shadows, he laid his hand on the cord regulating the rise and fall of the concealing curtain.

"Here she is!" he cried and drew the cord.

The canvas shook, gathered itself into great folds and disappeared in the shadows from which he had just stepped.

The air-car stood revealed—a startling, because wholly unique, vision.

Long did Sweetwater survey it, then turning with beaming face upon the watchful inventor, he uttered a loud Hurrah.

Next moment, with everything forgotten between them save the glories of this invention, both dropped simultaneously to the floor and began that minute examination of the mechanism necessary to their mutual work.

CHAPTER XXXVII

HIS GREAT HOUR

Saturday night at eight o'clock.

So the fiat had gone forth, with no concession to be made on account of weather.

As Oswald came from his supper and took a look at the heavens from the small front porch, he was deeply troubled that Orlando had remained so obstinate on this point. For there were ominous clouds rolling up from the east, and the storms in this region of high mountains and abrupt valleys were not light, nor without danger even to those with feet well planted upon mother earth.

If the tempest should come up before eight!

Mr. Challoner, who, from some mysterious impulse of bravado on the part of Brotherson, was to be allowed to make the third in this small band of spectators, was equally concerned at this sight, but not for Brotherson. His fears were for Oswald, whose slowly gathering strength could illy bear the strain which this additional anxiety for his brother's life must impose upon him. As for Doris, she was in a state of excitement more connected with the past than with the future. That afternoon she had laid her hand in that of Orlando Brotherson, and wished him well. She! in whose breast still lingered reminiscences of those old doubts which had beclouded his image for her at their first meeting. She had not been able to avoid it. His look was a compelling one, and it had demanded thus much from her; and—a terrible thought to her gentle spirit—he might be going to his death!

It had been settled by the prospective aviator that they were to watch for the ascent from the mouth of the grassy road leading in to the hangar. The three were to meet there at a quarter to eight and await the stroke and the air-cars rise. That time was near, and Mr. Challoner, catching a glimpse of Oswald's pallid and unnaturally drawn features, as he set down the lantern he carried, shuddered with foreboding and wished the hour passed.

Doris' watchful glance never left the face whose lightest change was more to her than all Orlando's hopes. But the result upon her was not to weaken her resolution, but to strengthen it. Whatever the outcome of the next few minutes, she must stand ready to sustain her invalid through it. That the darkness of early evening had deepened to oppression, was unnoticed for the moment. The fears of an hour past had been forgotten. Their attention was too absorbed in what was going on before them, for even a glance overhead.

Suddenly Mr. Challoner spoke.

"Who is the man whom Mr. Brotherson has asked to go up with him?"

It was Oswald who answered.

"He has never told me. He has kept his own counsel about that as about everything else connected with this matter. He simply advised me that I was not to bother about him any more; that he had found the assistant he wanted."

"Such reticence seems unpardonable. You have—displayed great patience, Oswald."

"Because I understand Orlando. He reads men's natures like a book. The man he trusts, we may trust. To-morrow, he will speak openly enough. All cause for reticence will be gone."

"You have confidence then in the success of this undertaking?"

"If I hadn't, I should not be here. I could hardly bear to witness his failure, even in a secret test like this. I should find it too hard to face him afterwards."

"I don't understand."

"Orlando has great pride. If this enterprise fails I cannot answer for him. He would be capable of anything. Why, Doris! what is the matter, child? I never saw you look like that before."

She had been down on her knees regulating the lantern, and the sudden flame, shooting up, had shown him her face turned up towards his in an apprehension which verged on horror.

"Do I look frightened?" she asked, remembering herself and lightly rising. "I believe that I am a little frightened. If—if anything should go wrong! If an accident-' But here she remembered herself again and quickly changed her tone. "But your confidence shall be mine. I will believe in his good angel or—or in his self-command and great resolution. I'll not be frightened any more."

But Oswald did not seem satisfied. He continued to look at her in vague concern.

He hardly knew what to make of the intense feeling she had manifested. Had Orlando touched her girlish heart? Had this cold-blooded nature, with its steel-like brilliancy and honourable but stern views of life, moved this warm and sympathetic soul to more than admiration? The thought disturbed him so he forgot the nearness of the moment they were all awaiting till a quick rasping sound from the hangar, followed by the sudden appearance of an ever-widening band of light about its upper rim, drew his attention and awakened them all to a breathless expectation.

The lid was rising. Now it was half-way up, and now, for the first time, it was lifted to its full height and stood a broad oval disc against the background of the forest. The effect was strange. The hangar had been made brilliant by many lamps, and their united glare pouring from its top and illuminating not only the surrounding treetops but the broad face of this uplifted disc, roused in the awed spectator a thrill such as in mythological times might have greeted the sudden sight of Vulcan's smithy blazing on Olympian hills. But the clang of iron on iron would have attended the flash and gleam of those unexpected fires, and here all was still save for that steady throb never heard in Olympus or the halls of Valhalla, the pant of the motor eager for flight in the upper air.

As they listened in a trance of burning hope which obliterated all else, this noise and all others near and distant, was suddenly lost in a loud clatter of writhing and twisting boughs which set the forest in a roar and seemed to heave the air about them.

A wind had swooped down from the east, bending everything before it and rattling the huge oval on which their eyes were fixed as though it would tear it from its hinges.

The three caught at each other's hands in dismay. The storm had come just on the verge of the enterprise, and no one might guess the result.

"Will he dare? Will he dare?" whispered Doris, and Oswald answered, though it seemed next to impossible that he could have heard her:

"He will dare. But will he survive it? Mr. Challoner," he suddenly shouted in that gentleman's ear, "what time is it now?"

Mr. Challoner, disengaging himself from their mutual grasp, knelt down by the lantern to consult his watch.

"One minute to eight," he shouted back.

The forest was now a pandemonium. Great boughs, split from their parent trunks, fell crashing to the ground in all directions. The scream of the wind roused echoes which repeated themselves, here, there and everywhere. No rain had fallen yet, but the sight of the clouds skurrying pell-mell through the glare thrown up from the shed, created such havoc in the already overstrained minds of the three onlookers, that they hardly heeded, when with a clatter and crash which at another time would have startled them into flight, the swaying oval before them was whirled from its hinges and thrown back against the trees already bending under the onslaught of the tempest. Destruction seemed the natural accompaniment of the moment, and the only prayer which sprang to Oswald's lips was that the motor whose throb yet lingered in their blood though no longer taken in by the ear, would either refuse to work or prove insufficient to lift the heavy car into this seething tumult of warring forces. His brother's life hung in the balance against his fame, and he could not but choose life for him. Yet, as the multitudinous sounds about him yielded for a moment to that brother's shout, and he knew that the moment had come, which would soon settle all, he found himself staring at the elliptical edge of the hangar, with an anticipation which held in it as much terror as joy, for the end of a great hope or the beginning of a great triumph was compressed into this trembling instant and if—

Great God! he sees it! They all see it! Plainly against that portion of the disc which still lifted itself above the further wall, a curious moving mass appears, lengthens, takes on shape, then shoots suddenly aloft, clearing the encircling tops of the bending, twisting and tormented trees, straight into the heart of the gale, where for one breathless moment it whirls madly about like a thing distraught, then in slow but triumphant obedience to the master hand that guides it, steadies and mounts majestically upward till it is lost to their view in the depths of impenetrable darkness.

Orlando Brotherson has accomplished his task. He has invented a mechanism which can send an air-car straight up from its mooring place. As the three watchers realise this, Oswald utters a cry of triumph, and Doris throws herself into Mr. Challoner's arms. Then they all stand transfixed again, waiting for a descent which may never come.

But hark! a new sound, mingling its clatter with all the others. It is the rain. Quick, maddening, drenching, it comes; enveloping them in wet in a moment. Can they hold their faces up against it?

And the wind! Surely it must toss that aerial messenger before it and fling it back to earth, a broken and despised toy.

"Orlando?" went up in a shriek. "Orlando?" Oh, for a ray of light in those far-off heavens For a lull in the tremendous sounds shivering the heavens and shaking the earth! But the tempest rages on, and they can only wait, five minutes, ten minutes, looking, hoping, fearing, without thought of self and almost without thought of each other, till suddenly as it had come, the rain ceases and the wind, with one final wail of rage and defeat, rushes away into the west, leaving behind it a sudden silence which, to their terrified hearts, seems almost more dreadfu to bear than the accumulated noises of the moment just gone.

Orlando was in that shout of natural forces, but he is not in this stillness. They look aloft, but the heavens are void. Emptiness is where life was. Oswald begins to sway, and Doris, remembering him now and him only, has thrown her strong young arm about him, when—What is this sound they hear high up, high up, in the rapidly clearing vault of the heavens! A throb—a steady pant,—drawing near and yet nearer,—entering the circlet of great branches over their heads—descending, slowly descending,—till they catch another glimpse of those hazy outlines which had no sooner taken shape than the car disappeared from their sight within the elliptical wall open to receive it.

It had survived the gale! It has re-entered its haven, and that, too, without colliding with aught around or any shock to those within, just as Orlando had promised; and the world was henceforth his! Hail to Orlando Brotherson!

Oswald could hardly restrain his mad joy and enthusiasm. Bounding to the door separating him from this conqueror of almost invincible forces, he pounded it w th impatient fist.

"Let me in!" he cried. "You've done the trick, Orlando, you've done the trick."

"Yes, I have satisfied myself," came back in studied self-control from the other side of the door; and with a quick turning of the lock, Orlando stood before them.

They never forgot him as he looked at that moment. He was drenched, battered, palpitating with excitement; but the majesty of success was in his eye and in the bearing of his incomparable figure.

As Oswald bounded towards him, he reached out his hand, but his glance was for Doris.

"Yes," he went on, in tones of suppressed elation, "there's no flaw in my triumph. I have done all that I set out to do. Now—"

Why did he stop and look hurriedly back into the hangar? He had remembered Sweetwater. Sweetwater, who at that moment was stepping carefully from his seat in some remote portion of the car. The triumph was not complete. He had meant—

But there his thought stopped. Nothing of evil, nothing even of regret should mar his great hour. He was a conqueror, and it was for him now to reap the joy of conquest.

CHAPTER XXXVIII

NIGHT

Three days had passed, and Orlando Brotherson sat in his room at the hotel before a table laden with telegrams, letters and marked newspapers. The news of his achievement had gone abroad, and Derby was, for the moment, the centre of interest for two continents.

His success was an established fact. The second trial which he had made with his car, this time with the whole town gathered together in the streets as witnesses, had proved not only the reliability of its mechanism, but the great advantages which it possessed for a direct flight to any given point. Already he saw Fortune beckoning to him in the shape of an unconditional offer of money from a first-class source; and better still,—for he was a man of untiring energy and boundless resource— that opportunity for new and enlarged effort which comes with the recognition of one's exceptional powers.

All this was his and more. A sweeter hope, a more enduring joy had followed hard upon gratified ambition. Doris had smiled on him;—Doris! She had caught the contagion of the universal enthusiasm and had given him her first ungrudging token of approval. It had altered his whole outlook on life in an instant, for there was an eagerness in this demonstration which proclaimed the relieved heart. She no longer trusted either appearances or her dream. He had succeeded in conquering her doubts by the very force of his personality, and the shadow which had hitherto darkened their intercourse had melted quite away. She was ready to take his word now and Oswald's, after which the rest must follow. Love does not lag far behind an ardent admiration.

Fame! Fortune! Love! What more could a man desire? What more could this man, with his strenuous past and an unlimited capacity for an enlarged future, ask from fate than this. Yet, as he bends over his letters, fingering some, but reading none beyond a line or two, he betrays but a passing elation, and hardly lifts his head when a burst of loud acclaim comes ringing up to his window from some ardent passer-by: "Hurrah for Brotherson! He has put our town on the map!"

Why this despondency? Have those two demons seized him again? It would seem so and with new and overmastering fury. After the hour of triumph comes the hour of reckoning. Orlando Brotherson in his hour of proud attainment stands naked before his own soul's tribunal and the pleader is dumb and the judge inexorable. There is but one Witness to such struggles; but one eye to note the waste and desolation of the devastated soul, when the storm is over past.

Orlando Brotherson has succumbed; the attack was too keen, his forces too shaken. But as the heavy minutes pass, he slowly re-gathers his strength and rises, in the end, a conqueror. Nevertheless, he knows, even in that moment of regained command, that the peace he had thus bought with strain and stress is but momentary; that the battle is on for life: that the days which to other eyes would carry a sense of brilliancy—days teeming with work and outward satisfaction— would hold within their hidden depths a brooding uncertainty which would rob applause of its music and even overshadow the angel face of Love.

He quailed at the prospect, materialist though he was. The days—the interminable days! In his unbroken strength and the glare of the noonday sun, he forgot to take account of the nights looming in black and endless procession before him. It was from the day phantom he shrank, and not from the ghoul which works in the darkness and makes a grave of the heart while happier mortals sleep.

And the former terror seemed formidable enough to him in this his hour of startling realisation, even if he had freed himself for the nonce from its controlling power. To escape all further contemplation of it he would work. These letters deserved attention. He would carry them to Oswald, and in their consideration find distraction for the rest of the day, at least. Oswald was a good fellow. If pleasure were to be gotten from these tokens of good-will, he should have his share of it. A gleam of Oswald's old spirit in Oswald's once bright eye, would go far towards throttling one of those demons whose talons he had just released from his throat; and if Doris responded too, he would deserve his fate, if he did not succeed in gaining that mastery of himself which would make such hours as these but episodes in a life big with interest and potent with great emotions.

Rising with a resolute air, he made a bundle of his papers and, with them in hand, passed out of his room and down the hotel stairs.

A man stood directly in his way, as he made for the front door. It was Mr. Challoner.

Courtesy demanded some show of recognition between them, and Brotherson was passing with his usual cold bow, when a sudden impulse led him to pause and meet the other's eye, with the sarcastic remark:

"You have expressed, or so I have been told, some surprise at my choice of mechanician. A man of varied accomplishments, Mr. Challoner, but one for whom I have no further use. If, therefore, you wish to call off your watch-dog, you are at liberty to do so. I hardly think he can be serviceable to either of us much longer."

The older gentleman hesitated, seeking possibly for composure, and when he answered it was not only without irony but with a certain forced respect:

"Mr. Sweetwater has just left for New York, Mr. Brotherson. He will carry with him, no doubt, the full particulars of your great success."

Orlando bowed, this time with distinguished grace. Not a flicker of relief had disturbed the calm serenity of his aspect, yet when a moment later, he stepped among his shouting admirers in the street, his air and glance betrayed a bounding joy for which another source must be found than that of gratified pride. A chain had slipped from his spirit, and though the people shrank a little, even while they cheered, it was rather from awe of his bearing and the recognition of that sense of apartness which underlay his smile than from any perception of the man's real nature or of the awesome purpose which at that moment exalted it. But had they known—could they have seen into this tumultuous heart—what a silence would have settled upon these noisy streets; and in what terror and soul-confusion would each man have slunk away from his fellows into the quiet and solitude of his own home.

Brotherson himself was not without a sense of the incongruity underlying this ovation; for, as he slowly worked himself along, the brightness of his look became dimmed with a tinge of sarcasm which in its turn gave way to an expression of extreme melancholy—both quite unbefitting the hero of the hour in the first flush of his new-born glory. Had he seen Doris' youthful figure emerge for a moment from the vine-hung porch he was approaching, bringing with it some doubt of the reception awaiting him? Possibly, for he made a stand before he reached the house, and sent his followers back; after which he advanced with an unhurrying step, so that several minutes elapsed before he finally drew up before Mr. Scott's door and entered through the now empty porch into his brother's sitting-room.

He had meant to see Doris first, but his mind had changed. If all passed off well between himself and Oswald, if he found his brother responsive and wide-awake to the interests and necessities of the hour, he might forego his interview with her till he felt better prepared to meet it. For call it cowardice or simply a reasonable precaution, any delay seemed preferable to him in his present mood of discouragement, to that final casting of the die upon which hung so many and such tremendous issues. It was the first moment of real halt in his whole tumultuous life! Never, as daring experimentalist or agitator, had he shrunk from danger seen or unseen or from threat uttered or unuttered, as he shrank from this young girl's no; and something of the dread he had felt lest he should encounter her unaware in the hall and so be led on to speak when his own judgment bade him be silent, darkened his features as he entered his brother's presence.

But Oswald was sunk in a bitter revery of his own, and took no heed of these signs of depression. In the re-action following these days of great excitement, the past had re-asserted itself, and all was gloom in his once generous soul. This, Orlando had time to perceive, quick as the change came when his brother really realised who his visitor was. The glad "Orlando!" and the forced smile did not deceive him, and his voice quavered a trifle as he held out his packet with the words:

"I have come to show you what the world says of my invention. We will soon be great men," he emphasised, as Oswald opened the letters. "Money has been offered me and—Read! read!" he urged, with an unconscious dictatorialness, as Oswald paused in his task. "See what the fates have prepared for us; for you shall share all my honours, as you will from this day share my work and enter into all my experiments. Cannot you enthuse a little bit over it? Doesn't the prospect contain any allurement for you? Would you rather stay locked up in this petty town—"

"Yes; or—die. Don't look like that, Orlando. It was a cowardly speech and I ask your pardon. I'm hardly fit to talk to-day. Edith—"

Orlando frowned.

"Not that name!" he harshly interrupted. "You must not hamper your life with useless memories. That dream of yours may be sacred, but it belongs to the past, and a great reality confronts you. When you have fully recovered your health, your own manhood will rebel at a weakness unworthy one of our name. Rouse yourself, Oswald. Take account of our prospects. Give me your hand and say, 'Life holds something for me yet. I have a brother who needs me if I do not need him. Together, we can prove ourselves invincible and wrench fame and fortune from the world.'"

But the hand he reached for did not rise at his command, though Oswald started erect and faced him with manly earnestness.

"I should have to think long and deeply," he said, "before I took upon myself responsibilities like these. I am broken in mind and heart, Orlando, and must remain so till God mercifully delivers me. I should be a poor assistant to you—a drag, rather than a help. Deeply as I deplore it, hard as it may be for one of your temperament to understand so complete an overthrow, I yet must acknowledge my condition and pray you not to count upon me in any plans you may form. I know how this looks—I know that as your brother and truest admirer, I should respond, and respond strongly, to such overtures as these, but the motive for achievement is gone. She was my all; and while I might work, it would be mechanically. The lift, the elevating thought is gone."

Orlando stood a moment studying his brother's face; then he turned shortly about and walked the length of the room. When he came back, he took up his stand again directly before Oswald, and asked, with a new note in his voice:

"Did you love Edith Challoner so much as that?"

A glance from Oswald's eye, sadder than any tear.

"So that you cannot be reconciled?"

A gesture. Oswald's words were always few.

Orlando's frown deepened.

"Such grief I partly understand," said he. "But time will cure it. Some day another lovely face—"

"We'll not talk of that, Orlando."

"No, we'll not talk of that," acquiesced the inventor, walking away again, this time to the window. "For you there's but one woman;—and she's a memory."

"Killed!" broke from his brother's lips. "Slain by her own hand under an impulse of wildness and terror! Can I ever forget that? Do not expect it, Orlando."

"Then you do blame me?" Orlando turned and was looking full at Oswald.

"I blame your unreasonableness and your overweening price."

Orlando stood a moment, then moved towards the door. The heaviness of his step smote upon Oswald's ear and caused him to exclaim:

"Forgive me, Orlando." But the other cut him short with an imperative:

"Thanks for your candour! If her spirit is destined to stand like an immovable shadow between you and me, you do right to warn me. But this interview must end all allusion to the subject. I will seek and find another man to share my fortunes; (as he said this he approached suddenly, and took his papers from the other's hand) or—" Here he hastily retraced his steps to the door which he softly opened. "Or" he repeated—But though Oswald listened for the rest, it did not come. While he waited, the other had given him one deeply concentrated look and passed out.

No heartfelt understanding was possible between these two men.

Crossing the hall, Orlando knocked at the door of Doris' little sitting-room.

No answer, yet she was there. He knew it in every throbbing fibre of his body. She was there and quite aware of his presence; of this he felt sure; yet she did not bid him enter. Should he knock again? Never! but he would not quit the threshold, not if she kept him waiting there for hours. Perhaps she realised this. Perhaps she had meant to open the door to him from the very first, who can tell? What avails is that she did ultimately open it, and he, meeting her soft eye, wished from his very heart that his impulse had led him another way, even if that way had been to the edge of the precipice—and over.

For the face he looked upon was serene, and there was no serenity in him; rather a confusion of unloosed passions fearful of barrier and yearning tumultuously for freedom. But, whatever his revolt, the secret revolt which makes no show in look or movement, he kept his ground and forced a smile of greeting. If her face was quiet, it was also lovely;—too lovely, he felt, for a man to leave it, whatever might come of his lingering.

Nothing in all his life had ever affected him like it. For him there was no other woman in the past, the present or the future, and, realising this—taking in to the full what her affection and her trust might be to him in those fearsome days to come, he so dreaded a rebuff—he, who had been the courted of women and the admired of men ever since he could remember,—that he failed to respond to her welcome and the simple congratulations she felt forced to repeat. He could neither speak the commonplace, nor listen to it. This was his crucial hour. He must find support here, or yield hopelessly to the maelstrom in whose whirl he was caught.

She saw his excitement and faltered back a step—a move which she regretted the next minute, for he took advantage of it to enter and close behind him the door which she would never have shut of her own accord. Then he spoke, abruptly, passionately, but in those golden tones which no emotion could render other than alluring:

"I am an unhappy man, Miss Scott. I see that my presence here is not welcome, yet am sure that it would be so if it were not for a prejudice which your generous nature should be the first to cast aside, in face of the outspoken confidence of my brother: Oswald. Doris, little Doris, I love you. I have loved you from the moment of our first meeting. Not to many men is it given to find his heart so late, and when he does, it is for his whole life; no second passion can follow it. I know that I am premature in saying this; that you are not prepared to hear such words from me and that it might be wiser for me to withhold them, but I must leave Derby soon, and I cannot go until I know whether there is the least hope that you will yet lend a light to my career or whether that career must burn itself to ashes at your feet. Oswald—nay, hear me out—Oswald lives in his memories; but I must have an active hope—a tangible expectation—if I am to be the man I was meant to be. Will you, then, coldly dismiss me, or will you let my whole future life prove to you the innocence of my past? I will not hasten anything; all I ask is some indulgence. Time will do the rest."

"Impossible," she murmured.

But that was a word for which he had no ear. He saw that she was moved, unexpectedly so; that while her eyes wandered restlessly at times towards the door, they ever came back in girlish wonder, if not fascination, to his face, emboldening him so that he ventured at last, to add:

"Doris, little Doris, I will teach you a marvellous lesson, if you will only turn your dainty ear my way. Love such as mine carries infinite treasure with it. Will you have that treasure heaped, piled before your feet? Your lips say no, but your eyes—the truest eyes I ever saw—whisper a different language. The day will come when you will find your joy in the breast of him you are now afraid to trust." And not waiting for disclaimer or even a glance of reproach from the eyes he had so wilfully misread, he withdrew with a movement as abrupt as that with which he had entered.

Why, then, with the memory of this exultant hour to fend off all shadows, did the midnight find him in his solitary hangar in the moonlit woods, a deeply desponding figure again. Beside him, swung the huge machine which represented a life of power and luxury; but he no longer saw it. It called to him with many a creak and quiet snap,—sounds to start his blood and fire his eye a week—nay, a day ago. But he was deaf to this music now; the call went unheeded; the future had no further meaning, for him, nor did he know or think whether he sat in light or in darkness; whether the woods were silent about him, or panting with life and sound. His demon had gripped him again and the final battle was on. There would never be another. Mighty as he felt himself to be, there were limits even to his capacity for endurance. He could sustain no further conflict. How then would it end? He never had a doubt himself! Yet he sat there.

Around him in the forest, the night owls screeched and innumerable small things without a name, skurried from lair to lair.

He heard them not.

Above, the moon rode, flecking the deepest shadows with the silver from her half-turned urn, but none of the soft and healing drops fell upon him. Nature was no longer a goddess, but an avenger; light a revealer, not a solace. Darkness the only boon.

Nor had time a meaning. From early eve to early morn he sat there and knew not if it were one hour or twelve. Earth was his no longer. He roused, when the sun made everything light about him, but he did not think about it. He rose, but was not conscious that he rose. He unlocked the door and stepped out into the forest; but he could never remember doing this. He only knew later that he had been in the woods and now was in his room at the hotel; all the rest was phantasmagoria, agony and defeat.

He had crossed the Rubicon of this world's hopes and fears. but he had been unconscious of the passage.

CHAPTER XXXIX

THE AVENGER

"Dear Mr. Challoner:

"With every apology for the intrusion, may I request a few minutes of private conversation with you this evening at seven o'clock? Let it be in your own room.

"Yours truly,

"ORLANDO BROTHERSON."

Mr. Challoner had been called upon to face many difficult and heart-rending duties since the blow which had desolated his home fell upon him.

But from none of them had he shrunk as he did from the interview thus demanded. He had supposed himself rid of this man. He had dismissed him from his life when he had dismissed Sweetwater. His face, accordingly, wore anything but a propitiatory look, when promptly at the hour of seven, Orlando Brotherson entered his apartments.

His pleasure or his displeasure was, however, a matter of small consequence to his self-invited visitor. He had come there with a set purpose, and nothing in heaven or earth could deter him from it now. Declining the offer of a seat, with the slightest of acknowledgments in the way of a bow, he took a careful survey of the room before saying:

"Are we alone, Mr. Challoner, or is that man Sweetwater lurking somewhere within hearing?"

"Mr. Sweetwater is gone, as I had the honour of telling you yesterday," was the somewhat stiff reply. "There are no witnesses to this conference, if that is what you wish to know."

"Thank you, but you will pardon my insistence if I request the privilege of closing that door." He pointed to the one communicating with the bedroom. "The information I have to give you is not such as I am willing to have shared, at least for the present."

"You may close the door," said Mr. Challoner coldly. "But is it necessary for you to give me the information you mention, to-night? If it is of such a nature that you cannot accord me the privilege of sharing it, as yet, with others, why not spare me till you can? I have gone through much, Mr. Brotherson."

"You have," came in steady assent as the man thus addressed stepped to the door he had indicated and quietly closed it. "But," he continued, as he crossed back to his former position, "would it be easier for you to go through the night now in anticipation of what I have to reveal than to hear it at once from my lips while I am in the mood to speak?"

The answer was slow in coming. The courage which had upheld this rapidly aging man through so many trying interviews, seemed inadequate for the test put so cruelly upon it. He faltered and sank heavily into a chair, while the stern man watching him, gave no signs of responsive sympathy or even interest, only a patient and icy-tempered resolve.

"I cannot live in uncertainty;" such were finally Mr. Challoner's words. "What you have to say concerns Edith?" The pause he made was infinitesimal in length, but it was long enough for a quick disclaimer. But no such disclaimer came. "I will hear it," came in reluctant finish.

Mr. Brotherson took a step forward. His manner was as cold as the heart which lay like a stone in his bosom.

"Will you pardon me if I ask you to rise?" said he. "I have my weaknesses too." (He gave no sign of them.) "I cannot speak down from such a height to the man I am bound to hurt."

As if answering to the constraint of a will quite outside his own, Mr. Challoner rose. Their heads were now more nearly on a level and Mr. Brotherson's voice remained low, as he proceeded, with quiet intensity.

"There has been a time—and it may exist yet, God knows—when you thought me in some unknown and secret way the murderer of your daughter. I do not quarrel with the suspicion; it was justified, Mr. Challoner. I did kill your daughter, and with this hand! I can no longer deny it."

The wretched father swayed, following the gesture of the hand thus held out; but he did not fall, nor did a sound leave his lips.

Brotherson went coldly on:

"I did it because I regarded her treatment of my suit as insolent. I have no mercy for any such display of intolerance on the part of the rich and the fortunate. I hated her for it; I hated her class, herself and all she stood for. To strike the dealer of such a hurt I felt to be my right. Though a man of small beginnings and of a stock which such as you call common, I have a pride which few of your blood can equal. I could not work, or sleep or eat with such a sting in my breast as she had planted there. To rid myself of it, I determined to kill her, and I did. How? Oh, that was easy, though it has proved a great stumbling-block to the detectives, as I knew it would! I shot her—but not with an ordinary bullet. My charge was a small icicle made deliberately for the purpose. It had strength enough to penetrate, but it left no trace behind it. 'A bullet of ice for a heart of ice,' I had said in the torment of my rage. But the word was without knowledge, Mr. Challoner. I see it now; I have seen it for two whole weeks. I did not misjudge her condemnation of me, but I misjudged its cause. It was not to the comparatively poor, the comparatively obscure man she sought to show contempt, but to the brother of Oswald whose claims she saw insulted. A woman   should have respected, not killed. A woman of no pride of station; a woman who loved a man not only of my own class but of my own blood—a woman, to avenge whose unmerited death I stand here before you a self-condemned criminal. That is but justice, Mr. Challoner. That is the way I look at things. Though no sentimentalist; and dead to all beliefs save the eternal truths of science, I have that in me which will not let me profit, now that I know myself unworthy, by the great success I have earned. Hence this confession, Mr. Challoner. It has not come easily, nor do I shut my eyes in the least to the results which must follow. But I can not do differently. To-morrow, you may telegraph to New York. Till then I desire to be left undisturbed. I have many things to dispose of in the interim."

Mr. Challoner, very white by now, pointed to the door before he sank again into his chair. Brotherson took it for dismissal and stepped slowly back. Then their eyes met again and Mr. Challoner spoke his first word:

"There was another—a poor woman—she died suddenly—and her wound was not unlike that inflicted upon Edith. Did you—"

"I did." The answer came without a tremour. "You may say and so may others that I was less justified in this attack than in the other; but I do not see it that way. A theory does not always work in practice. I wished to test the unusual means I contemplated, and the woman I saw before me across the court was hard-working and with nothing in life to look forward to, so—"

A cry of bitter execration from Mr. Challoner cut him short. Turning with a shrug he was about to lift his hand to the door, when he gave a violent start and fell hastily back before a quickly entering figure of such passion and fury as neither of these men had ever seen before.

It was Oswald! Oswald, the kindly! Oswald, the lover of men and the adorer of women! Oswald, with the words of the dastardly confession he had partly overheard searing hot within his brain! Oswald, raised in a moment from the desponding invalid to a terrifying ministrant of retributive justice.

Orlando could scarcely raise his hand before the other's was upon his throat.

"Murderer! doubly-dyed murderer of innocent women!" was hissed in the strong man's ears. "Not with the law but with me you must reckon, and may God and the spirit of my mother nerve my arm!"

CHAPTER XL

DESOLATE

The struggle was fierce but momentary. Oswald with his weakened powers could not long withstand the steady exertion of Orlando's giant strength, and ere long sank away from the contest into Mr. Challoner's arms.

"You should not have summoned the shade of our mother to your aid," observed the other with a smile, in which the irony was lost in terrible presage. "I was always her favourite."

Oswald shuddered. Orlando had spoken truly; she had always been blindly, arrogantly trustful of her eldest son. No fault could she see in him; and now—

Impetuously Oswald struggled with his weakness, raised himself in Mr. Challoner's arms and cried in loud revolt:

"But God is just. He will not let you escape. If He does, I will not. I will hound you to the ends of this earth and, if necessary, into the eternities. Not with the threat of my arm—you are my master there, but with the curse of a brother who believed you innocent of his darling's blood and would have believed you so in face of everything but your own word."

"Peace!" adjured Orlando. "There is no account I am not ready to settle. I have robbed you of the woman you love, but I have despoiled myself. I stand desolate in the world, who but an hour ago could have chosen my seat among the best and greatest. What can your curses do after that?"

"Nothing." The word came slowly like a drop wrung from a nearly spent heart. "Nothing; nothing. Oh, Orlando, I wish we were both dead and buried and that there were no further life for either of us."

The softened tone, the wistful prayer which would blot out an immortality of joy for the one, that it might save the other from an immortality of retribution, touched some long unsounded chord in Orlando's extraordinary nature.

Advancing a step, he held out his hand—the left one. "We'll leave the future to itself, Oswald, and do what we can with the present," said he. "I've made a mess of my life and spoiled a career which might have made us both kings. Forgive me, Oswald. I ask for nothing else from God or man. I should like that. It would strengthen me for to-morrow."

But Oswald, ever kindly, generous and more ready to think of others than of himself, had yet some of Orlando's tenacity. He gazed at that hand and a flush swept up over his cheek which instantly became ghastly again.

"I cannot," said he—"not even the left one. May God forgive me!"

Orlando, struck silent for a moment, dropped his hand and slowly turned away. Mr. Challoner felt Oswald stiffen in his arms, and break suddenly away, only to stop short before he had taken one of the half dozen steps between himself and his departing brother.

"Where are you going?" he demanded in tones which made Orlando turn.

"I might say, To the devil," was the sarcastic reply. "But I doubt if he would receive me. No," he added, in more ordinary tones as the other shivered and again started forward, "you will have no trouble in finding me in my own room to-night. I have letters to write and—other things. A man like me cannot drop out without a ripple. You may go to bed and sleep. I will keep awake for two."

"Orlando!" Visions were passing before Oswald's eyes, soul-crushing visions such as in his blameless life he never thought could enter into his consciousness or blast his tranquil outlook upon life. "Orlando!" he again appealed, covering his eyes in a frenzied attempt to shut out these horrors, "I cannot let you go like this. To-morrow—"

"To-morrow, in every niche and corner of this world, wherever Edith Challoner's name has gone, wherever my name has gone, it will be known that the discoverer of a practical air-ship, is a man whom they can no longer honour. Do you think that is not hell enough for me; or that I do not realise the hell it will be for you? I've never wearied you or any man with my affection; but I'm not all demon. I would gladly have spared you this additional anguish; but that was impossible. You are my brother and must suffer from the connection whether we would have it so or not. If it promises too much misery—and I know no misery like that of shame—come with me where I go to-morrow. There will be room for two."

Oswald, swaying with weakness, but maddened by the sight of an overthrow which carried with it the stifled affections and the admiration of his whole life, gave a bound forward, opened his arms and—fell.

Orlando stopped short. Gazing down on his prostrate brother, he stood for a moment with a gleam of something like human tenderness showing through the f are of dying passions and perishing hopes; then he swung open the door and passed quietly out, and Mr. Challoner could hear the laughing remark with which he met and dismissed the half-dozen men and women who had been drawn to this end of the hall by what had sounded to them like a fracas between angry men.

CHAPTER XLI

FIVE O'CLOCK IN THE MORNING

The clock in the hotel office struck three. Orlando Brotherson counted the strokes; then went on writing. His transom was partly open and he had just heard a step go by his door. This was nothing new. He had already heard it several times before that night. It was Mr. Challoner's step, and every time it passed, he had rustled his papers or scratched vigorously with his pen. "He is keeping watch for Oswald," was his thought. "They fear a sudden end to this. No one, not the son of my mother knows me. Do I know myself?"

Four o'clock! The light was still burning, the pile of letters he was writing increasing.

Five o'clock! A rattling shade betrays an open window. No other sound disturbs the quiet of the room. It is empty now; but Mr. Challoner, long since satisfied that all was well, goes by no more. Silence has settled upon the hotel;—that heavy silence which precedes the dawn.

There was silence in the streets also. The few who were abroad, crept quietly along. An electric storm was in the air and the surcharged clouds hung heavy and low, biding the moment of outbreak.

A man who had left a place of many shadows for the more open road, paused and looked up at these clouds; then went calmly on.

Suddenly the shriek of an approaching train tears through the valley. Has it a call for this man? No. Yet he pauses in the midst of the street he is crossing and watches, as a child might watch, for the flash of its lights at the end of the darkened vista. It comes—filling the empty space at which he stares with moving life—engine, baggage car and a long string of Pullmans. Then all is dark again and only the noise of its slackening wheels comes to him through the night. It has stopped at the station. A minute longer and it has started again, and the quickly lessening rumble of its departure is all that remains of this vision of man's activity and ceaseless expectancy. When it is quite gone and all is quiet, a sigh falls from the man's lips and he moves on, but this time, for some unexplainable reason, in the direction of the station. With lowered head he passes along, noting little till he arrives within sight of the depot where some freight is being handled, and a trunk or two wheeled down the platform. No sight could be more ordinary or unsuggestive, but it has its attraction for him, for he looks up as he goes by and follows the passage of that truck down the platform till it has reached the corner and disappeared. Then he sighs again and again moves on.

A cluster of houses, one of them open and lighted, was all which lay between him now and the country road. He was hurrying past, for his step had unconsciously quickened as he turned his back upon the station, when he was seized again by that mood of curiosity and stepped up to the door from which a light issued and looked in. A common eating-room lay before him, with rudely spread tables and one very sleepy waiter taking orders from a new arrival who sat with his back to the door. Why did the lonely man on the sidewalk start as his eye fell on the latter's commonplace figure, a hungry man demanding breakfast in a cheap, country restaurant? His own physique was powerful while that of the other looked slim and frail. But fear was in the air, and the brooding of a tempest affects some temperaments in a totally unexpected manner. As the man inside turns slightly and looks up, the master figure on the sidewalk vanishes, and his step, if any one had been interested enough to listen, rings with a new note as it turns into the country road it has at last reached.

But no one heeded. The new arrival munches his roll and waits impatiently for his coffee, while without, the clouds pile soundlessly in the sky, one of them taking the form of a huge hand with clutching fingers reaching down into the hollow void beneath.

CHAPTER XLII

AT SIX

Mr. Challoner had been honest in his statement regarding the departure of Sweetwater. He had not only paid and dismissed our young detective, but he had seen him take the train for New York. And Sweetwater had gone away in good faith, too, possibly with his convictions undisturbed, but acknowledging at last that he had reached the end of his resources. But the brain does not loose its hold upon its work as readily as the hand does. He was halfway to New York and had consciously bidden farewell to the whole subject, when he suddenly startled those about him by rising impetuously to his feet. He sat again immediately, but with a light in his small grey eye which Mr. Gryce would have understood and revelled in. The idea for which he had searched industriously for months had come at last, unbidden; thrown up from some remote recess of the mind which had seemingly closed upon the subject forever.

"I have it. I have it," he murmured in ceaseless reiteration to himself. 'I will go back to Mr. Challoner and let him decide if the idea is worth pursuing. Perhaps an experiment may be necessary. It was bitter cold that night; I wish it were icy weather now. But a chemist can help us out. Good God! if this should be the explanation of the mystery, alas for Orlando and alas for Oswald!"

But his sympathies did not deter him. He returned to Derby at once, and as soon as he dared, presented himself at the hotel and asked for Mr. Challoner.

He was amazed to find that gentleman already up and in a state of agitation that was very disquieting. But he brightened wonderfully at sight of his visitor, and drawing him inside the room, observed with trembling eagerness:

"I do not know why you have come back, but never was man more welcome. Mr. Brotherson has confessed."

"Confessed!"

"Yes, he killed both women; my daughter and his neighbour, the washerwoman, with a—"

"Wait," broke in Sweetwater, eagerly, "let me tell you." And stooping, he whispered something in the other's ear.

Mr. Challoner stared at him amazed, then slowly nodded his head.

"How came you to think—" he began; but Sweetwater in his great anxiety interrupted him with a quick:

"Explanations will keep, Mr. Challoner. What of the man himself? Where is he? That's the important thing now."

"He was in his room till early this morning writing letters, but he is not there now. The door is unlocked and I went in. From appearances I fear the worst. That is why your presence relieves me so. Where do you think he is?"

"In his hangar in the woods. Where else would he go to—"

"I have thought of that. Shall we start out alone or take witnesses with us?"

"We will go alone. Does Oswald anticipate—"

"He is sure. But he lacks strength to move. He lies on my bed in there. Doris and her father are with him."

"We will not wait a minute. How the storm holds off. I hope it will hold off for another hour."

Mr. Challoner made no reply. He had spoken because he felt compelled to speak, but it had not been easy for him, nor could any trifles move him now.

The town was up by this time and, though they chose the east frequented streets, they had to suffer from some encounters. It was a good half hour before they found themselves in the forest and in sight of the hangar. One look that way, and Sweetwater turned to see what the effect was upon Mr. Challoner.

A murmur of dismay greeted him. The oval of that great lid stood up against the forest background.

"He has escaped," cried Mr. Challoner.

But Sweetwater, laying a finger on his lip, advanced and laid his ear against the door. Then he cast a quick look aloft. Nothing was to be seen there. The darkness of storm in the heavens but nothing more.—Yes! now, a flash of vivid and destructive lightning!

The two men drew back and their glances crossed.

"Let us return to the highroad," whispered Sweetwater; "we can see nothing here."

Mr. Challoner, trembling very much, wheeled slowly about.

"Wait," enjoined Sweetwater. "First let me take a look inside."

Running to the nearest tree, he quickly climbed it, worked himself along a protruding branch and looked down into the open hangar. It was now so dark that details escaped him, but one thing was certain. The air-ship was not there.

Descending, he drew Mr. Challoner hastily along. "He's gone," said he. "Let us reach the high ground as quickly as we can. I'm glad that Mr. Oswald Brotherson is not with us or—or Miss Doris."

But this expression of satisfaction died on his lips. At the point where the forest road debouches into the highway, he had already caught a glimpse of their two figures. They were waiting for news, and the brother spoke up the instant he saw Sweetwater:

"Where is he? You've not found him or you wouldn't be coming alone. He cannot have gone up. He cannot manage it without an assistant. We must seek him somewhere else; in the forest or in our house at home. Ah!" The lightning had forked again.

"He's not in the forest and he's not in your home," returned Sweetwater. "He's aloft; the air-ship is not in the shed. And he can go up alone now." Then more slowly: "But he cannot come down."

They strained their eyes in a maddening search of the heavens. But the darkness had so increased that they could be sure of nothing. Doris sank upon her knees.

Suddenly the lightning flashed again, this time so vividly and so near that the whole heaven burst into fiery illumination above them and the thunder, crashing almost simultaneously, seemed for a moment to rock the world and bow the heavens towards them. Then a silence; then Sweetwater's whisper in Mr. Challoner's ear:

"Take them away! I saw him; he was falling like a shot."

Mr. Challoner threw out his arms, then steadied himself. Oswald was reeling; Oswald had seen too. But Doris was there. When the lightning flashed again, she was standing and Oswald was weeping on her bosom.

Anna Katharine Green – A Concise Bibliography

The Leavenworth Case (1878)
A Strange Disappearance (1880)
The Sword of Damocles: A Story of New York Life (1881)
The Defence of the Bride, and other Poems (1882)
X Y Z: A Detective Story (1883)
Hand and Ring (1883)
The Mill Mystery (1886)
7 to 12: A Detective Story (1887)
Risifi's Daughter, A Drama (1887)
Behind Closed Doors (1888)
Forsaken Inn (1890)
A Matter of Millions (1891)
The Old Stone House and Other Stories (1891)
Cynthia Wakeham's Money (1892)
Marked "Personal" (1893)
Miss Hurd: An Enigma (1894)
The Doctor, His Wife, and the Clock (1895)
Doctor Izard (1895)
That Affair Next Door (1897)
Lost Man's Lane: A Second Episode in the Life of Amelia Butterworth (1898)
Agatha Webb (1899)
The Circular Study (1900)
A Difficult Problem (1900)
One of my Sons (1901)
The Filigree Ball: Being a Full and True Account of the Solution of the Mystery Concerning the Jeffrey-Moore Affair (1903)
The Amethyst Box (1905)
The House in the Mist (1905)
The Millionaire Baby (1905)
The Chief Legatee' (1906)
The Woman in the Alcove (1906)
The Mayor's Wife (1907)
The House of the Whispering Pines (1910)
Three Thousand Dollars (1910)
Initials Only (1911)
Masterpieces of Mystery (1913)
Dark Hollow (1914)
The Golden Slipper, and Other Problems for Violet Strange (1915)
To the Minute; Scarlet and Black: Two Tales of Life's Perplexities (1915)
The Mystery of the Hasty Arrow (1917)
The Step on the Stair (1923)